## 'You are an ...
sir!'

'Beyond redemption, my darling. . .well almost. You could reform me.'

A slight blush added colour to her cheeks as she placed yet another flower in the arrangement.

'I never looked upon you as a possible mistress, you know.'

She released her breath in a tiny resigned sigh. 'I should prefer not to discuss what passed between us that morning.'

'If that means you'll put the unfortunate episode behind you and begin afresh, then I'll never mention it again.'

**Anne Ashley** was born and educated in Leicester. She lived for a time in Scotland, but now lives in the West Country with two cats, her two sons and a husband, who has a wonderful and very necessary sense of humour. When not pounding away at the keys of her typewriter, she likes to relax in her garden, which she has opened to the public on more than one occasion in aid of the village church funds.

**Recent titles by the same author:**

THE EARL OF RAYNE'S WARD

# LADY LINFORD'S RETURN

Anne Ashley

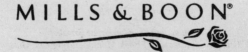

MILLS & BOON®

First published in Great Britain 1997
Harlequin Mills & Boon Limited,
Eton House, 18-24 Paradise Road, Richmond, Surrey TW9 1SR

© Andrea Bunney 1997

ISBN 0 263 80197 7

Set in Times 10 on 11½ pt. by
Rowland Phototypesetting Limited
Bury St Edmunds, Suffolk

04-9707-78829

Printed and bound in Great Britain by
Caledonian International Book Manufacturing Ltd, Glasgow

# Chapter One

Viscount Linford winced as the over-zealous application of the door-knocker echoed loudly round the hall to disturb the quiet confines of his library. His violet-blue eyes narrowed as he sipped his wine. He knew of only one person to set up such a hammering on a door. Unless he was very much mistaken, his peace and quiet was about to be shattered by the entrance of his most convivial of relatives.

The door opened, and an almost apologetic Peplow announced the arrival of Lady Barnsdale. The Viscount rose from the comfort of his favourite armchair, and moved with languid grace across to the decanters, his hand hovering between the Madeira and burgundy.

'How lovely to see you, Aunt Henrietta!' he greeted her warmly, as she swept into the room with a rustle of satin petticoats and much bobbing of the preposterously large plumes adorning her bonnet.

'Don't lie, Linford!' she responded in her usual forthright manner. 'If you had wanted to see me, you would have taken the trouble to inform me of your return to town. And I'll take a glass of Madeira.'

'You always somehow manage to discover my whereabouts, Hetta, without my having to enlighten you,' he returned blandly, handing her the wine before seating

5

himself opposite. 'Your army of spies has been remarkably diligent today, however. I arrived less than three hours ago.'

Her lips twitched. 'I know that. Amy Fitzpatrick saw you tooling your curricle into the Square.' She eyed him narrowly for a moment as she sampled the excellent wine. 'Rather an odd time to decide to come to London. The Season's almost half over. What brings you here? Or shouldn't I ask?'

'You shouldn't, but I've never known that stop you before.'

'Ha! You've a new barque of frailty under your protection, I'll be bound!' She gave vent to an unladylike snort. 'Heard all about that Parisian strumpet you had with you last year.'

He raised his eyes to stare blindly at an imaginary spot on the wall behind her, his mind's eye conjuring up a pleasant vision. 'A delightful little armful she was to be sure but, like all the others, palled after a time.'

This drew forth another derisive snort from his favourite relative. 'Think I don't know that? There ain't been one of 'em that's meant a groat to you. That's why it amazed me when you let that Standish chit go without putting up a fight. You could have had that gel, Linford. She was very fond of you.'

'But she was in love with the Earl,' he countered. 'And if you imagine I went abroad last year nursing a broken heart, you're far-and-away out.'

'Then why did you suddenly take it into your head to go?'

His frown, rarely seen by her, creased his high forehead, and for a moment she thought he would stubbornly refuse to satisfy her curiosity, but then he said, 'I did not fall in love with Rebecca Standish, even though she is a darling, but I might easily have done so. She did, however, force me to take stock of my situation. Things cannot possibly remain as they are.'

His frown disappeared as one black brow rose mockingly. 'What could I have offered her, after all. . .a *carte blanche*?'

Lady Barnsdale eyed him thoughtfully. His wife's mysterious disappearance had been a continuous torment. He had hidden his distress and feelings of guilt behind a veneer of cynicism and feigned indifference; but she knew: he had never been able to hide his anxiety from her.

'It's been six years, Dominic,' she said with rare gentleness. 'Even if she is alive, which I doubt, you don't imagine, surely, that you could discover what has become of her, now? You tried everything humanly possible before and to no avail.'

'I know, but I must try again.' He gazed down into the contents of his glass. 'If I should discover that she is dead, at least I can arrange for her body to be brought back to Linford Hall and placed in the family vault. And if by some chance she is still alive. . . Well, it will be as she chooses. But at least I can ensure she wants for nothing.'

'She's more likely to want another stab at being Viscountess Linford!' she retorted.

'If that is the case, why hasn't she returned?' he countered.

'Unless she's dead, I can think of no reason. But—but, Linford, if she isn't, you cannot wish, surely, to saddle yourself with that halfwitted creature again? Why, you'll breed a passel of moonlings!'

He gave a sudden shout of laughter. 'What on earth makes you suppose that I married a halfwit? Because I tell you, now, if that's what you've been thinking all these years, you couldn't have been more wrong. Rachel, my dear, was an intelligent girl. Shy, certainly, but that was all.'

She was slightly taken aback, but recovered in an instant. 'Well, you cannot deny the gel wasn't normal. Granted, I stayed with you for a few days only after your marriage, but she hardly spoke above half a dozen words to me the whole time I was there. And she went around all the time carrying a rag doll. . .a doll, at sixteen! I ask you!'

This drew a betraying twitch to his well-shaped lips. 'Yes, I can quite understand your thinking that rather strange. It certainly irked me at the time, I'll admit. It wasn't until after she had disappeared that I began to understand—began to realise what an appalling existence the poor child had endured during her short life.'

She looked at him searchingly. 'I recall your saying her father was something of a miserly recluse. Was her life so very bad?'

'Yes, it was,' he answered with unusual vehemence. 'Abominable!'

Lady Barnsdale watched him rise to his feet and go across to stand before the fireplace, every muscle in his tall, powerful frame seeming to grow taut as he stared down at the empty hearth. She was not a woman easily brought to tears, but at that moment she could have wept, knowing only too well that her stubborn stupidity had caused him years of needless pain.

She had watched Linford grow into the image of his father. She had adored her elder brother, but had deplored his weaknesses. He had spent a fortune on his pretty, frivolous wife and, when she had died, he had continued to squander it on his son.

Her nephew had been thoroughly spoilt and indulged, his every whim having been satisfied by his doting parent. Her nephew had needed to be brought to see the error of his ways; had needed to be taught self-discipline and restraint; but he had not deserved to be saddled with the shocking mountain of debts left by his father.

Sighing audibly, she leaned back against the red velvet upholstery of the sofa. She had been in a position to help, and had been willing to do so, providing her nephew had been prepared to mend his ways. She had desperately wanted him to settle down and marry. God, what a blind idiot she had been!

He had married, right enough, but not to one of the highly finished articles that had adorned the Season each year. Instead, he had married a wealthy merchant's daughter, a sad, drab lump of a thing with no conversation and even less wit.

'If only I had not been so stubborn!' She did not realise she had spoken aloud until she looked up to find him staring down at her. 'If I had loaned you the money when you came to see me that day, I could have saved you all these years of anguish.'

His smile was tender. 'No, Aunt Hetta. You mustn't blame yourself. You were right to have refused. Had you obliged, I should have continued to be the empty-headed fool I was in those days, caring for nothing and for no one, except my own selfish pleasures.'

He sipped his wine thoughtfully, his mind going back six long years to a certain cold day in February. 'When I received that letter from Roderick Weston, I thought it a godsend. I had seen my neighbour perhaps half-a-dozen times in my life before I called on him that day. From his sick-bed, he told me he would settle my every debt, providing I married his daughter. There she sat by the bed, head bent, saying not a word.'

His shout of laughter had a bitter edge. 'I hardly noticed her at all, and yet I didn't hesitate. Three weeks later, in that same drab bedchamber, we were married. When I left in the carriage afterwards, with my sixteen-year-old bride beside me and Weston's promissory note in my hand, I knew which meant more to me.'

Again he paused to sip his wine. 'Weston had told me that the settlement of my father's debts was only part of what I would eventually receive if I married his daughter. Believe me, Hetta, when I tell you I was satisfied with that alone. Weston lived for less than a month after the ceremony. His lawyers caught up with me here, in London. The old man cut up to the tune of a further half-million.

'Yes, Aunt,' he went on, smiling at her astonished look, 'half a million. And yet the miserly old rogue never spent a penny on that house of his, nor on poor Rachel.'

'What a scoundrel!' she exclaimed.

'And worse. It wasn't until after she had disappeared that I discovered the miserable existence the poor child had endured. From the day her mother ran off with that London fribble, the poor girl was a virtual prisoner, confined to that house and its grounds.

'From the day she was four years old, she saw no one except the various governesses engaged to educate her, her only friends the cook and housekeeper, and the vicar who came to see her twice a week to teach her both Latin and Greek. It's hardly surprising the poor child had little conversation. But halfwitted she most certainly was not.'

'Good God, Linford! I had no idea.' She shook her head. 'That poor child. . .that poor, poor child.'

His lips twisted into a self-deprecating sneer. 'And look at the bargain she got in a husband! I couldn't wait to get back here. As soon as cousin Matilda arrived at the Hall to look after my child bride, I upped and left, and returned to my dissolute life.'

'Yes—quite!' She moved uncomfortably in her seat. 'There's little to be gained by dwelling on the might-have-beens. We cannot change what has happened. We must put our heads to—' She broke off as the rapping of the door-knocker echoed round the hall once more. 'That will be Cheffy. I asked him to meet me here. We're calling on the Barringtons later.'

The door opened and a tall, rather portly gentleman in his late fifties strolled into the room, his round, podgy face wreathed in smiles as he shook the Viscount's hand.

'Good to see you back again from your travels, Linford!'

'He's been back three months and more,' Lady Barnsdale put in before her nephew could return the greeting. 'Been with those wretched brats of his, if I know anything.'

She turned to her long-time friend, who had eased his large bulk down on the sofa beside her. 'I'm glad you're early, Cheffy. You may be of some help. Linford is going to have another stab at trying to discover what became of that wife of his. Though how in the world he intends going about it defeats me.'

She looked frowningly up at her nephew as he handed Cheffy a glass of burgundy. 'Are you getting the Runners on the job again?'

'No,' he replied without a moment's hesitation. 'That would be futile, now. After all these years, I doubt they would be interested. No, I've learned of a man who takes on such cases—missing persons, lost family heirlooms—those sorts of things. He's coming here to see me tomorrow.'

The Honourable Charles Cheffingham drew in a deep breath, straining the seams of his dazzling waistcoat to dangerous limits. 'Don't see what I can do, m'boy, but I'll help if I can.'

'I should like you both to think back very hard, and tell me anything about Rachel that you particularly remember. Ashamed though I am to admit it,' the Viscount went on, running his hand through his thick, slightly waving black hair, 'I hardly remember her at all, not enough to give an accurate description. My one vivid recollection is that she had green eyes.'

'Yes, she did. Very fine eyes they were too, with lovely long, curling dark lashes,' Mr Cheffingham concurred. 'Matched her hair.'

'You mean she had dark hair?' his lordship ventured, hopefully.

'No, green. . .well, greenish. Demmed odd sort of a colour. Remember thinking so at the time.'

'Green?' Lady Barnsdale echoed, incredulous. 'It's my belief, Cheffy, you're a bit top-heavy.'

'Not had more than a bottle of claret and a glass or two of port all day,' he assured her, slightly affronted by the slanderous accusation. 'Not even bright in the eye! And I tell you the chit had queer greenish-coloured hair.'

'Utter rot! Her hair was sort of a—a dirty brown colour,' she argued, looking up at her nephew. 'Reminded me of the sweepings from a filthy stable.'

'How delightful!' his lordship muttered, seating himself opposite again, wishing fervently that he had never broached the subject in the first place, but forged on stoically. 'Let us reiterate—Rachel certainly had green eyes, and her hair—her hair, shall we say for argument's sake, was brownish in colour. Now, is there anything else you remember about her?'

Lady Barnsdale shrugged. Like her nephew, she remembered little about the young Viscountess, but Cheffy, for all his seeming insouciance, was in fact extremely observant.

'She was a clever little puss, as I recall,' he astounded Lady Barnsdale by remarking. 'I mind the day after we had arrived at the Hall, when you and Linford went off somewhere, and I came across her in the library, reading a book about some Greek whatnot that had the unfortunate habit of creeping up behind a fellow when he was least expecting it. Fate or some such thing.'

'Not Fate, Cheffy—Nemesis.'

'I do believe you're right, Linford. Nemesis—yes, that's the one! Told me all about it, she did.' He shook his head. 'Sad business, m'boy. Your wife was a taking little thing when she was animated. If she had had a few decent rags on her back, she would have been very pretty. Nice and plump she was. Just how I like 'em! Plenty of flesh on the bone. Not like that new-found widowed friend of yours, Hetta. What a skinny wench she is!'

'Emily is not skinny,' she countered. 'She's slender, I grant you, but she has a lovely figure.'

'She's certainly eyeable, I'll give her that. And that hair! Most beautiful red hair I've ever seen.'

Lady Barnsdale glanced surreptitiously in her nephew's direction. 'I'd like you to meet her, Linford. Don't get along with many females, as you know. I've always preferred the company of men. But Emily Stowen is different, somehow. Liked her from the moment we met.'

The Viscount had been attending with only half an ear. He had no intention of going out of his way to meet one of his aunt's middle-aged cronies, and had no hesitation in telling her so.

'Didn't come to London to socialise, Hetta. I don't intend staying above a couple of weeks, three at the most, so it's unlikely I'll meet your friend. Besides which, can't abide red-haired women. I'm partial to blonde hair, and find several shades of brown quite pretty. But red hair I deplore!'

Lady Barnsdale finished off the wine in her glass, and rose to her feet. 'Just as you like, Linford. But we shall be at the Rayne ball tonight, if you should change your mind. Which reminds me. The delightful Countess asked me to invite you, if you happened to be in town. The gel still has a soft spot for you, you rogue.

'Come along, Cheffy,' she added, turning to her escort, 'otherwise we'll be late, and I want to leave the Barringtons' gathering in plenty of time to dress for the ball tonight.'

His lordship escorted his visitors to the front door but, as he watched them climb into Cheffy's well-sprung town carriage, he had no expectations of seeing them again that day.

He dined at his club that evening, and remained for a while, playing cards with several acquaintances, but soon grew bored with the entertainment, even though he was, in fact, winning. He decided to leave.

Declining the porter's offer to call a chair, he placed his curly-brimmed hat at an angle on his head, and set off at a brisk walk, his mind deep in thought. His conversation with his aunt and Cheffy that afternoon had forcibly borne in upon him just what a momentous task it was going to be trying to discover what had become of his child bride.

It seemed doomed to failure from the start; deep down, he entertained no real expectations of success, but he was still determined to try. The individual on whom he pinned all hopes had been highly recommended. He was a man, seemingly, who achieved results, and he prayed that the task he was about to set him would not prove to be the ex-Runner's first failure.

His depressing thoughts ran along these lines for some time, his mind's eye unsuccessfully trying to conjure up a clear vision of his young wife. It was not until he was suddenly hailed by an acquaintance from an open window of a passing carriage that he became aware of his surroundings.

He was a mere five minutes' walk away from Berkeley

Square, and the town residence of his friend the Earl of Rayne, and his lovely young wife. He hovered on the brink of indecision for a moment, then crossed the road in the direction of the Square.

His lack of invitation card proved no bar, and he was admitted without hesitation by a liveried footman, who relieved him of his hat and cloak. As he strolled up the staircase the sounds of laughter and chatter, and the strains of music, grew steadily louder. He checked suddenly at the head of the stairs, his frown descending.

What on earth had possessed him to call? He must have been mad! He was in no mood for indulging in inconsequential chatter, or for being polite to people whom he had no earthly wish to see. He turned, about to retrace his steps, when a high-pitched shriek arrested him, and he turned again to see the lovely Countess tripping lightly towards him.

'How good it is to see you, Dominic!' She entwined her arm round his, thereby giving him little choice but to accompany her into the large, brightly lit ballroom. 'Your aunt said you had arrived in town. I'm so glad you found time to join our little gathering.'

He smiled down at her. She really was an enchanting creature. The Earl of Rayne was an exceedingly lucky man to be able to call such a darling his own.

'And it's good to see you again, Becky. But it's high time that husband of yours taught you how to behave,' he informed her with mock severity. 'Shrieking like a banshee is not at all the correct behaviour for a peer of the realm's wife.'

Not in the least abashed, she twinkled up at him. 'You always remind me so much of Drum when you scold. That, I suppose, is why I adore you so much,' she confessed, before tripping lightly away to greet more late-comers.

'Flirting with my wife again, Linford?' The Earl came sauntering towards him, his smile of welcome a trifle crooked. 'It's as well for you that I now consider you a friend, otherwise I should be very tempted to call you out.'

The Viscount's eyes glinted in response. 'This time last year you would not have called me so. In fact, you will admit you were mighty pleased to see the back of me, if you're honest.'

The Earl, laughing, gave him a hearty slap on the back. 'My judgement, then, must have improved greatly in the past twelve months. I cannot deny it was at Rebecca's insistence that we descended on you in Paris after our honeymoon, but your subsequent stay in Gloucestershire during the winter was at mine.'

'You have a darling for a wife, Rayne, and I have never tried to hide my regard for her, nor shall I. But I believe you must realise, now, that I was never any real threat. How could I have been,' his lips twisted into a bitter smile, 'circumstanced as I was. . .as I am?'

The Earl looked deeply into his violet eyes. The Viscount had confided in him during his stay at Rayne. He understood, fully, his friend's reasons for trying to discover the whereabouts of his wife, and had gone so far as to furnish him with the name of a man who might be of use in his endeavours.

'You must have made contact with Stubbs by now, Dominic. I hope his investigations bear fruit. But if not, for God's sake, man, bury the past! You cannot continue to live under this heavy burden of guilt.'

Linford sighed. 'The guilt, no matter the outcome, may possibly never leave me. But if nothing comes of these enquiries, I shall set my lawyers on having the marriage annulled. And then, I suppose,' he added without any degree of enthusiasm, 'look about me for another wife.'

'Well, you won't find one amongst this insipid lot, not

unless your taste has deteriorated,' the Earl returned, gazing down the ballroom at the swirling dancers, and at those ladies who, not so fortunate, but still hopeful for a partner, remained seated beside their chaperons. His lips curled suddenly into another crooked smile. 'But you might try a look in the room set out for cards some time this evening.'

'Oh?' The Viscount caught the amused twinkle in his companion's dark eyes. 'I might just do that. Is that deplorable aunt of mine here yet, by any chance?'

'Yes. She, too, is playing cards, I believe. Which reminds me. You haven't met——' He broke off as he noticed his wife signalling him frantically to greet yet more late-comers. 'Duty calls. We'll talk again later. Or, better still, come and dine with us tomorrow evening.'

The Viscount watched him walk away, and then wandered about the room, ignoring the hopeful glances cast his way by doting mamas as he spoke to various acquaintances. It was some time before he entered the salon adjoining the ballroom, which had been set out for cards.

Raising his quizzing glass, he scanned the various tables. There were several young ladies present, but none worth a second glance from what he could see. He was beginning to think that his friend had been indulging in some private jest when he noticed Lady Barnsdale seated at a corner table, and wandered over to her.

'Ah! So you decided to come, after all,' was his aunt's greeting. 'Well, as you're here, you may as well meet Mrs Stowen. Emily, this is my reprobate of a nephew.'

The Viscount had not thus far looked at his aunt's companion, who was seated with her back to the door, but at this inelegant introduction felt obliged to acknowledge her. He turned, but the polite utterance he had been about to make died in his throat as he stared down at one of the most lovely countenances he had ever seen.

Large almond-shaped eyes, framed in thick, curling

lashes, were raised to his, and just for a moment he thought he could detect a flicker of something resembling contempt in their beautiful green depths, but then it was gone, and he felt certain he must have been mistaken.

Smiling, she placed her cards face down on to the table, and held one slender white hand out to him. 'How do you do, sir? Your aunt speaks of you so often that I feel I know you already.'

'And not a mite of good,' that irrepressible lady put in. 'But, then, I've never been one to lie, have I, Linford?' she added, watching him bow gracefully over the slender fingers.

'I can always rely on you, Hetta, to vilify me,' he responded, reluctantly releasing his hold on the ravishing creature before him. 'Is this your first visit to London, Mrs Stowen?'

'No, sir. I have visited the metropolis once before, many years ago, but this has been a much longer stay.'

He frowned slightly. 'I cannot help feeling I have met you somewhere before.'

One white shoulder rose in a graceful shrug. 'It's certainly possible, if you're a frequent visitor to the West Country. I live quite retired there, my lord.'

'And what a waste! Do you not agree, Linford?' Lady Barnsdale smiled up at him, secretly pleased by his evident appreciation of her new-found friend. Then, out of the corner of her eye, she noticed someone trying to attract her attention.

'Lady Somerville desires speech with me. Will you both excuse me for a few minutes? You'll be quite safe in Linford's company, Emily. He cannot abide red hair,' she added mischievously, and chuckled at her nephew's flashing look of annoyance as she sped away.

'May I remain to keep you company until my incorrigible aunt returns, Mrs Stowen?'

At her nod of assent, he sat down, and found himself unable to take his eyes off the exquisite creature seated opposite. From her lustrous dark red hair, which resembled the colour of mahogany, crowning her queenly little head in beautifully arranged curls, to the ruby necklace encircling her slender throat, she was a vision to behold. Not perhaps the most beautiful woman he had ever seen, but certainly captivatingly lovely.

If there was a slight flaw—and as yet he was not prepared to call it so—it was her mouth, which drooped down slightly at the corners, giving her a rather petulant, childlike appearance when she was not smiling.

He watched her tapering fingers encircle the stem of her wineglass and raise it to her lips. 'Am I right in thinking you haven't known my aunt very long?'

'We met for the first time a little over six weeks ago.'

'And you do not find her sharp tongue and astringent comments a trifle off-putting?' he quizzed.

'No, for I, too, am not averse to plain speaking.'

Indeed? his lordship mused, one dark brow rising speculatively. He subjected her to a further prolonged, searching stare. Anyone looking at her might be forgiven for thinking that such a fragile-looking creature would wilt beneath the merest harshly spoken word. Just went to prove that one should not judge by appearances, he decided. Not only that—now he came to study her more closely, he could detect a certain stubborn determination about that softly rounded chin of hers.

'In that case you must have a great deal in common with my aunt.'

'It would be more accurate to say certain things in common.' Again she sipped her wine, unblushingly taking stock of his handsome features. 'Henrietta is extremely fond of you, my lord. There isn't a time when we're together when your name is not brought up in the conversation.'

'How exceedingly tiresome for you!'

She smiled at the dry tone. 'Not at all. I find her disclosures—shall we say—extremely illuminating. I understand that you have been on the Continent recently?' she went on with such a rapid change of subject that he suspected her former remark of containing some hidden meaning, but thrust the suspicion aside.

'I spent several months last year in Paris.'

'How I envy you! I have never left our shores, and would dearly love to travel, to see all those places I've read so much about in books. Now that I am without encumbrance, I may well do so.'

The Viscount noticed his aunt returning and, although he would have liked to remain conversing longer, reluctantly got to his feet.

'Can I persuade you to partner me in a dance, Mrs Stowen?'

'I shall be delighted, sir, but first I must be sporting enough to give your dear aunt the opportunity of retrieving some of her losses,' she responded, gesturing to the pile of gold sovereigns at her elbow.

'Until later, then, ma'am.'

His aunt watched him re-enter the ballroom, thinking it a highly fortunate circumstance that she had been called away at such an auspicious moment. Things could not have worked out better had they been contrived!

'Did my nevvy keep you entertained, my dear?'

'Moderately so, ma'am. Your deal, I believe.'

Reaching for the pack, Lady Barnsdale dealt two new hands. 'He arrived in town earlier today. Been with those confounded brats of his, if I know anything.'

Emily raised puzzled eyes from the contemplation of the cards in her hand. 'Brats?'

'I call 'em that.' Lady Barnsdale snorted loudly. 'He calls them his children. Picks them up all over the place.' She shook her head. 'Mad! He ought to leave them where they are. But, oh no, not Linford! He takes them into his home, feeds, clothes and, would you believe, educates the little blighters.'

Emily regarded her companion in stunned silence for a moment. 'Are you seriously trying to tell me, ma'am, that your nephew takes his—that he has children at his home?'

'No, not his home, precisely, but nearby. He's installed them in the house his wife grew up in, only a few miles from Linford Hall.' She glanced down at her cards, thereby missing the angry flash in her young friend's large eyes. 'Rather surprised to see him here tonight. When I visited him earlier, he was in a very pensive mood. He's decided to have another stab at trying to discover what became of that wife of his.'

'I understood you to say that she was dead, ma'am.'

Lady Barnsdale shrugged. 'It's what I think. After all, Emily, what other explanation could there possibly be for her not returning?'

Her young friend looked steadily across the table at her. 'She might not consider the position of Viscountess Linford as such a privileged one.'

'If that's the case, what on earth is he to do if he does find her?'

'Divorce presents itself as the best option for such a mismatched pair.'

'Yes, but will he?' Lady Barnsdale's sigh was audible. 'He's more likely to take her back to Linford Hall, and try to make a go of it.'

This drew a gurgle of laughter from her young companion. 'Perhaps the lady in question just might have a thing or two to say on that score, ma'am. I recall your telling me that she was a simple, very biddable girl, but people change, Henrietta. If she had had the least desire to return, she would have done so by now. It stands to reason that she has made a new life for herself and one, moreover, with which she must be content.'

'You're a sensible girl, Emily.' Lady Barnsdale smiled fondly at her. 'And you may very well be right. I shall always feel indebted to Rachel. Her disappearance changed him, almost overnight, from a thoughtless care-for-nobody into a sensible, considerate man. Rachel was the making of him, though she will probably never know it.'

Her smile was replaced by a worried frown. 'But he still possesses a determined, stubborn streak, a characteristic of generations of the Carlton male. Callous though it might sound, I should feel much easier in my mind if he does discover that she has died.'

'It is quite evident to me, ma'am, that you are worrying unnecessarily, and it is equally evident that you have lost interest in the game, for I have won yet again. I suggest, therefore, that we repair to the other room.'

Their emergence was noted by several persons, including Viscount Linford, who had been for several minutes conversing with Mr Cheffingham.

'Ah! So you've met her, have you?' Cheffy watched as the younger man's eyes followed the lovely widow's progress across the room. 'Ravishing creature, ain't she, Linford? Been causing many a male heart to flutter since her arrival in town. But the mysterious Mrs Stowen shows no interest in any man.'

The Viscount drew his eyes away from his aunt's companion and fixed them on Cheffy's jovial face. 'What makes you call her mysterious?'

'Well, m'boy, nobody seems to know anything about her. And the name Stowen—never come across it before! She's deep, that one. Reminds me of an iceberg.'

'I found her charming, not cold in the least.'

'Ain't talking about cold, m'boy. But ain't icebergs those things with more below the surface than above? More to 'em than meets the eye. Just like the widow!'

'And in that you probably have the answer. She is a widow, Cheffy. Possibly, she believes herself to be vulnerable and, therefore, is reticent and wary with strangers.'

'You might be right—I don't know.' Cheffy shook his head. 'But I've been in her company a dozen times and more, and still know next to nothing about her. And another thing,' he went on, not giving Linford the chance to come to the lovely young widow's defence again. 'It was a demmed queer way she got to know your aunt. Fainted in the path of Hetta's carriage when your aunt was taking an airing in the park one afternoon. Sounds contrived to me.'

Amusement glinted in the Viscount's eyes. 'If I didn't know better, Cheffy, I'd say you were jealous of the young widow. You don't, perhaps, feel you're in danger of losing your exalted position as my aunt's closest friend?'

'No such thing!' Cheffy retorted, with as much vehemence as a man of his amiable disposition could muster. 'Hetta and I have been friends for a good many years now. And *only* that, no matter what the *on dits* in the past were suggesting. I'm very fond of her, and shouldn't like to see her get hurt. She's more vulnerable than you might think.

'She's grown unaccountably fond of that gel, Linford, unaccountably fond. She's never had children of her own, and it's my belief she's beginning to look upon that young woman as the daughter she never had.'

This gave the Viscount food for thought, for he, too, would hate to see Hetta made unhappy. His aunt, however, was a shrewd judge of character, and he had no intention of interfering in what was, after all, her private concerns. Added to which, he rather thought that, being much

younger than Cheffy, he viewed Emily Stowen in a far
different light.

This did not mean, however, that such a level-headed
man as he, and one who, moreover, had had no little
experience of the opposite sex, could become captivated
by a pair of beautiful green eyes.

Why, then, a few minutes later, when his aunt came over
to inform them that Emily had gone home, complaining of
a sick headache, did the evening suddenly become quite
flat? He left the ball himself soon afterwards.

# Chapter Two

**P**eplow sniffed loudly as he stared down at the coarse-looking individual cluttering the recently swept front steps. Had his master not informed him to expect a caller at noon, precisely, and to admit him without delay, he would have had no hesitation whatsoever in ordering a person of such low birth to use the service entrance.

His many years with the Carlton family had, however, left its mark, and he obeyed his lordship's instructions without question. Showing the caller, whose broken nose indicated possible pugilistic tendencies, into the library, where his lordship sat awaiting him behind his desk, he furnished the 'visitor' with a glass of brandy before quietly leaving the room.

The Viscount, too, subjected his caller to a swift appraisal. However, unlike Peplow, he was immediately struck by the keen intelligence behind the grey eyes, and suspected that those same eyes were assessing him with equal swiftness.

'You received my letter, Mr Stubbs,' he began, 'so you must have some idea of the profoundly difficult task I am asking you to undertake. And honesty prompts me to admit that I do not hold out much hope of a successful outcome.'

Henry Stubbs said nothing, only delved into the pocket

of his rough homespun jacket to draw out a notebook. 'Ah, yes! Your young bride disappeared some six years ago, a mere six weeks after the wedding took place, leaving your ancestral abode, you believe, in the evening, but her absence wasn't discovered until the following day.'

'I know it appears strange, Stubbs, but when I tell you my wife was a very solitary girl, who spent most of her time alone in her room, reading, then you might begin to understand the reason behind the delay. A maid discovered her absence the following morning but, as her bed appeared to have been slept in, no alarm was raised.

'There was a distant cousin of mine, a Miss Matilda Cartland, residing at the Hall at the time, and she thought my wife had merely gone out for a walk. It wasn't until the afternoon was well advanced that my cousin became anxious and set up a search.'

His lordship paused for a moment to sip his wine, his expression thoughtful. 'It's my belief my wife didn't sleep in her bed that night, but left the house, undetected, in the early evening. Where she did, in fact, sleep, I have no way of knowing, but the following day, early in the forenoon, she was taken up, just west of Farnborough, by a carrier.

'He brought her to London, setting her down at Holborn late in the evening. He watched her stop at a corner and speak to a man. Then she set off in an westerly direction. And that was the last anyone saw of her.'

'Apart from your good self, had she any relatives or friends living here, my lord?'

'Numerous relatives, yes. But her father had no dealings with his family, and I know she did not seek shelter with any one of them. Nor did she attempt to make contact with her mother, who was in Ireland at the time. When, eventually, the lady did respond to my letter, she assured me that she had not set eyes on her daughter since the day she left her former husband's house twelve years before.

'Rachel did not seek refuge, either, with her mother's elder sister, Lady Torrington, who did, in fact, reside in London, but who has since died.' Once again he became thoughtful, then went on, 'Although Lady Torrington was very concerned about her niece, certainly more so than the girl's mother appeared to be, she had been denied all contact since the child was four years old. It's unlikely, therefore, that Rachel would have realised that she had an aunt.'

'Then, it's safe to assume, my lord, bearing in mind she was heading west, that she was coming here to you.'

'That possibility certainly occurred to me, but if that had, indeed, been her intention, she never arrived.' The Viscount looked directly across the desk into the ex-Runner's shrewd eyes. 'I left the house on that particular night at eleven o'clock, and did not return until the following morning. My butler assured me that no one called, and I do not doubt his word.'

Once again Mr Stubbs referred to his notes. 'You tell me you had the Runners on the case, but they came up with nothing. Also, you placed advertisements in newspapers throughout the land, offering a substantial reward for information leading to your wife's safe return.'

Lord Linford nodded. 'I had some response, but every sighting proved bogus. As the months passed, I began to think she must be dead, and yet. . .' He raised his eyes from the contemplation of the liquid in his glass. 'In all probability my wife is dead, but I would like proof. I was an only child, and would certainly wish the fruits of my own loins to succeed me, therefore, I need an heir.'

'Very understandable, my lord. As you've said yourself, after all these years it'll be no easy task, but Henry Stubbs ain't a man to turn his back on a challenge. I must pay a call at Bow Street—see if any of my old colleagues remembers anything about the case. But first, I'll just jot down a few particulars. How old is your wife, my lord?'

'She was sixteen when she disappeared.'

'That would make her, now, two and twenty. And I'll need a description of the young lady.'

The Viscount groaned inwardly. It really was hopeless. So hopeless, in fact, that he came perilously close to telling the man seated opposite to forget the whole thing, but checked himself at the last moment.

'I remained with my wife for a mere five weeks after our marriage took place, and after all these years my recollection is hazy, but what I can tell you is that she had green eyes, and her hair—her hair was sort of—er—brownish in colour.'

'Dark. . .? Mid. . .? Light brown?'

'Mid to—er—dark, I think.'

'Height?'

'She was of average height. Her head reached my shoulder. So, yes, average height. And she was a trifle on the plump side.'

Mr Stubbs's shoulders shook. 'Don't mean a thing, m'lord. My daughter Bessie was a plump little pigeon at that age. Puppy fat, my good lady calls it. But Bessie's as slender as can be now.' He scratched his grizzled head. 'The trouble with the ladies, m'lord, they can change their appearance so easily—dye their hair, paint their faces.'

The Viscount sighed audibly. 'We're balked from the start, Stubbs, and you know it.'

'No such thing, sir!' the ex-Runner countered before tossing the contents of his glass down his throat and rising to his feet. 'I'd like at some point to take a trip into Hampshire with you, and have a talk with folk who knew your wife well. But I'll start my enquiries here. I'll be in touch, but don't expect to hear from me for a week or two.'

As soon as Mr Stubbs had been shown out, the Viscount

ordered his curricle and pair to be brought round from the mews, and within half an hour was wending his way through the busy London streets, heading towards Hyde Park.

It was long before the fashionable hour when the cream of Society showed itself abroad but, as he saw when he turned his spirited pair into the gateway, the park was far from deserted.

After a leisurely circuit, stopping from time to time to converse with several acquaintances, he was heading back towards the gateway when a slender figure on the grass, walking with her maid, caught his attention and he drew up alongside.

'Why, Mrs Stowen! Fortune has favoured me this day! You have recovered from your headache, I trust?'

She came to stand beside the curricle, and smiled up at him. 'Yes, quite recovered, my lord, and very much enjoying this wonderful May sunshine.'

Her loveliness lost nothing in what for many women was the cruel light of day. She looked enchanting in her green walking dress and fashionable bonnet, those gorgeous mahogany-coloured locks peeking from beneath its rim.

'Can I not persuade you to take a drive with me, Mrs Stowen? As you say, it's a lovely afternoon and ought to be enjoyed.'

'I should like to very much, sir, but unfortunately cannot leave my maid to find her way back to Upper Wimpole Street alone. She knows London so very little, you see, and your curricle was hardly designed for three persons.'

'No, indeed. So, I have a far better solution.' He turned to his groom, perched on the back. 'Jem, I'd like you to see this young person safely home.' He tossed the young man a sovereign. 'Walk, or take a hackney carriage if you wish, and then return to Grosvenor Square.'

After a few quietly spoken words to her maid, Emily clambered up beside the Viscount. 'I think Alice will be all right,' she said, glancing over her shoulder to see the girl walking shyly beside the friendly groom. 'She's reticent with strangers, men in particular.'

His lordship cast her a swift, searching glance, before turning left out of the park and weaving his way along a busy Piccadilly. 'You show a deal of concern for your maid, ma'am.'

She shrugged. 'I suppose I do, but Alice is very young. She's been with me for four years. My aunt and I came upon her in Bristol, fleeing from her drunken father who had been in the process of selling her for the price of a night's drinking to one of his degenerate friends. She was only thirteen—thirteen and being forced into prostitution. It is a very cruel world we live in, sir.'

'It is, indeed, ma'am. But the girl has found a caring mistress in you.'

'I'm the lucky one,' she countered. 'She might be young, but she's an excellent abigail—hard-working, honest and, most of all, loyal.' She fell silent for a moment, allowing him to negotiate the narrow space between a wagon and a lumbering coach, and then praised his skill. 'I should feel quite nervous of trying to wend my way through all this mayhem.'

'Practice, ma'am. That's all it takes.' He glanced at her delightful profile, noting the small, straight nose, and the way her top lip jutted out slightly. Yes, she had a sweet mouth, sweet and very kissable, he ruminated, and then forced himself to concentrate on the road ahead. 'I recall your saying you hail from the West Country. Do you live alone, Mrs Stowen, or have you a relative to keep you company?'

'I live quite alone, now,' she replied, an unmistakable note of sadness creeping into her pleasant voice.

'I'm sorry. Have you been widowed long?'

'I am not a widow, sir,' she astounded him by responding. 'My husband is, unfortunately, very much alive and well.'

'But I understood that—'

'From Mr Cheffingham, I do not doubt,' she cut in, her smile returning. 'Wicked of me, really, but when I met your aunt for the first time, I did say that my husband was no longer with me. Which is perfectly true. We live quite separate lives, and are content to have it so. But I admit I did know my remark would be misconstrued. However, Henrietta now knows that my husband is still alive, but has promised not to betray my secret.'

'I do not consider myself slow-witted, ma'am, but I do not immediately perceive your reason for wanting people to think you a widow.'

'That is because you're a man, sir.'

'I'm extremely gratified that you recognise me as such,' he responded drily, drawing forth a delightful gurgle of laughter from his highly amused companion.

'Believe me, my lord, there was never any doubt in my mind on that score. But, to be serious for a moment. I came to London for—for several reasons.

'Widowhood shrouds me in a positive fog of respectability whereas, were it to become common knowledge that I live quite apart from my husband, estranged for some years, it would give rise to a deal of speculation. And I have no desire whatsoever to be the object of every addle-pated gossip-monger's vulgar conjecture.'

Having had experience of this himself years before, when his wife had mysteriously disappeared, Lord Linford could quite understand her reasoning and smiled to himself. 'I do not consider myself amongst their number. Your secret is safe with me, ma'am.'

Once again he had to force himself to concentrate on

the road ahead, his dark brows drawn together in puzzlement. How any man who had the great good fortune to
have such a lovely creature for his wife could allow her
to live quite separate from him defied understanding.

The husband must be totally demented, he decided,
unless, of course, he was old and infirm, and the physical
side of marriage was no longer of interest to him. But, even
so, she was intelligent enough to stimulate him mentally, if
she could no longer do so physically.

His curiosity got the better of him, and he found himself
asking, 'Is your husband many years your senior, ma'am?'

'He is somewhat older than I—yes, sir.'

'Have you lived apart for very long?'

'Oh, yes. For several years, now.'

Again his brows drew together. 'You must have been
married very young?'

'A veritable babe, my lord!' This time her laugh was
mirthless. 'Far, far too young to be tied to such a loathsome, dissipated roué.' At his shocked expression she
turned her head away, thereby hiding the glinting amusement in her large green eyes, and caught sight of a lady
mounted on a lovely dapple mare. 'What a darling creature! I wish I could have brought Firefly with me.'

'You enjoy that form of exercise?' he enquired politely,
though still somewhat scandalised by her shocking disclosures.

'Very much so. I ride most every day when at home.
Firefly is a darling filly, but has a tendency to be skittish
at times. She would not have coped with London's hustle
and bustle at all well, and it would have been cruel to
bring her here.'

'Then, might I suggest that you make use of one of my
hacks. I keep several horses here in London, one of which
is suitable for a lady to ride. You are welcome to make
use of him whenever you wish.'

'That is most kind, my lord, but I couldn't possibly presume on your generosity after so short an—'

'Don't be commonplace, ma'am!' he cut in sharply, and then smiled at the unmistakable flash of anger in her eyes. 'Believe me, the arrangement would be to our mutual benefit. My horses do not get nearly as much exercise as they require. So, we'll take it as settled. I'll call on you— shall we say, at noon tomorrow?'

'I really ought not to accept, but your kind offer is so very tempting. I do miss my daily ride.'

'Give in to temptation, ma'am,' he urged gently. 'You'll enjoy it.'

He tooled his curricle round London for perhaps half an hour, pointing out various landmarks to his interested companion, before reluctantly returning her to her home, bringing his bays to a halt before a house situated about halfway down Upper Wimpole Street.

'Thank you, my lord. That was most enjoyable. I am quite sensible of the fact that it is something of an honour to be taken up by one of London's most famous whips. Everything I experience after this will, I'm sure, seem quite tame in comparison.'

'I want none of your flattery, my girl!' he returned, an appreciative smile curling his lips at her impish teasing, as he offered her a gentle helping hand to alight. 'Until tomorrow.'

He returned to Grosvenor Square in a very contented mood, the depression of the morning having completely lifted. He tooled his curricle round to the mews, and entered his house a few minutes later to be met by his faithful retainer who informed him, somewhat ruefully, that a visitor awaited him in the library.

The Viscount's brows rose. 'But did you not explain to him that you were unaware of when I would return?'

'I did, my lord. But "she" insisted upon waiting.'

'I see. How long has my aunt been here?'

'A little under half an hour, sir,' Peplow answered, relieving his master of hat and gloves before opening the library door for him.

'My dear Hetta. And to what do I owe the pleasure of this unexpected visit?'

'No reason in particular.' She tossed the journal which she had been reading aside, and watched him seat himself in his favourite winged-chair. 'You left the ball so abruptly last night that I had no time to ask if you will be attending Lady Somerville's drum tomorrow evening.'

'I have not received an invitation.'

'I know that. She didn't realise until last night that you had arrived in town, and asked me to invite you. Will you go?'

'Perhaps,' was his non-committal response. 'Will Mrs Stowen be attending?'

'Naturally. A young widow who is both lovely and well bred is invited everywhere.'

'A widow?' One black brow rose mockingly. 'Come, come, my very dear Hetta.'

'Oh, I see. She's confided in you, has she?'

'Indeed, she has,' he admitted. 'I had the great good fortune in coming across her in the park earlier, and offered her a seat in my curricle.'

He paused and stared across at her consideringly. 'You seem inordinately fond of that young woman, Hetta. You'll forgive me for saying so, but it isn't like you to take a complete stranger under your wing. Lovely though she undoubtedly is, I suspect it is your sponsorship which opens the doors to Society for her.'

'Initially, perhaps,' she conceded, 'but not now. You know yourself, Linford, that Society for the most part is peopled by fools. Scandal and intrigue are its gods. And

Emily Stowen is certainly a mystery, a juicy morsel to be chewed over and savoured.'

He frowned slightly. 'Yes, there's certainly more to that young woman than meets the eye,' he agreed, remembering his conversation with Cheffy. 'And strange, too, the way you met. Fainting in the path of your carriage—rather odd, don't you think?'

Lady Barnsdale raised her eyes heavenwards. 'You had that from Cheffy, I don't doubt. Well, for your information, Linford, she didn't faint. She caught the heel of her shoe in her gown and tumbled. There's nothing strange in that. Done it myself a score of times! I do not deny that at the time I wasn't best pleased, and took her roundly to task for her clumsiness.'

She chuckled at the memory. 'Don't be fooled by that fragile femininity of hers, Nevvy. Rounded on me like a virago. She wasn't blessed with that colour hair for nothing, you know.'

So, darling Emily was blessed with a temper, was she? Well, he ought to have guessed that, he mused, recalling the unveiled flash of anger in her eyes when he had been mildly reproving earlier.

'Yes, she's certainly a lovely, intriguing little darling. I think it behoves me to become better acquainted with her. Emily Stowen will provide just the stimulating companionship I need to help me while away the time whilst I remain in London.' But even as he said it, he knew that the reason he had given for pursuing his acquaintanceship was far from the truth.

The following day he arrived at Upper Wimpole Street just before noon. He was admitted to the house by a middle-aged butler who led the way up a narrow flight of stairs, and showed him into a small parlour overlooking the street.

He stared about him, frowning slightly at the solid, but drab furnishings. On one wall hung a painting, a portrait of a woman, richly clad in the fashions worn during the previous century, which seemed strangely out of place in its cheerless surroundings.

He heard a faint click, and swung round to find Emily framed in the doorway, a smile of amusement hovering about her mouth.

'Admiring the richness of my home?' she quizzed.

His rueful expression betrayed him. 'Like the portrait, here, you seem strangely incongruous in such surroundings.'

'Why, thank you. I shall take that as a compliment.' Elegantly attired in a stylish bottle-green habit, with a cascade of white lace foaming at her throat, she came slowly towards him. 'The place is not to my taste, I'll admit. But I can scarcely blame my man of business, who hired it on my behalf for the duration of the Season. I left it rather late in deciding to come to London, and the properties in the more fashionable areas had been snapped up months before. It did have one advantage, however. The gentleman who owns the house was prepared to leave it fully staffed whilst he travelled abroad, which has been of immense benefit to me.'

His lordship nodded as he glanced at the portrait once more. 'And the painting—was that left here, too?'

'No, sir. I brought that with me from Somerset. Like my maid Alice, it is something I cannot bear to be parted from for very long.'

He caught the unmistakable note of sadness in her voice, and looked at her searchingly. 'A relative of yours, ma'am?'

'I called her aunt, but Lady Anne wasn't a relation of mine. She did, however, rear me, you might say. She nurtured me—remoulded me. She was the only human being I have ever truly loved.' Her eyes sparkled, but this time with unshed tears. 'She died last autumn. . .and the pain of loss is still as strong as ever.'

She shook her head, as though trying to shake off a melancholy that threatened to engulf her, then said, with a decisiveness that characterised her, 'Come, sir. The past with all its memories, both happy and sad, cannot be altered, but a lovely new day awaits us, and I am eager for my ride.'

She led the way down the stairs and out into the street, exclaiming over the fine mount that he had brought for her to ride. She allowed him to toss her effortlessly into the saddle, and they rode along side by side, with his lordship's groom at a discreet distance behind.

Long before they had reached the park, the Viscount had satisfied himself that she was a very fine horsewoman. She sat the hack with effortless grace, handling the mount with easy competence, her light hands, deceptively, in full control of the far-from-sluggish bay.

They drew no little attention from the passers-by, and she remarked on this as they entered the park, 'Anyone would think we were a pair of fairground freaks, my lord!'

He smiled. 'London is not accustomed to seeing me ride, ma'am. More often than not I take the curricle whenever I venture forth.'

'In that case, it is apparent that I have deprived you of your favourite pastime, sir.' She cast him one of those teasing looks to which he was rapidly growing accustomed. 'But do not expect me to apologise, for you did offer. No,' she amended, 'insisted would be more accurate, would it not? For all your aunt talks of you often, she omitted to inform me of the forceful—I might go so far as to say bullying—nature you possess.'

'If I do possess a bullying nature, then I'm glad of it. It has provided me with the pleasure of your company

again. And do not deny, ma'am, that you are enjoying
your ride.'

'I shouldn't dream of it,' she told him primly. 'But do
not resort to your cavalier tactics too often, my lord. I do
not respond at all well to force and might retaliate.'

He laughed outright at this, drawing more eyes to glance
in their direction, but he was oblivious to the stares; she
held his full attention.

She really was an adorable creature. Teasing and fun-
loving, she was sheer joy to be with. He could quite
understand why his aunt liked her so much. He liked her;
had been attracted to her from the first.

No, there was more to it than that, much more than just
a man's natural desire for a beautiful woman. For some
obscure reason he felt, strangely, drawn to her. Was she
a kindred spirit, perhaps? That might well prove to be the
case; but common sense told him that their friendship
would be of short duration only, and would of necessity
need to be terminated once the Season was over: she to
go her way; he to go his.

He was experienced enough and wise enough to keep
a tight rein on sentiment, and would part when the time
came with pleasant memories and a whole heart, he
decided, sublimely ignoring that tiny voice of reason that
warned him that level-headedness and experience were
poor weapons when pitted against the strong pull of attrac-
tion and the powerful hold of those more tender emotions.

# Chapter Three

Lord Linford drew his eyes away from the actors on the stage, and fixed his gaze on the slender white neck of the lady sitting slightly to the right and in front of him. How lovely she looked tonight, dressed as she was in a rich red gown with a beautiful necklace of rubies and diamonds adorning her swanlike neck.

Most women with hair that colour could never wear red, but on Emily it looked wonderful. . .

But then, he reminded himself, she always looked magnificent, no matter what she wore.

He withdrew his gaze, for a few moments allowing his eyes to wander over the boxes on the opposite side of the theatre, and smiled. When they had taken their seats, they had been the cynosure of all eyes, but he had grown accustomed to that during the past few weeks.

No matter whether riding together in the park, or swirling round a dance floor, they had always attracted a deal of attention, and had given rise to a deal of conjecture, he mused, his smile widening.

The curtain came down on the first act, and Lady Barnsdale joined in the rousing applause. 'Was that not excellent?' she exclaimed as she, too, gazed across the theatre. 'I do believe the delightful Lady Rayne is trying to gain your attention, Linford,' she informed him as the acclaim died away. 'Do go over to her box and see what she wants. You can take Cheffy with you.'

Smiling crookedly, Linford obediently rose to his feet. 'Come, Cheffy. We have received our *congé*.'

'Eh, what's that you say. . .? Oh, right, m'boy. I'm with you. Could do with stretching my legs.'

'I do believe the old fraud was asleep,' Lady Barnsdale opined when the gentlemen had left the box.

'Well, ma'am, you did sort of bully him into coming.' Emily offered in his defence.

'Do him good. He spends far too much time at the gaming tables. Besides, I wasn't prepared to come with just you and Linford. Makes me look like a chaperon.'

'I'm in no need of a chaperon, Hetta. I'm quite capable of looking after myself. And Linford poses absolutely no threat to me—I assure you.'

Lady Barnsdale frowned in puzzlement. Although the words had been spoken lightly enough, she suspected they contained some hidden meaning. Turning her head, she gazed into the box opposite which her nephew had just entered, and her frown vanished.

Oh, but wasn't he being circumspect! She could have laughed aloud; only by exercising the firmest control did she prevent herself from doing so.

Even though he paid Emily a vast amount of attention, it appeared that only a strong friendship had blossomed between them. Perhaps he had managed to hoodwink Society as a whole, but he could not fool her, and she wondered whether he realised, himself, just how deep his feelings towards Emily went.

Again, she became thoughtful. Of her lovely young friend's state of mind, she was not so sure. That she enjoyed Linford's society was patently obvious, but equally apparent was her seeming indifference to whether he was in her company or not. Lady Barnsdale frowned slightly over this. Added to which, Emily never spoke of him when he was not present.

If his name had been brought up in the conversation at all, it had been she, herself, who had raised it. Odd, that, she mused. Was it simply a case of out of sight, out of mind? Or was Emily merely trying to be sensible by keeping her emotions firmly in check, as there was no possible hope of a deeper relationship developing?

Therein lay the crux of the matter, she knew. Linford was still determined to discover what had become of his wife; and even if he should discover that she had died, Emily was still not free to marry him. She released her breath in a faint sigh. Fate could be so cruelly unjust! Here were two young people absolutely made for each other, yet both were locked in loveless, disastrous marriages.

'I have enjoyed this evening so very much,' Emily said, breaking into her friend's depressing thoughts. 'In fact, I have enjoyed the whole of the Season, and think it a pity that it must soon come to an end.'

Lady Barnsdale's smile returned. 'And so have I, my dear. I have not had such a pleasurable time for years, and feel quite depressed at the prospect of leaving you at the end of the week.'

'Ah, yes! I have been meaning to speak to you about that,' Emily responded, rubbing her fingers lightly over a tiny crease in her lovely gown. 'If the invitation still holds, I should like very much to attend your niece's wedding, and spend a little time with you at your home before I return to Somerset.'

Lady Barnsdale was delighted. Shortly after they had first met, she had invited Emily to stay with her, but had received a non-committal response. 'Nothing would give me more pleasure. In fact, if you have no desire to remain in London for Almack's closing ball next week, why not

accompany me back to Surrey? It will save you the hire
of a carriage, and the journey will be more pleasurable
with a companion.'

'An admirable suggestion!' Emily smiled that glowing
smile which made her look so ridiculously young that it
was difficult to believe she was a married woman in her
twenties. 'I have no desire to see the Season through to
its end. It is time I was leaving London.'

Again, Lady Barnsdale became thoughtful. How little
she knew of this vibrant young woman. In fact, she knew
little more about her, now, than she had a week after
their first encounter. Cheffy had often referred to Emily
as mysterious. She had frequently twitted him over it, but
now began to think that he might not be so wrong after all.

She was given no opportunity, however, to begin any
inquisition, even had she been so inclined, for the door to
their box opened and, until the curtain was about to rise
on the second act, they were visited by a never-ending
procession of young gentlemen, who had eyes only for
Emily, and several old friends of her own.

It was not until the intermission before the final act,
therefore, that she was able to inform her nephew of
Emily's decision to leave London at the end of the week.

Only for an instant did his handsome countenance betray
disappointment, then he smiled. 'She will be company for
you, Hetta. And even though you will be depriving me of
hers, I promise I shan't hold it against you.'

Common sense had warned that Emily's departure was
bound to happen sooner or later, but a lowness of spirits
suddenly descended upon him. When the play finally came
to an end, he saw the ladies safely installed in his elegant
town carriage, with Cheffy as escort, and then set off on
foot to his club.

He remained at White's for an hour or so before setting
off on foot again in a northerly direction. Presently, he

entered a small, but fashionable, dwelling in a quiet part of the city. The servant who admitted him displayed not the least surprise at seeing him on the doorstep at such a late hour. Handing over his hat and cloak, the Viscount mounted the narrow flight of stairs, and quietly entered a brightly furnished apartment on the first floor.

Branches of candles were strategically positioned so that most of their light was cast upon the figure of his mistress, reclining gracefully on the ornately carved *chaise longue*. Her guinea-gold curls were loosely dressed and lay caressingly on her shapely, rounded shoulders. Her eyelids were closed, but she was not asleep, for the fingers of her left hand were gently stroking the overfed pug lying beside her.

Suddenly she opened her large, limpid blue eyes wide, and said, with every vestige of surprise, 'Why, Dominic! I was not expecting you tonight.'

He moved slowly towards her, his smile faintly mocking. 'I did not realise, my dear, that I needed an appointment.'

Her red painted lips pouted prettily up at him as he removed her pet, whose low growl made clear its displeasure at being so rudely thrust on to the floor. Altering her position slightly, to allow him to sit beside her, sent her frothy pink negligée, which did nothing to hide her ample charms, sliding from one white shoulder.

Desire leapt into his violet eyes. For a few minutes he kissed her long and hungrily, before lifting her pliant, sensual body into his arms and carrying her into the bed-chamber.

His expert lovemaking left them both exhausted: she to sleep soundly; but he, surprisingly, to stare blindly at the silken canopy above his head. His bodily needs had been assuaged, and yet he felt strangely unfulfilled. The first light of a new day began to filter through the window, and he turned his head to stare at the woman sleeping peacefully beside him. The tangled bedcovers had slipped down, exposing her full breasts.

On all other occasions, the sight of her feminine charms had never failed to arouse him afresh, but this time nothing within him stirred, not even the desire to caress her again. She possessed a well-rounded, pleasing figure now, he thought, but if she wasn't very careful, in a few years she would end up like that pampered lap-dog of hers: fat and unappealing.

Raising himself on one elbow, he gazed about the bed-chamber. In the soft glow of flickering candle-light, the furnishings had looked rich and warm, but in the revealing light of day he found Sophia's taste faintly tawdry. Even her expensive perfume, which the night before he had found so intoxicating, seemed cheap and overpowering.

He released his breath in a long sigh. He was so tired of this life he led: keeping one mistress until he grew weary of her, and then moving on to the next. He wanted a wife. . .no, more than that—a friend, a helpmate to walk beside him through life, to share in its joys and its sorrows.

His eyes returned to his mistress once again; but it was not guinea-gold curls and a full, sensual mouth he saw, but a delicately featured face, with a mat of rich red hair fanning itself out across the pillow towards him. Had he been a callow youth, he would have believed himself to be infatuated. He was, however, no impressionable boy, and he could deny the simple truth no longer.

For the first time in his life, he had fallen deeply in love. At last he had found that one woman with whom he wished to spend the rest of his life, though she was married and so—God help him!—was he.

But even these obstacles to their happiness were not insurmountable. He and Emily belonged together. They were so right for each other, so suited in every way. And nothing and no one, least of all his errant wife and her obviously uncaring husband, would keep them apart!

Without rousing the woman beside him, he rose from the bed, hurriedly put on his clothes and quietly let himself out of the house. The early morning air was coolly refreshing after the stifling atmosphere of the bedchamber, but he could still discern Sophia's sickly-sweet perfume clinging to him like a second skin, and wrinkled his nose in distaste.

Their liaison was definitely at an end; there was no room in his life for any woman, now, but one. And Sophia had no cause to repine. Her reign had been short, certainly, a mere few months, but he had been generous, and was prepared to allow her the use of the house until the lease expired. By which time, he did not doubt, she would have found herself a new protector.

His arrival at Grosvenor Square coincided with the rising of his household. Letting himself into the house by way of the front door, he saw his impassive butler descending the stairs, and demanded the bath in his dressing-room be filled as soon possible.

Some time later, refreshed and free from that over-powering scent, he returned downstairs, and was in the process of consuming a hearty breakfast when Peplow entered the parlour, his countenance wooden.

'The individual who came to see you a little under a month ago, my lord, has returned.' He sniffed. 'I have shown him into the library.'

The Viscount's lips twitched. Loyal and diligent his butler might be, but he really was an unmitigated snob. 'Tell Mr Stubbs I shall be with him shortly,' he said pleasantly, but the instant the door had closed behind Peplow, he frowned.

He had heard nothing from the ex-Runner since their

first meeting. Had Stubbs discovered something at last? he wondered. Or had he merely come to say that any continuance of the investigations into Lady Linford's disappearance was futile? As he entered the library a few minutes later, he could not quell the hope that it was the latter admission his visitor had come to impart.

'Good to see you, Stubbs,' he said, not quite truthfully, but sounding genuine enough. 'Have you some news for me?'

'Yes, sir. I believe I have.'

The Viscount invited his visitor to resume his seat before seating himself opposite. 'What have you discovered?' he enquired, but with a decided lack of enthusiasm.

'I paid a visit to Bow Street,' the ex-Runner began, 'but the officers who had worked on the case could tell me little more than you had already. One aspect of this business had puzzled me from the start. Apart from the carrier who dropped your young wife in Holborn, no one appeared to have seen her.

'A female walking our streets at night, alone, isn't uncommon, especially amongst those engaged in a—er— certain profession. But your young wife, I'm sure, wouldn't have been taken for a woman of easy virtue. No, she was dressed in a plain grey cloak and gown. Hardly the raiment of a lady of the night.'

'Well?' his lordship prompted.

'I began to ponder on who might have been likely to see her. Who at that time of night would notice a young female abroad on her own?' He looked directly into the Viscount's fine eyes. 'Hackney carriage drivers, my lord. They're always on the look-out for a likely fare before calling it a night. So, I starts visiting those taverns many of 'em frequent of an evening, and sure enough, at the White Hart Inn, I gets lucky.

'A jarvey by name o' Ben Lowe recalled an incident,

some years back, involving a young female on her own.
He was travelling down a street near Bloomsbury Square,
about to finish for the night and go home, when he comes
upon an accident. A girl in a dark cloak had been knocked
down by a carriage.

'He stopped and went over to see if he could be of help.
Taken up for dead, he told me. The groom picks her up
off the road and places her in the carriage. Lowe watched
the carriage move off and turn left at the end of the road,
travelling east. He were about to return to his own carriage
when he notices this lying on the road.'

From beneath his coat, Stubbs drew out a rag doll, rather
faded and decidedly the worse for wear. 'Ever seen this
before, m'lord?'

'Yes, I believe I have,' he said slowly, 'or something
very like. My wife had just such a doll. It was one of the
items missing from her room.' He raised his eyes to look
at the ex-Runner keenly. 'Dead, you say. Was the
jarvey sure?'

Stubbs's brawny shoulders shook. 'My lord, you don't
know these people like I do. Taken up for dead can mean
anything. The girl might merely have fainted, or been
unconscious. Which wouldn't have been in any way
marvellous, considering the poor lass had been
knocked down.'

'Yes. Yes, of course.' The Viscount rose abruptly, and
began to pace the room, trying to assimilate what he had
been told. 'This carriage involved in the accident—could
the jarvey recall anything particular about it? Had it, perhaps, a coat of arms emblazoned on its doors?'

'I asked him that selfsame question, my lord. And no,
he couldn't say with certainty. But he recalled that it was
an old, but elegant, vehicle, pulled by a good quality team.
It contained just one occupant—a lady, certainly not
young, as he recalled, but elegantly attired.'

'Which suggests a person of some means.'

'It certainly does,' Stubbs concurred. 'And Lowe was in no doubt that she was a lady—well-spoken and very distressed by the incident. Having satisfied myself on this point, I thought it more than likely that the unknown female would have taken the young person home and sought medical help.

'I approached several well-to-do physicians round and about that area to ask if they'd been called out to an accident victim on that particular night in May six years ago, but to no avail. So now, my lord, I mean to start a new line of enquiry. I want to talk to those folks who knew your wife well. Someone she might have sought refuge with—a friend, or perhaps a favoured governess.'

Knowing far more about his wife's formative years than the ex-Runner did, the Viscount was decidedly sceptical, but agreed to accompany Stubbs into Hampshire. 'I shall probably leave here early next week.'

Stubbs got to his feet. 'I'll be ready when you are, sir, if you just send a message to my home. And the doll, sir?' he added as an afterthought, turning back at the door. 'Do you want to keep it?'

The Viscount smiled. 'I should imagine it has been well loved since the jarvey discovered it.'

'Yes, sir. He has a daughter.'

'Then return it to her. I'd be a brute, indeed, to deprive the child of her toy.'

Stubbs's visit had left the Viscount with much to think about. Had he not met Emily Stowen, he might have experienced hope and no little excitement at the prospect of a successful outcome to the investigations. But he had met Emily; whether or not he ever discovered what had become of Rachel was a matter of complete indifference to him now.

He ordered his curricle to be brought round from the

mews and, after paying a visit to those noted jewellers Rundell and Bridge, went straight to Upper Wimpole Street.

Emily, seated at the escritoire, looked up, surprised, as he entered the room. Setting aside the letter which she had been writing, she rose and moved gracefully towards him. 'Did we arrange to go riding this morning? If so, I must apologise, for it completely slipped my mind.'

'No, my dear, we did not.'

He captured her hands, holding them gently, yet firmly, in his own, whilst his eyes devoured her lovely face with its intelligent forehead and brightly sparkling eyes. Dressed demurely in sprigged muslin that emphasised her slender, yet shapely, figure, she was the antithesis of the merely sensual woman in whose bed he had lain only hours before. Even Emily's perfume was refined: a delicate fragrance which reminded him of a fresh spring garden.

He released his hold to delve into the pocket of his jacket, and drew out a small square box. 'For you, my dear,' he said softly, placing the gift in her hand. 'A mere token of my sincere regard.'

She looked briefly into his eyes, betraying both surprise and uncertainty in her own, before opening the box to reveal a glistening brooch, a circlet of rubies and diamonds.

'My lord, it—it's beautiful. But I cannot possibly accept such a—'

'Of course you can,' he interrupted gently and, lifting the brooch from its bed of velvet, pinned it to the bodice of her gown. 'Yesterday evening we had little opportunity for private conversation. My aunt, bless her, is a dear, but there are times I could wish her at Jericho.'

He took a hold of her upper arms this time. 'Mrs Stowen—Emily, you must realise how highly I regard you,

and the mere thought that we are soon to part distresses me
more than I can say.'

He pulled her unresistingly closer, and fastened his lips
over hers. It was like holding some wild, frightened bird.
He could feel the fluttering of her heart against his chest,
and was both surprised and delighted by the trembling lips
of innocence beneath his own. He raised his head, a knowing smile curling his mouth for a few brief moments before
capturing hers again with gentle and persuasive expertise.

'My darling girl,' he husked, resting his cheek against
her soft curls. 'Stay with me. Be mistress of my
house. . .my heart.'

Instantly she stiffened and, freeing herself from his hold,
walked slowly back across the room to stand by the
window. 'So, I can become mistress of your home, can I,
Lord Linford?' The deceptively soft and velvety voice was
edged with venom. 'When first I become mistress of its
master, no doubt.'

'Emily, you don't understand.' He made to move
towards her, but she swung round with such a look of
undisguised loathing in her eyes that the explanation he
had been about to offer died in his throat, and he remained
rooted to the spot.

'Oh, but I do. I understand perfectly.' Her lip curled
contemptuously. 'Why, you're even more loathsome than
even I had first thought! Your infamous behaviour is no
secret. London is strewn with your discarded mistresses.
Did you honestly suppose yourself capable of adding me
to their number?'

Her laugh was mirthless; before he realised what she
was about, she had torn his gift from her gown and had
hurled it across the room.

Her aim was unerringly accurate. The brooch caught
him just above his mouth, one sharp glinting stone
inflicting a small, but deep, cut, before dropping to the

floor at his feet. She watched in silence as he drew out a
pocket handkerchief and pressed it to his mouth, his eyes
betraying both anger and stunned disbelief as he stared
at the small red stain spreading slowly across the fine
white linen.

'You have learned two valuable lessons this day, my
lord,' she told him, her voice now icy cold. 'Firstly, not
every woman is glaringly abroad with her aim. And sec-
ondly, not all women are beguiled by your evident
masculine charms. I have been given little reason to like
men. And you, sir, are a prime example of the sex I despise.
And if in the future I should be misguided enough to take
a lover, I assure you that you are the very last—'

'Enough, madam!' he cut in sharply, his eyes as coldly
disdainful as her own. 'I see, now, I have been grossly at
fault.' Gathering together the shreds of his dignity, he
bowed with less than usual grace. 'If I have caused you
distress or embarrassment by coming here this day, then
I ask your pardon, and shall relieve you of my unwanted
presence.'

He left without another word, stalking from the house,
his body rigid with barely suppressed rage. The breakneck
speed with which he returned to Grosvenor Square left
the young groom in no doubt as to his master's state
of mind.

Nor was Peplow under any illusions when the Viscount
stormed across the hall and into the library, slamming the
door closed behind him with such violence that the vase
placed on the nearby table looked in danger of toppling
to the floor.

The stiff brandy his lordship poured himself brought
little solace, but after half an hour or so, during which
time he pulled Emily's character to shreds, bestowing upon
her every epithet that sprang to his ever-fertile mind, from
a conniving strumpet to a cold-hearted vixen, his temper

began to ebb, leaving him bitterly resentful and deeply hurt.

If only she had given him the opportunity to explain! He reached for the decanter again, his hand not quite steady, and carried it over to his desk. Seating himself, he poured out yet another drink, and sighed deeply. He had never considered Emily as a possible replacement for Sophia. Lord, that had been the last thing in the world he had wanted!

But for a while, of course, it would have been impossible for them to legalise their union. Obviously, she had misunderstood completely, and in truth he had not expressed himself very well. But she had given him no opportunity to explain. No, there was more to it than that, he realised suddenly. She had desired no explanation. It seemed almost as if she hated him. . .but why?

Had the man she had married been so cruelly uncaring that he had soured her to all other members of his sex? Had he merely used her for a while, and then discarded her like an unwanted mistress? That, of course, was the most obvious explanation, and yet, when he had kissed her, he could have sworn that she was a complete innocent: untouched by any man.

He sighed again. Speculation would avail him nothing, and it hardly mattered now, anyway. He had felt hurt and humiliated when he had stormed from the house. Utter rejection was a new experience for him and one, moreover, with which he had not dealt very well, he conceded, smiling ruefully.

But he could not leave matters as they stood. He loved her still, and even though she might never return his love, there was no reason why they should not in the future meet as friends.

He reached for a sheet of paper, and began to draft a letter of explanation and apology. After several abortive attempts, he managed to pen a missive which moderately pleased him. Sealing the letter with a wafer, he wrote out her name in bold characters, and was about to write her direction beneath when something suddenly struck him as rather odd. If one rearranged the letters in Emily's surname, it spelt Weston, his wife's maiden name.

'How very strange,' he murmured, just as the door opened and his butler entered.

'I am sorry to disturb you, my lord, but a package has just been delivered with instructions that it be given to you at once.'

The Viscount, his anger returning, scowled down at the small square box, which Peplow had placed on the desk. That confounded jade had the unmitigated gall to throw his gift back at him a second time! Be damned to her then! Sophia, at least, would be pleased to have it. It would serve as a farewell gift.

Tearing up his carefully penned missive, he quickly wrote two brief notes whilst his butler waited by the desk. 'Have these delivered by hand at once,' he ordered. 'The package is to go with the second. And make ready. . .we leave for Hampshire in the morning.'

The Green Man at Linfield was not situated on one of the main post roads, but was well maintained and always busy. Two days later when Lord Linford entered the tap, there were several customers leaning against the counter, drinking the excellent home-brew for which the hostelry was famed.

Nodding acknowledgement to the landlord, he went into the coffee room, where he discovered his quarry sitting in one corner, reading a copy of the *Morning Post*.

'Good day to you, Stubbs. I trust you passed a comfortable night? Though why you found yourself unable to stay with me up at the Hall, I don't know.'

'It was kind of you to offer, sir,' the ex-Runner responded, rising to his feet. 'but I wouldn't have learned anything there.'

'And have you discovered anything?'

'Not much,' Stubbs admitted. 'As you told me, no one seems to remember your wife very well, sir. I had a chat with one or two of the locals last night. From what I can make out, her father weren't much liked.'

During the journey back to Hampshire, the Viscount had disclosed many details of his wife's early life, so that Stubbs was well prepared not to meet with a resounding success to his enquiries.

'No, he wasn't,' he concurred, leading the way outside into the bright morning sunshine. 'We'll see what the Reverend Mr Hodges can tell us. Not that I expect him to divulge any more than he did six years ago, when I first approached him about it. But if anyone can help, he can.

'His house is next to the church. It's only a short step up the road, but I left my curricle at the stables here, if you prefer to ride?' he offered, as the older man walked with a slight limp.

'Kind of you, sir, but I can manage the walk. The old wound only plays me up from time to time, and when the weather's bad.'

'How did you come by it?' Linford asked, as they set off along the main street. 'Pistol wound?'

'That's right, sir.' Stubbs chuckled. 'All in the line of dooty, as you might say. Chipped off a piece of bone and left the old kneecap as stiff as bedamned. That's why I had to leave the Runners. Well, stands to reason, sir, they couldn't employ a body who weren't able to chase after the villains. And a desk job at Bow Street wouldn't have suited Henry Stubbs.'

The Viscount smiled at his companion's matter-of-fact attitude. 'You've certainly done well for yourself since.'

'Aye, I have that. Would have been in a very sorry state, though, if it hadn't been for the kind-hearted actions of a certain gentleman. Paid all the doctor's fees, saw to it that my wife and I wanted for nothing whilst I was laid up, and set me up in business, as you might say. Yes, Mr Ravenhurst was real good to me. One of the best men I know.'

Lord Linford's dark brows rose sharply. 'Would that be Marcus Ravenhurst?'

'Aye, sir. That's the gent. Do you know him?'

'Yes. We were up at Oxford together, and used to spar at Jackson's Boxing Salon. Haven't seen much of him in recent years, though.'

'No, you wouldn't, m'lord. Married to one of the sweetest fillies you could ever wish to meet. Dotes on her, he does. He's got the reputation of being a hard, uncaring individual, but he ain't like that at all.'

'You're a shrewd judge of character, Stubbs,' the Viscount told him, smiling, as they arrived at their destination.

Mr Hodges's home was a small, but attractive, stone-built house, surrounded by a well-tended, pretty garden. His housekeeper opened the door to them, greeting the Viscount warmly before leading the way down a narrow passageway to the small study.

The Rector, a sparse man in his early sixties, with a crop of thick white hair which waved back from a high, intelligent forehead, was seated behind his desk. As the door opened, he looked up, his smile of greeting mirrored in his kindly blue eyes as he put down his pen and got to his feet.

'Visitors for you, sir,' the housekeeper informed him, showing the Viscount and his odd companion into the room.

Lord Linford introduced Mr Stubbs, and then made known the reason for their visit.

'Sad business, my lord,' he said solemnly before inviting them to sit down. 'I do not see that I can be of more help than I was before, but ask away, gentlemen.'

'You knew my wife far better than I did. I'd be grateful if you would tell Mr Stubbs everything you remember about her.'

'Poor little Rachel Emily,' he murmured almost to himself, and the Viscount looked at him sharply.

'Emily?' he echoed.

'Why, yes, my lord. Christened her myself when she was little more than eight weeks old. Sweet little baby she was. Saw something of her in those early years whilst her mother still resided up at the house. Then I didn't set eyes on her again until she was. . .oh, twelve, thirteen. She looked forward to my twice-weekly visits.'

He shook his head sadly. 'Tells you something about the life she led, does it not, my lord, when the poor child looked forward to having Latin and Greek drilled into her?'

The Viscount did not respond to this, but asked, instead, if there was anyone in her childhood of whom she had been particularly fond, and with whom she might have sought shelter.

'Didn't have any friends, my lord, excepting the cook and housekeeper, that is.' Mr Hodges frowned suddenly. 'No, wait a moment. . .! Yes, there was someone, one of the governesses engaged to teach her. She was dismissed by Mr Weston shortly before I began my twice-weekly visits.'

He looked up as the door opened, and his housekeeper entered, carrying refreshments on a tray. 'Mrs Wentworth, what was the name of that governess who wrote to me, asking after Rachel?'

'Prentis, sir,' she responded, smiling faintly as she

placed the tray down on to the desk and began to pour out the wine. 'Fooled the old devil good and proper there, I did, my lord. He dismissed that woman simply because little Rachel had grown fond of her. Evil old miser! He ought to burn in hell for the way he treated that little mite.

'Yes, I know, Mr Hodges,' she went on at the reproving glance he cast her. 'It's wrong to speak ill of the dead, but I can't help the way I feel about that wicked so-and-so.'

'Would that be Mrs or Miss Prentis?' Mr Stubbs put in before the housekeeper could continue her diatribe.

'She weren't wedded, at least not then,' the housekeeper replied, handing him a glass of wine. 'She was real fond of Rachel. Wrote to the girl several times, but didn't receive a reply. I reckon that old demon destroyed the letters, because Rachel certainly never saw them. Miss Prentis was that concerned she wrote to Mr Hodges, here, asking after the girl, and he replied to the letter.'

Again her lips curled with satisfaction. 'But I took Miss Prentis's letter up to the house, and gave it to the poor child. Yes, I know, Mr Hodges,' she retorted as she received a further reproving glance from her master, 'deception is sinful, and I knew you wouldn't have approved, and that's why I never let on at the time.

'But that poor mite had little enough joy in her life, and if receiving a letter, now and then, from someone who cared about her brought a little happiness, well, I'm not sorry I did it. Miss Prentis wrote here to me, my lord, and I took the letters up to the house, and dealt with the ones Rachel sent in reply.'

'That was kind of you, Mrs Wentworth,' he told her, ignoring the clergyman's tut-tutting. 'Do you happen to remember Miss Prentis's direction?'

'I haven't received any letters from her since I wrote and told her about Rachel's disappearance, my lord. But she did find employment, after she left old Weston, at a

seminary in Bath. I'm sure I've kept a note of it somewhere. I'll go and look.'

'Before you go, Mrs Wentworth,' he said, arresting her
progress to the door. 'You appear to have known Rachel
very well. Could you give Mr Stubbs here a description
of her? I'm afraid the details I furnished were, to say the
least, vague.'

Raising her eyes, she stared at an imaginary spot on the
wall behind him. 'I can see the little one, now, sat at the
kitchen table with the housekeeper and cook. The image
of her lovely mama, she was, with that beautiful red hair
and those sparkling green eyes.'

'Red hair?' the Viscount echoed, not hiding his conster-
nation. 'But, Mrs Wentworth, Rachel's hair was—was a
sort of brownish colour, surely?'

The housekeeper stared at him in open-mouthed astonishment for several moments, then burst out laughing.
'Now you put me in mind of it, sir, she did do something
to her hair, not long before you was wed. I mind she came
here to see me soon after you had returned to London.
The one and only time she ever set foot in this house.

'I asked her what she'd done to herself. That old devil
of a father of hers was always passing some nasty remark
about her hair. Brought back memories of his wife, I suppose. So Rachel tried to change it. Bought a dye from a
peddler who passed the gate one day, she told me. Assured
her it would turn her hair a beautiful raven-black. Lord,
what a colour! Horrible greenish-brown it were. She did
look a fright.

'And she'd put on a deal of weight, as I recall. Not
surprising, though, considering the cook fed her nothing
but sweetmeats whenever the girl ventured down to the
kitchen.'

'You're sure her hair was red?' Mr Stubbs asked, frowning dourly in the Viscount's direction.

' 'Course I am! Unusual colour it were. Real dark red, not carroty-coloured. Always put me in mind of the table in the parlour, didn't it, Mr Hodges?'

He nodded, smiling. 'I am not one to take a deal of notice of a person's outward appearance, my lord. But that hair I can never forget. . .it was the colour of mahogany.'

'Oh, what am I about!' the housekeeper exclaimed suddenly. 'I can show you exactly what she was like, sir. When Mrs Weston took off all those years ago, the old man ordered all her personal belongings destroyed. But the housekeeper kept a miniature of her mistress. Hid it away, so the master wouldn't find it.

'When she left your service a couple of years back, my lord, the children up at the house having got too much for her, she came across the miniature whilst she was packing, and brought it here to me. Asked me to give it to Rachel, if ever she returned. I'll fetch it for you.'

The Viscount did not respond. He was in the grip of such an astonishing premonition that he did not even hear one single word of the conversation which passed between the other two men whilst Mrs Wentworth was out of the room.

She came back presently, and placed the miniature into his hand. He stared down at it in silence, his face draining of every vestige of colour.

There was the sound of a tiny crack as his long fingers curled round the delicate gilt frame. 'By God, I'll be hanged for murdering her yet!' he rasped suddenly through gritted teeth, drawing three pairs of startled eyes to turn in his direction. Swiftly, he rose to his feet. 'Your investigations are now at an end, Stubbs. . .I know, precisely, where my Viscountess is to be found.'

## Chapter Four

**E**mily smiled contentedly as she gazed about the sweetly perfumed rose garden. It had been yet another glorious June day. Rather too warm for any strenuous activity, perhaps, but now a light breeze was fanning the Surrey landscape, making the late afternoon stroll very pleasant.

Raising her eyes, she stared along the western aspect of the fine Tudor mansion. Set in a small area of parkland, the house had been erected by Thomas Barnsdale in 1536. Succeeding generations had added to the original building, thankfully without spoiling its appearance, so that it now boasted fourteen bedchambers and as many reception rooms.

A sigh escaped her as she transferred her gaze to her companion. 'It's none of my business, I know, but I cannot help feeling, Hetta, that you're making a big mistake in leaving here.'

'It wasn't a decision I made lightly,' she confessed. 'But the house is far too large for just me, Emily. It's a family home and needs children. Besides, it's too late now to change my mind.

'The new owner will be taking up residence in a few weeks. And I have been lucky in managing to find someone willing to purchase all the livestock at the home farm, and take the house with most of its furnishings, which I certainly shan't require, of course, when I purchase my house in Bath.'

'I wasn't suggesting you should remain here, Hetta. You are absolutely right—it is too large for you on your own. But you've lived in Surrey more than half your life. Your sister lives only three miles distant and Cheffy less than that. You'll be leaving many friends behind. Why not look for a smaller dwelling in the area?'

Lady Barnsdale's eyes narrowed suspiciously. 'Has Cheffy been talking to you? I thought as much,' she went on at her young friend's guilty expression. 'He's turning into a real mother hen. I'm quite capable of looking after myself. Good heavens! I've been doing so since my husband died. And Bath will suit me very well. Besides which, I shall be near you.'

'Not that close,' Emily countered. 'I live some thirty miles distant.'

'But you'll visit me, won't you?'

'Of course I shall, and I hope you will stay with me, but. . .' Emily entwined her arm round the older woman's '. . .do something for me, Hetta. Do not rush into buying a house there. Rent one for a few months. Use the time to decide if Bath suits you. It doesn't suit everyone, and I rather think with your temperament you'll find the place a trifle flat.'

'Very well, child. I'll take your advice.' Lady Barnsdale smiled fondly as she patted her friend's arm. 'I imagine it must be time for dinner. Shall we go back inside?'

The table had been laid, and an eager young footman was ready to serve as they entered the small informal dining-room. They had just seated themselves when they heard the unmistakable sounds of an arrival. One of Emily's finely arched brows rose questioningly, and Lady Barnsdale looked far from pleased.

'If that's Cheffy again, descending on us just as we're about to dine, I'll box his—' She broke off as the door opened, her grey eyes widening in astonishment. 'Great heavens. . .! Linford! What in the world brings you here?'

Emily's spoon dropped from her suddenly limp fingers, landing in her soup bowl with a clatter. She muttered under her breath as she dabbed at the splashes on the bodice of her gown with a napkin, and then bestowed such a dagger-look on the visitor, as he came towards the table, that he burst out laughing.

'My arrival does seem to have discomposed you both.' He placed a chaste salute on his aunt's cheek, and then turned to the younger woman. 'Mrs—er—Stowen, I trust I find you well?'

'Oh, we have had a wonderful two weeks together,' Lady Barnsdale said hurriedly, after a swift glance at her young friend's angry, set features. 'The time has simply flown by. Well, do sit yourself down, Linford. . . Grimshaw, set another place!'

She waited until her orders had been carried out, and her nephew had been served, before enquiring about the reason for the unexpected visit.

One black brow rose. 'Need you ask? My memory over certain things, I'll admit, has been known to be faulty. But I was under the distinct impression that there was shortly to be a celebration in the family.'

'Ha! And you so fond of your cousin Charlotte that you couldn't bear to miss her wedding, I suppose?'

'Quite so,' was his only response to this sally.

She eyed him suspiciously, her keen gaze noticing the slight blemish on his handsome face. 'What's that mark, Nevvy, just above your top lip?'

He dabbed at his mouth with a napkin whilst his eyes moved fleetingly in the younger woman's direction. 'I was attacked, quite unnecessarily I thought, by a vicious little cat.'

'Ha!' his irrepressible relative barked again. 'The two-legged variety, I'll be bound!'

'Really, Aunt Hetta! What will your young guest think?' His smile was not pleasant. 'Now, I put it to you—what do you do with a creature that turns on you for no reason, when only moments before she had been purring beneath your caressing touch?'

'Drown the blighter!' she answered unequivocally. 'Can't keep vicious animals about you, Nevvy. Besides, can't abide cats.'

Emily, who had sat silently eating her broth throughout the whole interchange, looked up at this, her lips curling into a decidedly mischievous smile. 'Oh, I don't know, Hetta. Cats do have their uses, you know. They are extremely adept at ridding one's home of unwanted pests, especially vermin.'

Linford's shoulders shook in silent, but appreciative, laughter. Then he changed the subject, asking his aunt if she still intended selling her four-year-old gelding.

'Interested, Dominic?'

'Yes. I've just sold two of my hacks, and I've always had a fancy for that grey of yours.'

The conversation continued along these lines for several minutes before becoming general. As soon as the meal was over, Lady Barnsdale invited Emily to join her in the drawing-room, leaving her nephew to his port. He did not linger long, and presently went across the hall to rejoin the ladies, one black brow rising mockingly when he discovered his aunt quite alone.

'Poor, darling girl. Succumbed to a sick headache, I suspect.'

Lady Barnsdale's lips twitched. 'I'll say this for you, Linford, you never need things explaining.' She became serious suddenly, watching him intently as he took the seat opposite. 'One thing I should like explained, though. . . What has happened between you two?'

Again his brow rose. 'What should have happened, pray?'

'I don't know, but something most certainly has. Emily has been with me, here, for two whole weeks, and each time I've mentioned your name, she's changed the subject.'

'Why not ask her?'

'I see. So you don't intend to satisfy my curiosity. Very well, but you can at least tell me, now that we're alone, what has really brought you here?'

'Family matters, ma'am. What else? And I certainly do want to take a look at that gelding.' He smiled at the infuriated look she cast him. 'By the by, I'm not inconveniencing you, I hope, by descending on you uninvited?'

'No, we've plenty of room. I've ordered a bedchamber made ready.' She sighed. 'I wish, now, I hadn't promised Augusta that I'd hold the wedding breakfast here, but her house is so much smaller that it would have been unkind to refuse. There'll be several people arriving tomorrow, including my very tedious brother, and his equally tedious wife, bringing with them their idiotish son.'

She looked at him steadily for several moments. 'I wish you would do something about that, Linford. I have never made any secret of the fact that your father was my favourite. I adored him. Clive I have never cared for overmuch. And when I think that that nincompoop of a son of his might one day take your place. . .well, it grieves me more than I can say.'

'It wouldn't please me overmuch.'

'Then, for heaven's sake, do something about it!' she snapped, but could not prevent a smile at the mocking glance he cast her. 'Oh, very well. So you have been trying. Have you discovered anything yet?'

'About what, pray?'

'Your wife, of course! Oh, Linford, you can be so infuriating at times!'

'When you get angry, my dear, you put me in mind of a ruffled hen,' he told her, but then relented. 'The man I engaged to investigate the matter is no longer working on my behalf. I paid him off. Very handsomely, as it happens.'

'Does that mean you've abandoned the idea? That you're no longer continuing the search for Rachel?'

'Quite correct.'

'Well, I cannot pretend I'm sorry, Linford. I thought it a nonsensical idea from the start.' She adopted a look of innocence as she stared down at her hands resting in her lap. 'I suppose you'll now be on the look out for a new wife?' There was no response, and she looked up to find his mocking smile had returned. 'Oh, very well. I cannot deny I had high hopes for you and Emily. . . Oh, Linford, she's so right for you!'

'I've never found your judgement faulty, Hetta.'

Like an excited child, she gave a crow of delight as she clapped her hands together. 'You'll need to make up your differences first, though. And don't try to tell me you haven't quarrelled, because I know you have.'

She paused, her eyes narrowing. 'You'll need to get her on her own. Yes, that would be best. She'll be at the church tomorrow morning, decorating it with flowers. I know it isn't the norm to do so, but it's such a plain little building that we decided a few flowers at the altar would brighten things up. Go to her there.'

Linford refused to commit himself.

But the next morning, after inspecting the gelding and informing his aunt that he would take him off her hands, he went to the church in which Charlotte was to be married the following day. It appeared deserted, and he was about to leave to search elsewhere, when he heard the sound of humming emanating from the vestry.

As if sensing that she was no longer alone, Emily turned from the table at which she was working to find the Viscount, his broad back propped against the doorpost, regarding her with an infuriatingly smug grin on his handsome face.

'What the hell are you doing here?' she snapped, making it abundantly obvious that she was anything but pleased to see him.

'Tut! Tut! Such language from a lady. And in the house of God, too! I am here to escort you home.'

'I do not require your escort, sir. So kindly remove yourself and find someone else to annoy.'

'You know, my darling, you really do deserve to be soundly smacked,' he informed her lightly. 'But I still think you adorable.'

Ignoring the tiny gasp of outrage, he walked slowly towards her. She did not attempt to move away as he reached her side, but continued to focus her attention on the flower arrangement on which she had been working before his arrival. He stared down at her lovely profile, noting the stubborn set of that determined little chin, and sighed.

'Come, let us call a truce, my darling. At least until this confounded wedding is over. It would make my aunt happy.'

She paused in the act of picking up a rose to glance up at him. 'Yes, I know it would,' she said softly. 'Very well, Linford. For Hetta's sake I'll agree to that. But kindly refrain from addressing me in that fashion. I am not "your" anything.'

'Are you not?' he purred silkily like a satisfied cat, and

this time her glance up at him was decidedly wary, but she regained her composure almost at once.

'If you are determined to stay, then you can make yourself useful by trimming those stems.'

He obediently picked up the knife, and for a short while they worked together in silence, but then he broke it to ask, 'How long do you intend remaining with Hetta?'

'I shall leave the day after tomorrow,' she answered without taking her eyes off the beautiful arrangement she was creating.

'Unfortunately, Alice contracted a severe chill before I left London, and I was unable to bring her with me. Although the housekeeper there has taken a marked shine to the girl, and has promised to take very good care of her whilst I'm away, I couldn't with a clear conscience abandon her for longer than is absolutely necessary.'

'May I make a suggestion, if you do not think it too presumptuous of me? I noticed the paint work is scratched on my travelling carriage, and intend returning it to the coachmaker for repair. I know Hetta has offered you the use of hers, but it would make sense, would it not, to return in mine as it will be making the journey anyway?'

'That is kind of you to offer, sir, but—'

'I shall not be returning to London,' he put in, 'if that is the objection which prevents you.'

She had the grace to blush at this, and did not attempt to deny the truth of it. 'Very well,' she said, after several moments' thought. 'I shall accept your kind offer. But how will you manage?'

'I'm taking Ramon off my aunt's hands. I shall take him back to Hampshire.'

'You'll ride?' She turned wide, startled eyes up to him. 'But it must be fifty miles or more!'

'I have not as yet entered upon my dotage, ma'am,' he informed her tartly, but with such a decided twinkle in his dark blue eyes that she gurgled with laughter, which in turn drew a warm smile to his well-shaped mouth. 'You are a darling, you know. I never meant to upset you.'

She reached for another bloom, her hand not quite steady. 'Hetta isn't much like her sister, is she?'

He smiled at the rapid change of subject. 'No, thank God! Whenever I see Aunt Augusta, which thankfully isn't often, she's either just recovering from an illness which very nearly took her off, or experiencing the symptoms of one which is sure to do so. Sickness and death are a neverending source of interest to her. What a Tragedy Jill the woman is! Still,' he shrugged, 'it cannot be much fun being married to that devilish dull husband of hers. And producing and rearing that brood of puling brats would destroy anyone's zest for life.' He frowned suddenly. 'How many has she now? Seven? Eight?'

'She has five children, sir,' she informed him, desperately trying to control a quivering lip. 'Charlotte is the eldest, and the one who is getting married tomorrow to a certain Mr Frederick Penrose, the Squire's youngest son, in case you have forgotten.'

'No, I hadn't forgotten, because Hetta never told me. She probably knew I would, though, so didn't think it worthwhile mentioning in the first place.'

Another gurgle of laughter escaped her. 'You are an abominable person, sir!'

'Beyond redemption, my darling. . .well, almost. You could reform me.'

A slight blush added colour to her cheeks as she placed yet another flower in the arrangement. 'Your uncle and family will be arriving this evening, I understand.'

'Yes, unfortunately. He's another I try to avoid whenever possible.'

'You do not appear to hold your family in very high esteem, my lord.'

'With the exception of Hetta, I'm quite content to consign them all to the Devil. I have never looked upon you as a possible mistress, you know.'

She released her breath in a tiny resigned sigh. 'I should prefer not to discuss what passed between us that morning.'

'If that means you'll put the unfortunate episode behind you and begin afresh, then I'll never mention it again.'

'Consider it forgotten,' she responded without a moment's hesitation.

The little church looked cheerful, decorated with the vases of beautifully arranged flowers. The ladies in the congregation, many of whom were dressed in the finest the famous London modistes had to offer, added their splendour to the occasion. Even the bride, who by no stretch of the imagination could be accounted a beauty, was unanimously thought to look charming in her cream-coloured gown and matching silk bonnet.

When the ceremony finally came to an end, the guests piled into the waiting carriages, and wended their way along the narrow lanes to Lady Barnsdale's home. A sumptuous wedding breakfast awaited them, laid out on the long table in the great hall.

When most of the delicacies had been consumed, the guests began to congregate into small groups, some to disappear into the room laid out for cards, whilst others, mainly the younger people present, went into the large salon where musicians, hired for the occasion, were playing a selection of country dances.

Lady Barnsdale broke off her conversation with a group of neighbours, and looked about her for Emily. She finally ran her young friend to earth in one of the smaller salons, sitting beside the bride's mother on a sofa, a look of comical dismay on her lovely face.

'Ah! There you are, my dear. You have a great deal to thank this young woman for, Augusta,' she said, turning to her woeful-looking sister, who had just been bemoaning the loss, forever, of her dear sweet daughter, sublimely disregarding the fact that Charlotte, after the honeymoon was over, would be living not two miles distant from her.

'It was she who arranged these beautiful flowers you see here, and those in the church. But I cannot allow you to monopolise Emily. There is someone simply dying to have speech with her,' and, so saying, she took hold of her young friend's arm, and then guided her from the room.

'Who desires speech with me, ma'am?'

Picking up two glasses off the tray a young footman held, Lady Barnsdale chuckled. 'I do. And do not deny that you needed rescuing.'

Emily's smile was a trifle rueful as she took the glass of champagne Lady Barnsdale held out. 'I was only saying to Linford, yesterday, that you and your sister are not much alike. In looks a little, perhaps, but not in character.'

'No, neither of us was blessed with any degree of beauty.' She glanced across the lofty hall to where her nephew stood with Cheffy, her brother and his son.

'I think I told you before that, in our family, it's the men who are blessed with all the looks. Linford's father was a handsome devil, and his son is his image. Clive, too, was a well-looking man, but has sadly gone to seed. Look at the girth on him! Why, I do believe he's bigger even than Cheffy! And as for Cedric. . .'

Emily looked at the young man, standing beside his taller and much broader cousin. He had inherited the Carlton colouring: black hair and blue eyes; but there the similarities between them ended. Even their tastes in dress were vastly contrasting: Linford was always impeccably,

but quietly, attired; whereas his young cousin aped
the dandy.

'You are not overly fond of Cedric, are you?'

'Oh, I've nothing against the boy, Emily. I consider him
a moonling, and it a complete waste of time his being up
at Oxford, but he's pleasant enough. No, it isn't that.'
She sighed audibly. 'I cannot envisage Clive ever taking
Linford's place, but it isn't beyond the realms of possibility
that Cedric might one day do so. And I just cannot bear
the thought of his stepping into Linford's shoes.'

Emily stared down into the contents of her glass.
'Linford is still a young man, Hetta. Time, yet, for him
to marry again and produce an heir.'

The older woman's lips curled into a secretive little
smile. 'Yes, I know. He's given up looking for his wife,
by the by. Did he tell you?'

'No, he didn't. But, then, he never has discussed her
with me.' One finely arched brow rose. 'He never stood
the remotest chance of finding her, you know. . . Never
will, unless she chooses to be found.'

'If that's the case, then I hope to God she never does
choose to be! They weren't in the least suited.'

'No, I know.'

Lady Barnsdale looked at her sharply. 'How do
you know?'

'You told me.'

'Did I?' She shrugged, and then looked over at her
favourite nephew again. 'Linford has frequently been
maligned unjustly, I consider, for his rakish habits, but
should he ever be fortunate enough to marry the woman
of his choice, I'm sure, like his father before him, he'll
be a faithful and devoted husband. And I desperately want
to see Linford happily married.'

She fixed her gaze on Emily again. 'He's leaving in the
morning. Did you know?'

'Yes, he did tell me that. And so, too, am I. I must go to my room presently, and begin packing.'

The following day, only Lady Barnsdale stood outside to bid Emily farewell. She did this tearfully and very unwillingly, but eventually allowed her young friend to enter the carriage, and then waved a final goodbye.

Resting her back against the plush velvet squabs, Emily sighed with relief. At last it was over: the pretence was finally at an end. She would be in London in a few hours, and back in Somerset by the end of the week. She must put Linford and past hurts behind her once and for all, and begin afresh.

This was a pleasant prospect, and yet she had, surprisingly, felt a little hurt when he had left his aunt's home without bothering to seek her out to say farewell. He had, no doubt, left very early because he had a long ride ahead of him.

She ought, she supposed, to feel guilty at depriving him of his exceedingly comfortable travelling carriage, but she did not. No, not a whit! After all, she mused, smiling rather wickedly, who had more right to travel in his lordship's carriage than she, his wife—Rachel Emily Weston Carlton, Viscountess Linford?

She gurgled at the irony of it all as she removed her bonnet and tossed it on the seat beside her. It was going to be another hot, sultry day. Already, the coach felt stuffy and uncomfortable. She let down the windows, allowing what little breeze there was to pass through the equipage, and then leaned against the seat once again, her mind going back to a certain very sad autumn day the year before.

'You must go back and see your husband, child. You must do the honourable thing. Promise me. . .'

Lady Anne Norton's words came back so clearly that she might have been sitting on the seat beside her. Rachel's

vision became blurred with unshed tears. How could she
have refused a dying woman's last request?

How could she have said 'nay' to the woman who had
picked her up off a London street, and who had taken her
into her home, bestowing such loving care on her that in
the space of six years she, the miserable and unloved girl,
had changed into an elegantly poised and happy young
woman? She had not refused. Of course she had not; but
honesty prompted her to admit that she had scarcely done
the honourable thing.

It would have been a simple matter to write to Viscount
Linford, to inform him that she was still very much alive
and well, and to suggest an annulment to a marriage which
ought never to have taken place. But, no—some perverse
little demon had prompted her to go to London and to
seek him out. Her appearance had changed so drastically
that she had experienced no qualms at all at being
recognised.

Smiling, she shook her head, marvelling at her own
simplicity. Meeting Lady Barnsdale had been contrived
easily enough. And that, she realised now, had been a
great error of judgement on her part.

She had needed Hetta as a passport into Linford's
society, but she had not allowed for the possibility that
she might genuinely grow fond of a woman whose very
presence had terrified her six years before. Henrietta was
an outrageously outspoken, darling woman who was going
to be sadly hurt when she discovered the truth, as discover
it she must. . .

And what of Linford? Would he, too, be hurt when he
received the letter that she must now write, or merely
angry? He was capable of great anger. He had been furious
when she had thrown his gift back at him; and she was
rather glad that when he did eventually discover the truth,
she would be many miles away, safe in her Somerset home.

What on earth had possessed her to go to London in the first place? she asked herself. Why had she contrived to get near him again? Rampant curiosity, she was honest enough to admit. After their long separation, she had wanted to see if he, too, had changed very much. He had not. He was as handsome as he had been at the age of four and twenty when they had married; if anything, a little more so, now that age had matured his features slightly.

Her frown descended as she recalled that auspicious first meeting at the Rayne Ball. She had been instantly aware that he had found her desirable. A sudden thirst for revenge had been all-consuming. How she had wanted to hurt him as much as he had hurt her six years ago! She had wanted him to fall desperately in love with her, and then, her purpose achieved, she would have walked out of his life without so much as a backward glance.

The desire had remained with her for, perhaps, a week after that first meeting. Loath though she was to admit it, even to herself, but there had been times when they had been together, riding in the park or dancing, when she had almost forgotten who he was and, more especially, what he was—a callous, unfeeling rake of a husband who had left her with his empty-headed cousin, whilst he had caroused in the arms of his mistress!

Hurt welled, and she hated herself for experiencing it, still, after all these years. Linford meant nothing to her, and the sooner she was free of him, the better!

She turned her head to stare at the passing countryside, and forced herself to think about the next few days when she would be fully occupied in making arrangements for her return journey to Somerset, but after a while the gentle rocking of the comfortable carriage had its effect, and her eyelids grew heavy and eventually closed.

She was rudely awoken by a sudden and violent jolting, which very nearly sent her sprawling on to the floor. 'What on earth. . .?' she muttered, staring out of the windows at the high hedges on either side of the narrow, deeply rutted lane. They had not travelled along this road to Hetta's home, surely? She felt certain they had not. The journey into Surrey had been made along much wider roads for the most part, and none with such an uneven surface.

Rising from the seat, she poked her head out of the window. 'Jem! Jem!' she called, knowing the groom quite well after the many times he had ridden with Linford and herself in the park. 'This is not the road to London, I'm sure.'

His head appeared over the side of the carriage. 'No, ma'am, it ain't. There were a fallen tree back along, and we was forced to turn off the main road. Sorry about the bumps, ma'am. It won't be long before we're on a better surface.'

Sure enough, after another two miles or so, they came to a junction, and the carriage turned left on to a much smoother road, wide enough for two carriages to pass. Catching sight of a milestone, Rachel peered out of the window and looked back to read 'FARNBOROUGH 10 MILES'.

Farnborough? They were in Hampshire and, what was worse, travelling in the totally wrong direction. She was about to call to Jem again, to demand an explanation, when the coach turned off the road, and came to a halt outside a small wayside inn. The offside door was suddenly thrown wide, and a large figure loomed in the aperture.

'What in the world are you doing here?' she demanded, wide-eyed with astonishment.

# *Chapter Five*

Viscount Linford stood regarding her, unsmiling, for endless moments, then, grasping her wrist, pulled her towards him, and lifted her effortlessly out of the coach.

'Come,' he said curtly, taking a firm hold of her arm. 'A light luncheon awaits us within, and I do not wish to delay. We still have a fair way to travel before evening.'

Somewhat bemused, Rachel allowed him to lead her willy-nilly into the inn, across the coffee room and into the small, private parlour, where a young woman had just finished placing several dishes on to the table.

'Thank you, Margaret. I shall call if I require anything further.' The Viscount waited until the door had closed behind her before pulling out one of the chairs. 'Come, madam, seat yourself! You must be hungry by now.'

'I do not understand you, sir.' She regarded him frowningly, her green eyes betraying her genuine bewilderment. 'Are you trying to tell me that you have decided to travel to London, after all?'

His smile as he began to carve the chicken was not pleasant. 'We are not going to London, Rachel. We are going home to Linford Hall.'

Rachel. . .? He had called her by her given name! Fearing her legs would give way, she slumped down on to the chair which he had drawn out for her. He knew! But how? She glanced briefly into eyes that looked mockingly down at her.

'I'm glad you possess the sense not to try to deny it. It would be futile, my dear, believe me.'

'How long have you known?' she asked, her voice not quite steady.

'Not very long.' Again his smile was far from pleasant. 'Have the satisfaction of knowing that, during our time together in London, I never for one moment suspected that you were my errant Viscountess.

'What amusement you must have derived from my crass stupidity! And, my dear, I was stupid. Unbelievably so! I thought there was something familiar about you the very first time we met. And your name, Stowen—I had never come across it before. Very clever, that. You are to be congratulated. Even when I had worked out that little conundrum, idiot that I am, it still never dawned on me.'

She reached for the wine he had poured her and took a large swallow, hoping it might help to calm her nerves and gather together her scattered wits. 'How did you find out?'

'The Rector's housekeeper, Mrs Wentworth, knew you very well when you were a child. That hair of yours was your undoing. I have never come across quite that shade of red before. Her description left me in little doubt, even before she presented me with a miniature of your mother. You bear a marked resemblance to her—did you know?'

He placed several slices of chicken on her plate. 'Come, eat! You are looking decidedly pale, and I do not wish you to fall into a decline even before I have restored you to your home.'

This brought the colour back into her cheeks. 'Linford Hall has never been my home, nor shall it ever be! I am returning to London.'

He made no response to this, but sat himself down, and began to help himself liberally from the various dishes, much to her intense annoyance.

'A gentleman would not sit gorging himself in the presence of a lady,' she informed him tartly.

'Don't be tiresome, Rachel. I've told you already, I do not wish to delay longer than necessary.'

'You may do as you please,' was her bored response. 'In fact, the sooner you leave, the better. I assume one can arrange the hire of a carriage from here?'

'I've no idea, but it hardly matters. Like it or not, madam wife, I am taking you home. Besides,' he shrugged, 'there is absolutely no reason for you to return to London. Alice, together with all your belongings, is awaiting you at the Hall.'

For a few moments, all she could do was gape across the table at him in outraged disbelief, then she stood up quickly, very nearly sending the chair toppling to the floor.

'How dare you! How. . .oh!' Words failed her. She began to pace up and down the small room, her slender body rigid with barely suppressed rage.

'You make quite a magnificent spectacle, my darling, when you're angry,' he informed her infuriatingly. 'But like any other display, it does have its limitations, so do be sensible and come and sit down.'

She chose to ignore him. So, after a few moments, he rose from the table, and moved slowly towards her. Then, before she realised his intention, he wrapped one powerful arm round her slender waist and carried her, ineffectually struggling, back to the table, where he dumped her none too gently down on to the chair, one shapely hand on her shoulder keeping her there.

'Now, listen to me very carefully,' he said, an unmistakable thread of menace in his deceptively soft voice. 'You and I shall be in each other's company a considerable time this day, and I have no intention of putting up with childish temper tantrums. So, behave yourself, and eat your food like a good girl, and we shall get along just fine.'

She watched him, a malevolent glint in her green eyes, as he returned to the seat opposite. God, how she hated him! How dared he manhandle her in that odious fashion! It was a totally new experience and one, moreover, that she did not care for in the least.

With deceptive meekness she began to eat the food on her plate, whilst her mind worked furiously. That he had every intention of taking her back to his ancestral home was obvious. What wasn't so clear was why. Was it some perverted form of revenge because she had succeeded in hoodwinking him for so long? Or merely wounded masculine pride because she had dared to run away from him in the first place?

Well, it hardly mattered, she told herself. She had to get away. She cast a brief glance towards the door, measuring the distance. Should she make the attempt now? Would the innkeeper and his wife aid her?

'I wouldn't even think of attempting it, if I were you,' he advised her, so accurately reading her thoughts. 'Tom and his wife are old friends of mine.' He watched her slender, tapering fingers curl round the stem of her glass. 'And I wouldn't advise you to throw that, or anything else at me ever again, my darling, otherwise you might find my retaliation both humiliating and unpleasant.'

She merely raised the glass to her lips, eyeing him measuringly over its rim for a moment before taking a sip of the rich red liquid.

'Your threats leave me unmoved, Linford. Nothing loathsome you did would ever surprise me. What does surprise me, though, is that you wish me to return with you. Our marriage is over. It has been over for six years. An annulment is what we both want, and that shouldn't be too difficult to obtain for a man in your position.'

He finished off the food on his plate, and then sat back in his chair, his expression unreadable. 'Why this unaccountable hatred, Rachel?' he asked unexpectedly. 'Has it something to do with the money your father left to me and not to you?'

She stood up, unable to meet that searching stare, and this time when she went across the room to stare out of the window, he made no attempt to bring her back.

'Yes,' she said at length, 'the money. He gave everything to you, and nothing to me, his own flesh and blood.'

The door opened, and the young innkeeper, whom Rachel had glimpsed when she had first entered the hostelry, came in to inform the Viscount that his carriage was ready and awaiting him at the door.

'Thank you, Tom.' Linford rose to his feet. 'Come, madam. It is time we were on our way.'

His lofty assumption that she would willingly acquiesce angered her further. 'I have no intention of accompanying you anywhere, sir. So, do not let me detain you further,' she informed him haughtily, and before she could avoid those strong, shapely hands, he had picked her up once more and, under the amused eye of the innkeeper, tossed her ignominiously over one powerful shoulder.

'Oh, how dare you! Put me down at once, do you hear!' she screamed, pummelling his back with her small fists.

He brought the flat of his hand down hard on the seat of her dress. 'I heard you. And so, I suspect, did the entire inn.' He delved into the pocket of his jacket, and tossed a purse to the innkeeper. 'Thank you, Tom. I'll see you next time, when I sincerely trust my wife behaves in a more ladylike manner.'

This stricture drew Rachel's attention, and she stopped her ineffectual struggling to peer awkwardly at the innkeeper. 'Don't just stand there, goggling, you fool! Do something! This oaf is—ouch!' she cried as she received a second hard slap on the rear.

'Accept my apologies for this very unseemly behaviour, Tom.' He raised his eyes heavenwards. 'It's the hair, you know,' and, so saying, carried his still manfully struggling and indignant Viscountess out of the room, leaving the innkeeper smiling broadly.

'Tom! Tom!' His pretty young wife came rushing into the room. 'Ought we to do something? That lady said as how his lordship were abducting her.' She frowned up at her highly amused husband. 'Do you think she really is his wife?'

'She's his wife, right enough. Believe me, Meg, I've no doubts on that score.'

Rachel, meanwhile, was regarding her husband in seething indignation as the carriage pulled out of the inn yard. 'I have never been so humiliated in my life!' she snapped, her face still crimson with embarrassment.

'No?' One jet black brow rose. 'Then, all I can say is that you've been singularly fortunate. And I did warn you, my darling, that I wouldn't tolerate any displays of childish temper, so you've only yourself to blame.'

He leaned back against the seat, regarding her thoughtfully for a moment. 'Your life before our marriage was, to say the least, cheerless. But I seriously suspect that during our years apart you've been thoroughly spoilt and indulged.'

The fact that there was more than a grain of truth in what he had said only made her more angry, and she turned her back on him, wincing slightly as she moved in her seat. The thin material of her light summer dress and underthings had offered scant protection against his hard, punishing slaps.

No one, not even her father, had ever dared to lay a hand on her before. Her eyes narrowed. She would make him pay for that humiliation no matter how long it took! she vowed determinedly.

Her vengeful deliberations ran along these lines for quite some time, but then common sense prevailed, and she focused her mind on how to extricate herself from her unfortunate predicament. Escape, of course, was the only solution. She had sufficient funds in her reticule for a night's lodging and the hire of a carriage to return her to London.

No, she thought suddenly, that was pointless now, as Alice and her belongings had been removed. Curse his impudence! Somerset must be her goal. But she couldn't possibly leave Alice behind—certainly not to the tender mercies of this dissolute rake.

She turned her head, and was incensed further to discover him rocking gently with the movement of the carriage, his eyes closed. Not only was he ill-mannered enough to eat in her presence, he had the sheer effrontery to fall asleep in it, too! She made herself more comfortable in her corner, and promptly did the same.

She finally awoke when the carriage made a sharp left-hand turn and slowed down to enter a gateway. Blinking the sleep from her eyes, she turned her head to find her tormentor staring at her, an infuriatingly smug smile curling his lips.

'No one seeing you looking so sweetly angelic in sleep would believe what a sharp-tongued little vixen you are. You've saved me the trouble of waking you. We are almost home, my love.'

Ignoring his first uncalled-for remark, she stared interestedly out of the window at the park. The lime trees which edged the driveway offered pleasant relief from the hot June afternoon sun, but blocked much of the view, and it was not until the driveway swept gracefully down in a wide arc that she caught her first glimpse of the pleasant greystone Elizabethan house, which had been her home for those few short weeks.

Fleetingly, her mind went back to the first time she had seen it, when her husband had brought her here in his carriage, after that simple ceremony conducted in her father's bedchamber. What hopes she had experienced then! Thankfully, she was not so gullible now, and experienced no such joyful expectations.

She reached for her bonnet, which had lain on the seat beside her from the start of the most unpleasant journey, and placed it on her slightly dishevelled locks, tying its bright green ribbon in a coquettish bow beneath her chin.

The carriage came to a halt, Linford jumped out and, after letting down the steps, offered her a helping hand to alight. Suppressing the urge to slap his hand way, she accepted this courtesy with as much grace as she could muster. She did not doubt that she had given much amusement to the coachman and groom by her unseemly departure from the inn, and had no intention of amusing them further.

As she reached the front entrance, the door opened, as if by magic, and she suffered a further severe shock when she saw all the servants standing in line, awaiting her inspection.

The butler stepped forward and bowed. 'My lady, may I say what a pleasure it is to welcome you back into this house.'

'Thank you, Peplow,' she responded graciously, remembering so well the many kindnesses which the grey-haired retainer had bestowed upon her all those years ago.

'May I present you to the housekeeper, Mrs Litton, who has been with us almost a year.'

Rachel found herself confronted by an unsmiling, angular woman in her late forties. Her brown hair, liberally streaked with grey, was confined beneath a starched white cap, and the chatelaine, dangling from the waist of her severe black dress, jingled as she dropped a stiff curtsy and moved down the long line, presenting the other servants.

'Mrs Litton will show you to your room, my dear,' his lordship said when the last of his household had been presented. 'We'll dine at six, quite informally in the small parlour, if that meets with your approval?'

How she longed to say that she would not dine with him anywhere! But as she was the focal point of many pairs of interested eyes, all seemingly watching her closely, waiting for that breach of etiquette which would prove her unsuitable for the exalted position of mistress of such a fine house, she refrained, and merely nodded before following the gaunt-looking housekeeper up the wide staircase.

'Your suite of rooms is this way, my lady.'

Rachel, who had been about to turn left at the head of the stairs, frowned as she meekly followed Mrs Litton to the west wing. Evidently she had been allocated a different room from the one she had used when she had first arrived at the Hall.

The housekeeper threw wide a door, and Rachel found herself standing in a large, airy bedchamber, beautifully decorated in shades of pale green and cream; but she scarcely noticed her surroundings as her eyes instantly fell on the slight figure of her young abigail.

'Alice!' She went over to her, smiling brightly. 'I trust you are fully recovered now from your chill?'

'Yes, Miss Em—I mean, my lady,' Alice corrected, casting a furtive glance at the tall figure by the door whose steely-grey eyes and sharp ears missed nothing.

'I shall instruct that hot water and fresh towels are brought up to you, my lady,' Mrs Litton said woodenly. 'Will there be anything else?'

'I shall ring if I require anything.' Thus disposing of

the housekeeper, she turned to her young maid again, giving her a quick hug before taking off her bonnet, and casting it down on to the bed. 'How long have you been here, Alice?'

'A little over a week, Miss Em. Jem brought me in his lordship's carriage.' She raised puzzled young eyes to her mistress's face. 'Is it true you're married to his lordship?'

'Yes, Alice,' she responded. Unfortunately, all too true, she added silently to herself. She forced a smile. 'I was married when I was younger than you are now. The marriage was not—not a happy one, and so I went to live with Lady Anne.'

'Did Lady Anne know you was married?' the young abigail asked, still puzzled, remembering clearly that that gracious lady had always referred to Viscountess Linford as Miss Emily.

'Yes, she knew.' Rachel's eyes moved to the wall opposite, where the portrait of her beloved benefactress had been hung. Those kindly eyes smiled down at her so calmly as though to reassure her that everything would be all right.

A chambermaid, entering with a pitcher of warm water, put an end to any further questions Alice might have asked, for which Rachel was thankful. She had not as yet formulated any plan of escape. Linford, loathsome creature that he was, was no fool, and it would be a grave mistake to underestimate him. She did not doubt that for a while to come her movements would be closely watched.

This did not mean, however, that if by some chance an opportunity for escape presented itself, she would hesitate to use it; but she was under no illusion that getting herself and Alice safely away would prove an easy task. Best keep her young maid in ignorance for a while, she decided. Let her assume, as no doubt the rest of the servants did, that there had been a reconciliation between master and mistress.

Alice was very young and, although Rachel trusted her implicitly, the girl might betray her mistress's true state of mind quite unwittingly.

For the next hour Rachel concentrated on preparing herself to dine with her husband. She emerged from the dressing-room feeling refreshed and much calmer than she had for some considerable time. She sat down at the dressing-table and, whilst Alice was arranging her hair, took stock of her surroundings.

It really was a most delightful bedchamber, bright and cheerful with its green silk drapes and bed hangings. 'Where does that lead, Alice?' she asked, gesturing to the door at the far end of the room.

'To his lordship's bedchamber, Miss Em.'

Rachel stiffened before her green eyes narrowed to slits. There was no lock, no sign of a bolt, even. Unless, of course, it was bolted on the other side. That was something which she would rectify without delay. She would have a bolt, sturdy and strong, put on her side!

'What dress do you want to wear, Miss—I mean, my lady? Do you want the pretty primrose silk?'

'I left that in Somerset, Alice. Don't you remember?'

'No, it's here, miss,' the young abigail cheerfully informed her in all innocence. 'All your clothes are here. The master brought them from Somerset. And he brought Firefly, too.'

Brushing past her maid, Rachel went over to one of the wardrobes and threw wide its door. It was all too true. Unalloyed fury coursed through her veins. Damn the man! What right had he to enter her home? And what were the servants about to let him walk off with her belongings that way?

Her eyes narrowed. She recalled, now, that on one particular occasion when Linford had called to take her riding, her man of business had been with her. Like a fool she had introduced Mr Thwaite to the Viscount. What a blunder! He must have sought out Mr Thwaite in London, and discovered the exact location of her West Country home. The only other possibility, of course, was that he had obtained the information from Lady Barnsdale.

In seething silence, she finished dressing. She did not care a whit, now, how she looked just to dine with him; but when she made her way down the stairs, half an hour later, her appearance was faultless.

Peplow, waiting in the hall, showed her into the parlour, where her husband stood by the window, staring out across the park. The resentful look she cast him as he came towards the table left him in little doubt concerning her mood; but throughout the entire meal she responded politely to his conversational remarks, betraying none of her inner turmoil before the servants, and he admired her for that.

When the meal was finally over, he did not remain at the table to savour the port, but followed her out into the hall. 'There are one or two matters I wish to discuss with you, my dear, before you retire for the evening. If you would care to accompany me into the library?'

'No, I shouldn't, as it happens,' she did not hesitate to inform him, now they were out of earshot of the servants, 'but I suppose I must. You hold all the cards, Linford. But do not make the mistake of underestimating your opponent. I am no mean player.'

He opened the door for her, and she entered the library. It had occurred to her whilst dressing for dinner that she did not remember his ancestral home at all well, but the library she did recall vividly. She had spent many hours in this book-lined room during her few short weeks at the Hall.

Memories came flooding back as she glanced at the well-stocked shelves, the dark red velvet drapes and the large oak desk, behind which she had discovered her young husband sitting on several occasions when she had dared to venture into his sanctum.

She felt no such fears, now, in his presence, as she sat in one of the comfortable chairs by the hearth, only anger and bitter resentment. 'What is it you wish to say to me?'

He smiled at the curt tone as he went over to the table on which the decanters stood. 'Not over your sulks yet, my darling?'

'I am not sulking, Linford,' she countered hotly. 'Though, God knows, no one has more right to do so! Not only have you brought me here against my will, but you've had the cursed impudence to gain entry into my home and remove my belongings.'

'This is your home, Rachel,' he responded smoothly, pouring out two glasses of wine. 'And I assumed you would want your things about you.'

'You assumed no such thing!' she retorted, but accepted the glass he held out to her graciously enough, and then watched him narrowly as he seated himself in the chair opposite. 'And if you imagine that bringing my personal effects to this house will keep me here, you are far and away out.'

'I'm well aware of that,' he responded smoothly. 'Now, do you think we could possibly continue this discussion with a little less heat?' He leaned back in his chair, eyeing her lovely, angry face over the rim of his glass. 'You have, I don't doubt, already decided to run away from me again. Put it from your mind, Rachel. That course of action will avail you nothing.'

'And what alternative do I have? I've no intention, whatsoever, of remaining here with a man I find utterly loathsome.' He made no response to this, and she looked at him thoughtfully. 'Why have you brought me here, Linford. . .? Revenge?'

'Don't you know?' he countered softly, then smiled at the wary look she cast him. 'No, not for revenge, my darling, though no one has more right to extract it than I. Do you know that, when you ran away from me all those years ago, I was branded, in some quarters, a wife murderer? My friends, my true friends stood by me, but there were many who did not. It wasn't a pleasant experience, I assure you, and one I have no intention of repeating.

'So, I've formulated a course of action which will prove, I sincerely trust, beneficial to us both. May I be permitted to tell you what I have decided?'

'I can hardly wait,' she responded sarcastically, but a spark of interest had ignited, and she was prepared to listen to what he had to say.

'It is by way of a proposition.' He gazed down into the contents of his glass. 'If you are willing to remain here with me—shall we say, for a period of six months?— acting the part of a dutiful wife whenever in the presence of others, then I shall, after that time has elapsed, set my lawyers on obtaining an annulment to our marriage.

'News of your return, if I am not very much mistaken, will spread throughout the county like wildfire. People will assume that we are trying for a reconciliation, and if—when you leave, they will assume the reconciliation has failed. Divorce, my dear, is still very much frowned upon, but with our combined gall I'm sure we shall ride out the tide of censure. You, then, will be free to go where you please, and I. . .'

His words trailed away, and she looked at him searchingly for a few moments before rising and going over to stare out of the window.

What he had proposed was beneficial to her. This way she could enter any society she chose. She would not need to hide herself away, ostracising herself from the world at large for fear of being discovered. But could she trust him?

She turned to look at him again. 'What you suggest makes sense, Linford. But I still do not understand why you are prepared to take this course of action.'

'You believe me to be a callous individual. And, perhaps, you have just cause to feel as you do. But I want an heir, Rachel. A child conceived from the union of two people very much in love, just as I, myself, was conceived.'

Her eyes narrowed as she studied his handsome features keenly. 'You said I must act the part of a dutiful wife. I would like to know, precisely, what these duties include.'

Amusement glinted in his dark blue eyes as he raised them from the contemplation of his wine. 'You will be mistress of this house for as long as you remain my wife. You may make any changes you deem necessary. All my servants are at your command. In return, I shall expect you to take on the duties of hostess whenever I invite relatives or friends to stay. I insist upon courtesy at all times to my neighbours and tenants, and—'

'I am not, as a rule, ill mannered, Linford!' she cut in sharply, and his smile returned.

'No, you are not, as you proved, admirably, when you entered this house. The welcoming committee was not at my behest, I assure you. It was at Peplow's instigation.' He looked at her strangely, his expression unreadable. 'He, at least, remembered you.'

This drew a reluctant smile to her lips as she resumed her seat. 'How fortunate, then, that I did not accept any one of your several invitations to dine at Grosvenor Square. Although,' she continued, a decidedly mischievous twinkle in her eyes, 'it would not have been without its amusing side had I done so.'

'Minx!' His deep rumble of laughter echoed round the room. 'I must get to know you all over again,' he said, his amusement fading. 'The shy girl I married has gone forever, I suspect. The delightfully poised Mrs Stowen is only a part of your character. What manner of woman is Rachel Emily Carlton, Viscountess Linford?'

Feeling acutely uncomfortable under his searching scrutiny, she finished off her wine, and placed the glass down on to the table by her chair before rising to her feet once again. 'I am rather tired, sir, so I shall bid you good night.'

She was genuinely fatigued after the traumas of the day, but found, as she climbed into bed after dismissing Alice, that sleep eluded her.

Linford had given her much to think about. If he was genuine, and he had given her no reason to suppose that he was not, she would need to remain here only until the end of the year. The New Year would bring a new life— not immediately, of course. The annulment must come first, but afterwards she could go where she pleased. She could travel abroad. Foreign lands held no fears for her; only confinement filled her with dread.

Tossing the bedcovers aside, she padded across the deeply piled carpet, and began to relight the candles, her mind recalling, vividly, Linford's words to her after her unseemly exit from the inn. He had reminded her of her childhood. Her smile was bitter as she reached for her robe and sat down at the dressing-table. Yes, she had been a very unhappy little girl: lonely and unloved.

Her father's cruelty had not been physical, but mental. She had been made to pay for her mother's desertion every day of her young life. He had treated her with complete indifference, going for days without seeing her, sometimes weeks when he had paid a visit to London on one of his numerous business trips before his health had begun to fail.

When he had instigated her marriage to the Viscount, it had not been done, she felt certain, with any regard whatsoever for her future well-being, but as a means of revenge on Linford's father, a man whom he had avidly disliked.

She reached for her hairbrush, and began absently to pull it through her long, lustrous hair. Just what the dis-agreement between the two men had been over, she did not know; but she recalled, vividly, overhearing the servants saying that Linford's father was never again to be admitted into the house.

What better revenge, she mused, could her father have extracted than to thrust his unloved offspring upon his enemy's son? But her father hadn't had it all his own way. His nonentity of a daughter had from somewhere found the courage to leave the man who had married her merely for money.

Her smile turned rueful as she recalled Linford's other words. She had, indeed, been thoroughly spoilt during their long separation. And she had loved every minute of it! She blessed Providence for inducing her to walk into the path of Lady Anne Norton's carriage on that never-to-be-forgotten night. No two people could have needed each other more.

Lady Anne's marriage had not been blessed with chil-dren. On that fateful night, the elderly widow had been given the child for which she had always longed; and the lonely, desolate girl had been given the motherly love of which she had been deprived for so many years.

The sound of a firm tread on the passageway outside her room brought her out of her thoughts. There was a soft tap on the door, and then it swung open to reveal the tall figure of her husband, almost filling the aperture.

'What do you want?' she demanded, sudden panic add-ing a sharpness to her voice.

Closing the door quietly, the Viscount came slowly towards her. 'I saw the light under your door, and thought, perhaps, you had gone to sleep, leaving the candles burning.'

'As you see, I have not.'

'Indeed, no. And yet you informed me you were tired. I shall not tolerate lies, Rachel.'

She found his nearness disturbing, and looked up into eyes which glinted ominously. He had been drinking heavily, she suspected. 'It was not a lie.' She rose to her feet and moved away, trying to suppress the fear which rose within her at being alone with him here, in the intimacy of her bedchamber. 'I was tired, but found myself unable to sleep. It must be the strange surroundings.'

She turned round to look at him. 'Before you leave,' she added pointedly, 'perhaps you would be good enough to satisfy my curiosity over one thing? Why have I been allocated these rooms?'

'All your predecessors used these apartments, my dear.' His look was challenging. 'Where else should my Viscountess lay her weary head?'

'I was given a room in the east wing when you first brought me here.' She gave him back look for look. 'Was I not your Viscountess then?'

'I'll admit that was a grave error on my part. . .perhaps the biggest mistake I have ever made in my life. But you were very young, and I, foolishly as things have turned out, was merely trying to be kind.'

'Really?' Her lip curled. 'Well, you could hardly expect me to have ever credited you with that.'

'Vixen!' he exclaimed, his eyes smiling as he stared across the short distance which separated them. She looked so vulnerable, so very desirable with her slipperless feet peeking from beneath the hem of the modest nightgown, which covered almost all of her, yet failed to disguise the slender loveliness beneath.

Rachel turned away, her cheeks growing warm beneath

that all too knowing and appreciative gaze, and her eyes fell upon the door which connected their respective bedchambers.

'There's no lock on that door, sir,' she said accusingly, her voice harsher than it might otherwise have been in order to hide her acute discomfiture. 'If you wish me to remain in this bedchamber, and give any credence to this feigned reconciliation, then you will see to it that a sturdy bolt is fitted to my side first thing tomorrow!' Her face still averted, she did not see his expression darken suddenly. With the swiftness of a sleek jungle cat, he was beside her. Sweeping her into his powerful arms, he tossed her on to the bed, pinioning her wrists above her head, keeping her there.

Struggling valiantly, she kicked out with her bare feet, sending the modest nightgown riding up to her knees. Some detached part of his brain registered that he was being privileged to see far more of his lovely young wife than he had ever seen before, but he was far too angry to appreciate the slender, shapely limbs bared for inspection.

'Now, you listen to me!' he rasped through clenched teeth. 'There has never been any bar on that door, nor shall there ever be in my lifetime. There will never be any locks or bolts between us, you vixen, except those in your mercenary little heart!'

His body pressed so hard on hers made breathing difficult, and her young breasts ached beneath the cruel weight of his powerful chest. She stopped struggling to stare at his angry face, only a matter of inches away from her own, her eyes betraying both fear and defiance.

'I have never in my life forced my attentions on an unwilling female, and I do not intend to start with you,' he went on, his voice now losing its angry sharpness. 'I shall never come in to this room by way of that entrance unless bidden, but it shall never be to enter your bed. If this union of ours is ever to be consummated, you shall come to me.'

'The sun will rise in the west first!' she vowed, defiant to the last, almost spitting the words into his face.

His soft laugh, as he released his hold and rose from the bed, was full of genuine amusement. 'We shall see,' he responded softly as he opened the offending door, and then, still smiling, closed it quietly behind him.

# *Chapter Six*

**R**achel awoke the next morning heavy-eyed and not in the least refreshed, which was not surprising, considering she had spent half the night listening to her husband pacing up and down like some caged animal in the next room; expecting at any moment to see that offending connecting door thrown wide and to find him standing beside the bed, demanding his rights as her husband.

Not that she had any very clear idea concerning what those rights might involve. Having had no mother to instruct her on such matters, she had remained sublimely ignorant. Lady Anne had been of precious little help, either, although on one particular occasion she had said that Viscountess Linford had never been a wife in the true sense because she had never shared her husband's bed.

Rachel raised her eyes heavenwards. Whatever that was supposed to mean! Brushing these puzzling thoughts aside, she rang for Alice, and half an hour later went down to the room where she had dined the previous evening to find her husband, surprisingly, already seated at the table, going through his correspondence.

'I trust you slept well?' he enquired politely.

'Since you ask, no, I did not,' she answered tartly.

'You kept me awake half the night by prowling about your room.'

His smile was a trifle crooked as he watched her take the seat opposite and help herself to coffee. 'I apologise, my dear. I had a great deal on my mind. But you had nothing to fear. . . I've already told you that.'

He resumed his perusal of the letter in his hand, and she looked at him consideringly as she nibbled at a slice of bread and butter. It was rather strange, but she did not fear him, even though he had manhandled her quite roughly on more than one occasion.

Only last night, when he had tossed her on to the bed—holding her captive so effortlessly, it had seemed to her—had she been afraid of him or, perhaps, afraid of the unknown? Ignorant she might be, but it was obvious that whatever it was that changed an innocent damsel into a wife took place in the bedchamber.

He looked up suddenly and caught the prolonged, frowning scrutiny. One jet brow rose. 'From your expression, my love, I evidently do not pass muster this morning.'

'I wasn't so much assessing your outward appearance, Linford, as considering you as a whole, as you might say. And not very favourably, as it happens,' she admitted, and his shoulders shook.

'Honesty is always to be valued highly, but you might try tempering its bluntness with a little diplomacy, otherwise you could quite easily dent my masculine pride.'

'Ha!' she barked, mimicking Lady Barnsdale to perfection. 'I doubt that anyone could so much as scratch the surface of your overweening vanity. Besides which, I shall never again offer you the opportunity of branding me a liar.'

Once again his smile was crooked. 'You cannot deny,

Rachel, that since we met you have been, shall we agree, rather sparing with the truth.'

'Perhaps,' she conceded. 'But I always answered any questions you put to me truthfully, and have never told you a deliberate—' She checked herself on the admission she had been about to make, and lowered her eyes, unable to meet that searching scrutiny.

'So, you have lied to me.' His eyes narrowed. 'Over what, I wonder?'

Hurriedly finishing off her meagre repast, she rose from the table. 'If you will excuse me, I'd like to visit the stables to see Firefly.'

'Of course, my dear. You may do just as you please. But if you would be willing to forgo your ride this morning, I'd like to take you over to the vicarage. Mr Hodges and his housekeeper are both eager to see you again, and the sooner I introduce you to our neighbours, the better.'

She agreed to this and, later that morning, after changing her dress, accompanied him on what she suspected would be the first of numerous calls she would be forced to make during the next few days.

It was only the second time that she had sat beside him in his curricle. After that one and only drive about London, they had always ridden whenever they had ventured forth.

Once again, she found herself admiring the skill with which he tooled the equipage, and rather thought that she would like a racing curricle of her own. She would enjoy bowling along those narrow Somerset lanes on warm spring mornings, displaying her skill to her numerous friends there.

'You're very quiet, my dear. Not nervous at the prospect of seeing Mr Hodges again, surely?'

'Oh, no. I'm looking forward to it. As it happens, I was just considering purchasing a new equipage. I've tooled Anne's one-horse gig, so I'm not a complete novice, but after seeing all those ladies in London handling sporting carriages with such flair, I rather have a fancy for one of these, a racing curricle or, perhaps, a high-perch phaeton.'

'Oh, you do, do you? Well, you're not having one whilst I have any say in the matter!' he told her roundly. 'If you want to drive yourself about, I'll first need to satisfy myself that you're competent, and then, and only then, shall I purchase something for you. A new gig or, perhaps, a curricle, but not a racing model. And certainly not a high-perch phaeton!'

The arrogance of the man! How she would have dearly loved to box his ears soundly! 'I wasn't asking for permission, Linford,' she responded through clenched teeth. 'I neither need your permission, nor require you to purchase anything for me. I have sufficient funds of my own for my needs.' She cast him a frowning, sideways glance. 'Unless, of course, you've helped yourself to my second fortune.'

He winced slightly at this barb. 'The money and property left to you by Lady Anne Norton, Rachel, is yours and yours alone to do with as you wish,' he replied levelly. 'But for as long as you remain my wife, I am responsible for your well-being, and shall not permit you to break your fool neck by indulging in some hare-brained scheme.

'My offer to instruct you stands, but if I ever discover you've so much as given orders for my bays to be harnessed, you'll not sit with any degree of comfort for a sennight!'

She did not doubt for a moment that he would carry out his threat. Had she not already felt the strength of those shapely hands? Her bosom heaved. 'Don't worry, Linford. I would never dream of doing such a thing, nor shall I give you the pleasure of displaying the brutish side of your nature again. But if you ever dare to lay a hand on me just once more, this mockery of a reconciliation of ours is at an end!'

'Believe me, my darling, you cannot possibly wish for its termination more than I do,' he confounded her by responding, and she relapsed into a dignified silence.

Her welcome at the vicarage could not have been warmer. Mrs Wentworth no sooner set eyes on her than she promptly dissolved into tears; and even Mr Hodges's kindly blue eyes grew misty as he took her hand and patted it fondly.

'My dear, I cannot express my joy at seeing you safely reunited with your husband, so I shall not make the attempt. Suffice it to say, welcome home, my lady.'

Rachel was genuinely moved, and felt the strong desire for the second time that morning to box her husband's ears for forcing her to deceive this kindly man who had brought such comfort to her during her lonely childhood.

She stayed with him for a short time only, and then left him with the Viscount to discuss ways of raising funds for the urgent repairs to the church roof, whilst she went in search of Mrs Wentworth, whom she discovered sitting at the kitchen table, busily preparing vegetables.

Unlike Mr Hodges, the housekeeper was bursting with curiosity, and wanted to know where Rachel had been hiding herself for the past six years. She had her inquisitiveness satisfied over this.

When she tried to discover why Rachel had taken it into her head to go away in the first place, she speedily discovered that she was no longer dealing with the shy, biddable girl whom she had known so well, but a very poised and self-confident Viscountess whose brow rose haughtily at such impertinence, and she speedily changed the subject.

*       *       *

During the next few days the Viscount took his wife to visit all his tenants. He watched her avidly and found her behaviour faultless. She was courteous and friendly towards them all, but showed a marked preference for the Hughes family, who had farmed on his land for almost fifteen years.

They had two sons, the elder being a halfwitted giant of a man in his early twenties whose pale blue eyes looked out at the world with a sort of childlike innocence.

'Don't be afraid of Ben,' he had told her as they had ridden away from the Hughes' farmhouse. 'He's quite harmless, and literally wouldn't hurt a fly. He loves animals. His father allows him the use of the old barn in the five-acre field, and he's turned it into a sort of animal sanctuary.'

'I wasn't afraid of him, although his size is rather daunting,' she had admitted. 'And I should like to visit this animal sanctuary of his one day.'

As Linford had surmised, news of his wife's unexpected return quickly spread throughout the locality, and during those first days many of his neighbours, agog with curiosity, found an excuse to call at the Hall.

He could discern quite easily those who found favour in his young wife's eyes. The Halhams, bringing with them their three boisterous children, made an instant favourable impression; as did the young physician who had taken Dr Boyd's place when the aged practitioner had retired earlier that year.

The chill which Alice had contracted whilst in London had left her with a niggling cough, and Rachel had requested young Dr Gillis to call. Linford had never seen the serious, dedicated young man so much as smile until he entered the parlour to find him seated beside Rachel, laughing heartily at something that she had just said.

\*     \*     \*

The Viscount could detect just as easily anyone of whom Rachel was not particularly fond. Generally, she seemed to get along with most people quite well, but the instant he entered the parlour, a few days after the doctor's visit, he knew, instinctively, that she was far from enjoying the company of the latest visitors to descend on the Hall.

Colonel Maitland had purchased a house in the area some two years after Rachel's disappearance, bringing with him his wife and their four children. He was a rotund, jovial individual with whom the Viscount rubbed along quite well, but he disliked, intensely, the Colonel's out-spoken, self-opinionated wife.

He masterfully disguised his feelings, however, as he greeted the formidable matron and her two daughters, before seating himself beside his wife on the sofa.

Taking a hold of Rachel's hand, he squeezed it reassuringly. She made not the least attempt to draw away, and he could almost feel the tension leaving her. 'My poor darling. You must be fatigued to death with all the visitors you have received these past days, but you have coped admirably.'

Rachel thought she had, too, until today. It was only natural that Linford's neighbours and friends would be curious to discover if the rumour of his wife's unexpected return had any foundation. All had been friendly, and all had refrained from asking any personal questions.

The instant Peplow had announced the Maitland ladies, however, she had known, instinctively, that the robust, formidable woman who had swept majestically into the room ahead of her daughters was cast in an entirely different mould; and had come perilously close to losing her temper at the prying, not to say insolent, questions put to her before Linford's timely arrival.

'I've very much enjoyed meeting all your neighbours,

Linford, though I must confess I do find it a trifle daunting when I'm virtually accused of being an imposter.'

'Mama did not mean that,' Miss Maitland hurriedly assured him before her mother could open her mouth and cause more offence. 'It was just that we were so surprised when we learnt of your—er—sudden and unexpected return, my lady.'

Releasing his wife's hand, the Viscount drew out his delicately painted snuff box, and took a pinch of its contents before returning it to his pocket, whilst his gaze remained fixed on Mrs Maitland's forbidding countenance. She was unable to meet that faintly disdainful stare, and lowered her eyes.

'There was nothing sudden in my wife's return,' he told them levelly. 'We were together in London for several weeks before I brought her here, as you would have seen for yourself, Miss Maitland, had your grandmother's unfortunate demise not forced you to leave the metropolis almost before the Season had begun.'

'Yes, most unfortunate,' her mother agreed, regaining her composure. She was far from satisfied that the reconciliation was all that it seemed, but was sensible enough to refrain from prying further and, thereby, risking offence to their august neighbour. Hurriedly pulling on her gloves, she rose to her feet. 'Come along, my dears. There are several purchases we need make before returning home.'

'Oh, not yet, Mama!' The vivacious elder daughter turned her large, faintly reproving brown eyes up at Linford, who had also risen. 'You promised to show me your new gelding, my lord, and you never did ride over with him.'

'An unfortunate oversight on my part which I shall rectify immediately. With your permission, ma'am,' he said, turning to Mrs Maitland. 'Perhaps you, also, would care to accompany me to the stables? I have two new acquisitions which I am sure shall meet with your approval.'

Mrs Maitland had always considered herself no mean judge of horseflesh, and readily accepted the invitation, instructing her younger daughter to accompany them.

'No, no, Mama! Lucy isn't interested in horses,' Arabella said hurriedly. 'She can remain to keep her lady-ship company.'

Rachel smiled faintly at the deliberate exclusion as the door closed behind them, and then looked across at the younger sister. Both Maitland girls were blessed with dark, lustrous locks and large brown eyes, but there the similarities between them ended. Lucinda was a poor imitation of her vivacious elder sister, being smaller, plumper and far less pretty.

The poor girl had not said a word since entering the room. She had sat, head bent, eyes seemingly glued to the hands clasped nervously in her lap; feeling acutely embarrassed, Rachel guessed, by her relatives' sad lack of tact and breeding.

Rachel had disliked the elder sister on sight, suspecting her of being her fond Mama's pampered darling, but she was keeping an open mind with regard to the younger girl.

'You do not care for riding, Miss Lucinda?' she enquired in an attempt to break through the girl's embarrassed shyness.

'Oh, please call me Lucy, everyone does,' she said in a rushed, but pleasant voice. 'I always think I've done something wrong if people call me Lucinda. And I do ride, my lady, but—but not so well as Arabella.'

No, and no doubt you have been told over and over again that you do not do anything half so well as your pampered elder sister, Rachel thought, but said, 'We must go riding together some time. There are many places in the area I have not had the opportunity to visit.'

Shy brown eyes, wondering, assessing, held confident green ones for several moments, then, 'I should like to very much. Perhaps, if you're free tomorrow, we could ride over to see the ruined monastery near Trinsham? It isn't far.'

Rachel felt touched by this gesture of friendship on the young girl's part, and readily agreed.

When she arrived at the rendezvous the following afternoon, however, she was dismayed to find that not only Arabella was included in the party, but also two gentlemen, one of whom was, of all people, Cedric Carlton, Linford's young cousin.

'Good gad!' he exclaimed as she drew Firefly to a halt beside Lucy's mount. 'So it is you, Mrs Stowen! I didn't think I could have been mistaken with the description Miss Lucy furnished me with.'

Rachel wished fervently that the ground would open and swallow her up. How on earth was she supposed to cope with this ticklish situation? Five pairs of eyes were turned in her direction, betraying a wide range of feelings from bewilderment and smug satisfaction, to bold insolence from those of a hard-featured, stocky groom.

'How do you do, Cedric?' she said with remarkable aplomb, considering her heart was thumping so loudly against her ribcage that she felt certain everyone must hear it. 'What a joy it is to see you again! Linford omitted to inform me that you were acquainted with the Maitlands.' And I shall take the greatest pleasure imaginable in murdering him when I return to the Hall! she added silently.

'Oh, aye, aye. Friend of Harry's. Up at Oxford together, don't you know,' he informed her, still in some confusion.

'And you must be Harry Maitland.' Rachel reached out her hand to the faintly embarrassed young man. 'I would have known you anywhere. You bear a marked resemblance to your sister.'

'Yes, poor Lucy and I take after Father. Bella and little Charles have all the looks. They take after Mama's side of the—'

'What I would like to know,' Arabella put in rudely, 'is why you were going about calling yourself Mrs Stowen?'

Rachel, one finely arched brow rising haughtily, fixed her eyes on the elder sister. 'Yes, I dare say you would, and would suggest, therefore, that if vulgar curiosity ever gets too much for you, Miss Maitland, that you apply to my husband for the explanation.' She turned to Lucy. 'Shall we be on our way?'

'That's given you your own, Bella,' her brother said in an undertone, smiling as he stared at the two figures riding a little way ahead.

She flashed him an angry look. 'You may accept the so-called Lady Linford at face value, Harry, but I am not such a fool. It wouldn't surprise me to discover that she's an impostor.'

'Don't be foolish!' Harry scoffed. 'Why on earth would Linford try to pass off an impostor as his wife? No sense in it.'

'No, dash it! Wouldn't do that,' Cedric agreed. 'High stickler, is old Linford. Family honour and all that.' He frowned suddenly. 'But there's something havey-cavey about the whole business. No sight nor sound of his wife in six years, then she turns up out of the blue. Dashed odd!'

'Why don't you ask him, Cedric?' Arabella coaxed.

'Eh?' Cedric looked decidedly put out. 'No, no, couldn't do that, Bella. Linford's a fine enough fellow, but has a dashed nasty way with him if crossed. Besides, ain't any of my business.'

As far as Harry was concerned, that was an end to the matter. As they rode along, he began to tell Cedric of a cock-fight taking place the very next day, leaving his sister to follow in seething silence.

It was a glorious July afternoon with hardly a breath of wind; consequently, by the time they had reached the turn off to Trinsham, the gentlemen were feeling hot and thirsty, and were more than willing to forgo the dubious pleasure of walking round a 'ruined pile', as Harry phrased it, in favour of having their thirsts quenched at the Blue Boar, and arranged to meet back at the signpost in an hour.

Lucy watched them ride away with her, still, very disgruntled sister accompanying them. 'Poor Bella. She has certainly had her nose put out of joint by your arrival, my lady. She always considered herself the "Belle of the County".'

Rachel smiled. 'That is very flattering, Lucy, but as I am a married woman, I hardly pose any threat to your sister. I'm sure she could have any beau she chooses.'

'Not quite, my lady.'

Rachel looked at her sharply, noting the sudden rise of colour in the girl's cheeks, and then enlightenment dawned. Her brow rose. Well, well! So Arabella had designs on Linford, had she? That explained a great deal.

'No wonder your sister dislikes me so much.'

'She would have disliked you anyway, ma'am, simply because you're so beautiful.'

'You are determined to put me to the blush with your flattery, Lucy Maitland! And if we are to continue this friendship, you must stop it at once. And stop calling me ma'am! My name is Rachel.'

'Oh, I couldn't possibly call you that. Mama would never approve.'

'Very well. We shall compromise. When we are alone, you may call me Rachel, and when in the company of others, Lady Linford, but not ma'am. You make me feel like a matriarch!'

Lucy, gurgling with laughter, willingly agreed, and chatted away in a far less restrained way as they walked round the ruined monastery, which must have been a wonderful sight once, situated as it was on a slight rise.

When they had explored every crumbling wall, Rachel sat herself down on one of the large grey stones which had once formed part of the huge refectory, and said, 'My arrival has certainly caused no small stir. It isn't really surprising, either, that some people doubt my authenticity.'

'Don't pay any attention to Bella,' Lucy advised, sitting herself down beside Rachel. 'Most people are pleased there is now a mistress at the Hall. I was speaking to Mr Hodges this morning. He remembers you very well, and spoke of you to my mother and me with great fondness.'

'Dear Mr Hodges. He's one of the few people who knew me in those early years.' Rachel gazed across the open countryside to where a herd of cows sought shelter from the hot sun under a clump of trees. 'I was married very young. . .too young. I was nowhere near ready for matrimony, nor to assume the responsibilities of Viscountess Linford.'

'Is that—that why you went away?' Lucy enquired tentatively.

'In part yes.'

'But you're older, now. You won't go away again, surely?'

This was getting on to dangerous ground. Rachel had been more than willing to offer some explanation for the long estrangement from her husband, but felt honour-bound not to divulge the true state of affairs that now existed between Linford and herself.

He had, after all, promised an annulment, providing she acted the part of a dutiful wife, and she would not fail to keep her part of the bargain by divulging that the so-called reconciliation was pure farce.

On the other hand, though, she had no intention of telling a deliberate lie to this kind-hearted girl whom she was beginning to like more with every passing minute, and said, 'Certainly not today.' She got to her feet. 'But if I do not return to the Hall soon, his lordship will begin to think that that is precisely what I have gone and done.'

When they arrived at the turn-off to Trinsham, there was no sign of Lucy's brother. They waited for a while, but then headed homewards, believing that the others had tired of waiting and had gone on ahead. They arrived at the estate's boundary wall, still without catching sight of a soul, and Rachel suggested that they traverse the grounds, thereby cutting Lucy's journey home by a mile or so.

They were rounding a bend in the bridle-path, which skirted the wooded area of the park, when they spotted Arabella and her groom, still some little way ahead, circling Ben Hughes with their mounts. They were not close enough to hear what was being said, but when the groom suddenly kicked out with his stoutly shod foot, knocking Hughes to the ground, Lucy gasped in dismay, and Rachel's eyes flashed dangerously.

Digging her heel into Firefly's flank, she left Lucy behind. 'What on earth do you think you're doing?' she demanded angrily, bringing her filly to an abrupt halt by Arabella's mount.

'This fool refused to let me see what he has hidden beneath his shirt.' Arabella tossed her proud little head haughtily. 'Renfrew was merely obeying orders. And Linford will no doubt be exceedingly grateful to me, "my lady",' she went on with undue emphasis on the courtesy. 'This rogue, I suspect, has been poaching.'

Only by exercising the greatest restraint did Rachel prevent herself from lashing out at Arabella's smugly smiling face with her crop. 'Whatever my husband's views may be on the subject of poaching, I am certain that he would never countenance a spoilt, ridiculous child undertaking the duties of his gamekeeper.'

She had the satisfaction of seeing Arabella's cheeks stain crimson before turning her attention to the servant, noting the hardened cruelty in the dark brown eyes and the disdainful twist of full lips. 'Nor would he ever solicit the aid of a mindless thug. Get yourselves out of my sight and off this land before I lose my temper!'

Arabella's self-assurance plummeted beneath the angry contempt. 'Come, Renfrew. "Her ladyship" hasn't heard the last of this!' she snapped in a last act of defiance before cantering away.

'You had better go too, Lucy,' Rachel advised, her voice still harsh. 'I am sorry this disgraceful incident has marred what would otherwise have been a most pleasurable afternoon.'

Lucy, having arrived in time to hear the gist of what had passed between Rachel and Arabella, followed her sister without a word of farewell, looking rather sad and shamefaced. Rachel watched her for a few moments, and then turned her attention to Ben, who had scrambled to his feet, his arms protectively clasped across his great barrel of a chest, his eyes looking bewildered, fearful.

Kicking her foot free of the stirrup, she slipped to the ground and made to move towards him, but he backed away. 'It's all right, Ben. I'm not going to hurt you.'

Had he not looked so frightened, she might have laughed at the ludicrousness of her words. Here she was, telling this giant of a man, who must stand six feet six in his stockinged feet, not to be afraid of someone who nowhere near reached his shoulder.

'Do you not remember me?' she asked softly. 'I came to visit you the other day. I am Lady Linford.'

He stared at her strangely, intently, the vacant expression vanishing as he fixed his eyes on her mouth. He ceased backing away, and she came slowly towards him.

'Did that man hurt you?' Again his eyes were fixed on her lips, and she wondered if he had understood anything she had said. She felt at a total loss. How did one communicate with someone like Ben Hughes?

'Bad man,' he said suddenly, distinctly.

'Yes, he is a bad man, and he ought not to have kicked out at you that way. His lordship permits you on his land, does he not?'

She had spoken each word slowly, clearly, hoping that he would again understand, and was rewarded by a vigorous nodding of his large head. Then she noticed a sudden movement beneath his rough shirt, and groaned inwardly. Dear God! Surely Arabella Maitland hadn't been right after all?

In silent dismay Rachel saw a small furry head appear. Ben drew out the frightened animal whilst making the strangest cooing noises, like those of a dove, which seemed to soothe the trembling rabbit, held so gently in that massive hand.

Rachel then noticed its badly cut and bleeding front leg. Suddenly enlightenment dawned, and she smiled. 'You're taking him to your barn, aren't you?' she asked softly, so as not to alarm the poor frightened animal further, and was again answered by a nod of Ben's head. 'May I come too?'

She received no response to this at all, so decided to accompany him, anyway. Leading Firefly, she almost had to run to keep up with the young man's massive strides, whilst trying to keep up a one-sided conversation; consequently, she arrived at their destination, a short while later, hot and breathless.

The doors stood wide open, and she followed Ben into the barn. It took a few moments for her eyes to adjust themselves to the contrasting change in light; then she saw the rows of cages against the far wall, most of which

contained a variety of wild animals and birds. Many of
the doors had been left open, but the creatures, it seemed,
were reluctant to seek their freedom.

How strange, she thought as she watched the big man
place the injured rabbit on a rough wooden table. He
smeared its cut leg with some ointment, taken from a jar,
and then bound its leg up deftly with a strip of linen
bandage, possibly the remnants of a shirt or some other
garment purloined from his home.

The rabbit never attempted to escape throughout this
operation. It was almost as if it knew that the huge hands
that touched it would never do harm. That giant of a man
was so special. What a gift he possessed!

She continued to watch as Ben placed the rabbit in one
of the empty cages, gave it water and food, and then closed
the cage door. 'Will it be all right?' She received no
answer. Reaching out, she touched his shoulder, and he
turned to look at her. She repeated the question, and this
time received a broad grin and the customary nod.

Perplexed, she moved away to seat herself on the edge
of the table, and watched Ben go to each cage in turn to
add food, or replenish the small bowls with fresh water.
Apart from those strange sounds he made, which seemed
to have such a soothing effect on his patients, she had
heard him speak only once. Throughout the time they had
been walking together, he hadn't uttered a single word,
and yet she felt certain he understood everything she said.
At least. . .

Suddenly a thought struck her, so novel that she almost
dismissed it as ludicrous, but it persisted like some irritat-
ing itch. Balling her slender fingers, she thumped the table
hard, startling some of the animals and birds.

Ben did not even turn his head, but she saw him look
along the rows of cages, wondering, perhaps, what it was
that had suddenly startled his patients. Then he turned

to look at her questioningly. God in heaven! He wasn't halfwitted. . .he was deaf!

'What do you do with the animals once they are well?' she asked as he continued to stare at her. 'Do you set them free?' Again he nodded, and she went over to stand in front of him. 'You understand everything I say, don't you, Ben?' He nodded yet again. 'But you cannot hear what I say, so how do you know?'

For a moment he looked bewildered, and she thought she must have been mistaken, after all, but then he touched his lips with his fingertips.

She frowned. 'Are you trying to tell me that you know what I'm saying by the movement of my lips when I speak? Incredible!' she exclaimed at the all-too-familiar nod. 'You truly are an amazing man, Ben Hughes!'

He blushed fiery red, and she laughed up at him. 'I must go now, my friend. It's getting late, but may I come and see you again?'

He accompanied her outside to where she had tethered Firefly. The filly whinnied softly, but did not nuzzle her hand, but the tall man's beside her. Firefly had always been reticent with strangers. It had irked her immeasurably when Linford—curse him!—had gained the animal's confidence so easily; but she had never known Firefly take so quickly to a complete stranger.

Waving a last goodbye, Rachel cantered back along the track to where she had seen Ben knocked to the ground, and then turned Firefly on to the path leading through the wood, bringing her to a halt by the side of a large elm.

Some detached part of her brain registered that she was not alone in this wooded area of the park. She heard the sound of gunfire, but so deep in thought was she that she paid little heed.

She felt she must do something for Ben Hughes. She might, of course, be totally wrong in assuming he was

deaf, but she didn't think so. She would pay a call on Dr
Gillis, and get his opinion. She was determined to do all
she could for that amazing man before she left Hampshire
for good.

She gave Firefly the office to start. The filly had just
moved forward a pace or two when the sound of a shot
rang out. Rachel turned her head sharply, and saw to her
horror the splintered bark, and an evil rounded metal ball
embedded in the elm a matter of only inches away from
her head.

# Chapter Seven

'Why, Miss Em!' Alice swung round with a start as the bedchamber door slammed shut. 'Whatever's wrong? You look as white as a sheet.'

Rachel, still badly shaken over the incident in the wood, kept her back firmly pressed against the closed door. 'Someone has just tried to kill me, Alice,' she confided, still breathless from her breakneck return to the Hall. Fearing her legs might give way, she moved over to the *chaise longue* and slumped down on to the soft upholstery. 'It couldn't have been an accident. . . But who. . .? Why?'

Placing the gown, which she had so lovingly pressed, into the wardrobe, Alice, wide-eyed and fearful, hurried over to her mistress. 'What happened, Miss Em?'

'Someone took a shot at me whilst I was cutting through the wood. If I hadn't urged Firefly on just at that precise moment, I wouldn't be sitting here now.' She glanced up, and the sight of her young abigail's anxious expression calmed her, and she even managed a semblance of a smile. 'The gods were certainly on my side this day, Alice.'

'You must tell his lordship at once, my lady!'

Rachel frowned heavily. Sound advice, but supposing she had been wrong? Rising to her feet, she went over to the window, trying to recall in detail those dreadful moments. Could she possibly have been mistaken? It had all happened so quickly, after all. Furthermore, she had no desire to cause a stir, unless she was absolutely certain in her own mind of exactly what had taken place. Which meant, of course, a return to the wood.

She shuddered convulsively just as something caught her attention, and she turned her head slightly to see a man emerging from the home wood, a gun over his arm. He was some way away, but even from that distance she recognised her husband's graceful, long-striding gait. God in heaven. . .! Linford?

'No, Alice. Tell no one of this. One cannot go around making accusations unless one is perfectly sure.'

Deeply troubled, but forcing a smile, she ordered her bath to be filled, and was luxuriating in the rose-scented water when she became aware of the sounds of an arrival. In all probability it was only a neighbour come to call, and she had no intention of seeing anyone until she had gained control of her disordered thoughts.

As it happened, she could not have been more wrong. Peplow opened the door, and Lady Barnsdale, accompanied by Mr Cheffingham, entered the hall. The butler informed them that both master and mistress were changing for dinner, and showed them to the bedchambers always kept in readiness for their visits, before making his way to the west wing to inform his lordship of their arrival.

The Viscount smiled to himself as he went down to his library. The letter he had written to his aunt the week before had brought her hotfoot into Hampshire, as he had suspected it might. She wasted no time on civilities, either, as she swept into the room a short while later, with the ever-faithful Cheffy at her heels, but demanded to know what on earth had brought his wife back after all these years.

'I did, Hetta,' he answered infuriatingly, as he handed them both a glass of his excellent Madeira.

'You know perfectly well what I mean, Linford!' she snapped. 'I distinctly recall your telling me that you had given up the search for her.'

'Yes, very true,' he concurred. 'I had given up looking for her, my dear, because I knew precisely where she was to be found.'

Casting him a look of exasperation, she slumped down on to the couch. She was far from happy with this most unexpected turn of events, and had been in low spirits since receiving his letter. She was about to ask where his chit of a wife had been hiding herself when the door opened, and she swung round, the glass of wine almost dropping from her suddenly limp fingers.

It would have been difficult to say which of them looked more stunned by the other's unexpected presence. Lady Barnsdale's jaw dropped perceptively, much to her nephew's intense amusement, and his wife's eyes widened in astonishment.

Rachel regained her wits first, and came smilingly forward. 'What a pleasant surprise, Hetta! Linford omitted to inform me that you were coming to pay us a visit.'

'That was because I wasn't one hundred per cent certain of it myself, my love,' he responded smoothly, but with a devilish glint in the depths of his violet eyes.

Lady Barnsdale, at a complete loss, looked from one to the other. 'But—but I don't understand. What in the world are you doing here, Emily?'

'Plain as a pikestaff, m'dear!' Cheffy put in, bowing over the Viscountess's hand. 'May I say what a pleasure it is to see you safely restored to your husband's home, my lady.'

Lady Barnsdale, who had also risen at Rachel's entry, slumped back down on to the sofa, spilling most of the contents of her glass on to the richly coloured Axminster carpet.

'You should have warned her, Linford!' Rachel's voice was edged with censure as she relieved her friend of the glass. 'For heaven's sake, get her some brandy! She looks about to swoon.'

'I shall take leave to inform you, young woman, that I have never fainted in my life.' Hard-eyed and disdainful, Lady Barnsdale sat rigid in her seat. 'I need neither Linford's brandy, nor your solicitude!'

Dinner was announced, and Rachel, feeling acutely hurt by her friend's contemptuous attitude, watched as Linford offered his aunt a supporting arm, leaving Cheffy to escort her into the dining-room. She took her seat at the foot of the table, distress rapidly turning to anger as it became apparent that she was being deliberately excluded from the conversation.

She had borne much that day. Not only had she been forced to contend with Arabella Maitland's mischief-making, the unexpected appearance of Cedric Carlton and the disgraceful incident involving Ben Hughes, but also someone trying to put a period to her life—possibly the villainous wretch seated opposite! But be damned if she would be deliberately ignored at her own table!

The tenuous hold on her temper finally snapped. With one sweep of her slender arm she sent plates, glasses and cutlery crashing to the floor, and then stormed from the room in a swirl of pale-green silk.

'No, Dominic.' Lady Barnsdale grasped his arm as he made to rise from the table in angry pursuit. 'It is all my fault. Let me go to her.'

Linford sighed as he watched his aunt leave the room with far more grace than his wife had done, and then turned to the only other person at the table, who had continued to eat his dinner, just as though nothing untoward had occurred.

A reluctant smile curled his lips. 'Does nothing ever disturb you, Cheffy?'

'Eh. . .? What's that? No, bound to have happened.' He reached for his wine and tossed it back in one large swallow. 'Mind you, m'boy, you should have warned Hetta. Been a shock. Told you she's very fond of that gel. Been fretting herself to death since your wife left Surrey.'

Linford passed the dish of mushrooms, prepared in a particularly fine sauce, which Cheffy had been eyeing with relish, then sat back in his chair, studying the older man over the rim of his glass. 'It hasn't been a shock to you in the least, though, has it, my friend?'

'No,' Cheffy admitted, piling the mushrooms on to his plate. 'Can't say I knew for certain, though. There was something oddly familiar about her, but it was the hair that threw me. Never have seen hair of just that exact shade before. Would have remembered, you see.'

Linford's heavy frown returned. 'Yes, the hair,' he muttered darkly, drawing forth an amused chuckle from his imperturbable companion.

'Can't have hair that colour, m'boy, and not be blessed with a temper. And no shrinking violet would suit you. Best keep the one you have. You'll deal famously once she's settled.'

The Viscount's scowl vanished to be replaced by a crooked smile. 'You're a downy one, Cheffy, and no mistake.'

Lady Barnsdale, meanwhile, had reached Rachel's bed-chamber, and scratched lightly on the door. She received no response, so entered the room, anyway, to find her young friend staring out of the window.

'Recriminations, Hetta?' Rachel said softly, instinctively knowing who had entered. 'Come to take me roundly to task for my subterfuge? I shall hear you out with equanimity. I owe you that much, at least.'

She received no response and turned, then, to see Lady Barnsdale, eyes brimful with tears, seated on the *chaise longue*. She was at her side in an instant. 'No, not that, Hetta! I can cope with your harsh tongue, but not your tears.'

'You—you planned it all, didn't you?' she responded softly, falteringly. 'Our meeting. . .? Friendship?'

'The meeting, yes,' Rachel admitted, reaching for the older woman's hands and holding them gently in her own. 'But everything that happened afterwards was not at my contrivance. I never intended to grow so very fond of you—would never have believed such a thing possible.'

Her smile was crooked. 'When I first met you all those years ago, Hetta, you frightened me to death. How could I have possibly known I should come to regard you in the light of a dear friend? No, more than that. I would never have believed I could come to care for someone as I cared for Anne.'

Lady Barnsdale followed the direction of Rachel's gaze, and stared up at the portrait. She knew nothing of Lady Anne Norton, and asked Rachel to explain how she had come to know the kindly soul that smiled so serenely down from the painting.

Hesitantly at first, Rachel began her story, but soon became lost in the narrative. She related something of her lonely and unhappy childhood; of her hopes for the future when she had married the Viscount; of that near-fatal first meeting with Lady Anne and of how, under that wonderful woman's loving care, she had changed from a diffident drab of humanity into a happy, self-confident young woman.

'Were you so very unhappy with Linford in those first

short weeks of marriage?' Lady Barnsdale asked gently, when her young friend had come to the end of the revealing homily. 'Was he so very unkind to you that you felt the need to hide yourself away for six long years?'

'Unkind?' Rachel echoed, frowning slightly. 'No, Hetta, he wasn't unkind, precisely. Indifferent would be more accurate.' She rose and went over to the window once more, her eyes, instinctively, moving to the wooded area of the estate. 'After all, the only reason he married me was to get his hands on my father's fortune.'

There was no bitterness in the soft voice; she sounded, if anything, quite matter of fact. Lady Barnadale frowned, perplexed. 'Is that why you left him? Was it because your father left everything to Dominic?'

'Sour grapes, you mean?' Rachel laughed, a mirthless hollow sound. 'Oh no, Hetta. That wasn't the reason. Although it's what Linford surmises—what I've allowed him to believe.'

'Then why?' she demanded, knowing her young friend was keeping something of great significance to herself; something which had upset her so much that she had felt she could no longer remain with her husband. 'Although I care for my nephew deeply, I'm not blind to his faults, but I'm certain he would never have deliberately hurt you, as I see now he must have done.'

She was silent for so long that Lady Barnsdale thought that she was not going to answer. Then she said very softly, 'I left him because he destroyed a young girl's hopes, a young girl's dreams. I left him because he broke a young girl's heart. Do you truly want to know how he managed to do that, Hetta. . .?'

When Lady Barnsdale left the room some time later, she was both saddened and deeply troubled. Rachel had confessed all, even going so far as to impart details of her

abduction after she had left Surrey, and of the reason
behind her remaining at the Hall now.

Lady Barnsdale believed she knew her nephew's true
motive in bringing his wife back to his ancestral home,
and prayed with all her heart that the outcome would be
a happy one, but what she had learned from her young
friend left her with grave doubts.

After sending a message down to the gentlemen to say
that she was retiring early, Lady Barnsdale sought the
solitude of her allotted bedchamber. She had informed
Linford, already, that she intended making an early start
in the morning, as she had some last-minute arrangements
to make before she finally left Surrey for Bath.

Hopefully, he would not be suspicious over her not
rejoining them downstairs. But the simple truth was that
she did not trust herself not to interfere if she came face
to face with him soon after Rachel's appalling disclosure.

An indifferent night's sleep did not improve her state of
mind, and she rose the next morning still depressingly
troubled. She ordered a breakfast tray brought to her room,
and then went along to the west wing to bid farewell to
Rachel, who, for the first time since her arrival at the Hall,
had also taken breakfast in her room.

Their parting was both lengthy and tearful, but eventually Lady Barnsdale dragged herself away, and found the
gentlemen awaiting her in the hall.

'I cannot in all honesty say this has been an enjoyable
visit, Linford, and I'm not sorry to be leaving,' she told
him with brutal frankness, when Cheffy had gone outside
to the waiting carriage. 'I believe I understand your reasons
for bringing Rachel back here. I hope to God you do, too!'

She looked up at him; her eyes were hard and coldly
disdainful, he thought.

'I have no intention of interfering, and shall say only

this. . . If you ever hurt that child again, Linford, I will never forgive you as long as I live!'

She left him, then, without another word; without the customary hug and kiss; without so much as a smile of farewell; and he felt, understandably, hurt and not a little puzzled.

He took himself off to his library, and began to look through the papers his steward had left for his perusal, but found himself unable to concentrate, and eventually put them to one side, his eyes narrowing as he recalled Hetta's ill-natured leave-taking.

What had Rachel been saying to put his aunt in such a disagreeable frame of mind? His temper began to stir. What had that red-haired vixen been spewing forth to set Hetta against him so? He ought, he knew, to have written to his aunt explaining all, so that she had been well prepared for what she would discover at the Hall. That he had been, in part, responsible for her unhappy short visit only added fuel to his temper.

The library door opened, and Peplow entered with a letter delivered by hand. Linford, after requesting his butler to remain in case there was need of a reply, ran his eyes over the few hurriedly scrawled lines, his brow darkening as he muttered several choice and unrepeatable expletives.

'Is her ladyship in the house?' he demanded through clenched teeth.

'No, my lord, she went riding shortly after Lady Barnsdale's departure.'

'She did, did she?' his lordship muttered ominously. 'In that case, be good enough to inform her when she does return that I wish to speak to her at once.'

Peplow, who had grown very fond of his young mistress, for the first time ever carried out his lordship's orders most reluctantly, and half an hour later, still dressed in her habit, Rachel entered the library.

'You wished to speak to me, Linford?' Closing the door, she came towards the desk, where he sat busily writing a letter.

She was in no good mood herself. Not only had she not forgiven him for the previous evening's fiasco, but she had been over to the wood again and, locating that old elm tree without any difficulty, had the proof that she had not been fanciful. Her eyes hardened as she felt in her jacket pocket, and her fingers came into contact with the rounded piece of lead shot.

The Viscount looked up suddenly and caught the almost calculating expression on her lovely face. 'I neither know why you are looking at me like that,' he told her brusquely, 'nor do I want to know, particularly. But I do insist upon knowing what makes you think you have the right to countermand my wishes by ordering the Maitland girls off my land? Because of your audacity I have received what I can only describe as a damned impertinent letter from a neighbour!'

Rachel kept a tight rein on her temper, but it was an effort, and found release in sarcasm. 'Oh, have you, now.' Her lip curled. 'My heart bleeds for you, Linford. The high and mighty Lord of the County feels ill-used because he received an impolite missive. If that is the full sum of your grievances, sir, you should count yourself fortunate.'

Rising abruptly, the Viscount brought his fist down hard on to the desk. 'Damn it, madam! Do you think me unreasonable to expect an explanation?'

'I did not realise, sir, that that was what you were requesting.'

Ignoring the continued sarcasm, he looked at her closely for the first time. She looked pale and drawn, and his temper began to cool. 'Come, madam,' he said, all sharpness gone from his voice now. 'We can deal better than this.'

A sigh escaped him. 'You have every right to feel aggrieved over my aunt's impromptu visit. But believe me when I tell you that it was never my intention to upset either of you. I was wrong not to have explained fully to Hetta in my letter, and am sorry if my thoughtlessness caused you distress.'

She looked at him searchingly, but could detect nothing but regret in his violet eyes. He had been generous enough to apologise for his actions, so the least she could do was offer an explanation for her own. After all, she was here for a few short months only, and had no desire, whatsoever, to be the cause of a rift between him and one of his neighbours.

'I did order Miss Maitland off your land. And if I—I overstepped my authority, then I'm sorry, but I believed my actions were justified.' She could not prevent a twitching smile. 'Though I must admit, if I'm honest, I wasn't in the best of humours at the time.'

His own lips curled in response to the admission. 'May I be permitted to know what put you out of temper?' He thought for a moment that she would not satisfy his curiosity, but then, very reluctantly it seemed to him, she explained.

It was his turn to stare, and he did so for several thoughtful moments. She met that searching scrutiny without so much as a blink, and he was satisfied with what he saw.

'Thank you, my dear, for acting on my behalf. I shall deal with the matter from here on. You will not be troubled further. And, Rachel,' he added, arresting her progress to the door, 'you will not be troubled with any further unexpected visits from my relatives.'

At this she turned to look at him again, that unmistakable mischievous glint in her eyes. 'I wouldn't be too sure of that if I were you, Linford. I omitted to inform you yesterday, but your cousin Cedric is staying with the Maitlands,' and laughed at his comical look of dismay as she left the room.

Later that morning, she watched him, mounted on Ramon, galloping across the park, and wondered whether he intended paying a call on Colonel Maitland.

When he joined her in the dining-room for a light luncheon, he told her nothing of where he had been, but later that afternoon Peplow informed her that there would be two guests for dinner, and she was not in the least surprised to learn that these were none other than Cedric Carlton and Mr Harry Maitland.

The evening turned out to be the most enjoyable she had spent since her arrival at the Hall. The young gentlemen's light-hearted bantering proved to be a refreshing change from that icy-cold formality which usually prevailed at meal times. Linford, too, seemed different, somehow: far more relaxed; and behaved towards her just as he had done during those numerous occasions when they had been together in London.

After the meal was over, Rachel left the gentlemen to enjoy their port, and took herself off to the small salon. Expecting to be left to her own devices for some time, she occupied herself with some sewing, and was surprised when a short while later Harry Maitland entered the room.

'Linford's taken Cedric into the library to discuss something in private,' he informed her, coming smilingly forward. 'Which gives me the opportunity to apologise to you, my lady, for that disgraceful occurrence yesterday.'

Setting aside her work, Rachel asked him to sit down. 'You were in no way to blame, Mr Maitland, so there is absolutely no need to apologise.'

'Please call me Harry. Everyone does.' She readily agreed and he seemed to relax slightly. 'It was my fault, in part. I know what Arabella is, and should never have permitted her to ride home with just Renfrew as escort.'

'You cannot be held responsible for your sister's actions. She is nineteen, after all, hardly a child.'

'No, she isn't,' he agreed, frowning. 'The trouble is, she's been spoilt to death. She's Mama's pet, and anything she wants, she gets.' He smiled suddenly. 'That, hopefully, is now at an end. After Linford's visit, Papa was in a towering rage. Never seen him take on so before. He's normally the most even-tempered, good-natured soul, except when he's suffering from the gout, of course.

'Had us all lined up before him in the library, demanding to know what rigmarole we'd been spinning about you to Mama. Lucy and I hadn't a clue what he was talking about. It was all Arabella's mischief-making, of course. Spun Mama some yarn about you deliberately excluding her from the visit to the monastery, and being high-handed when you discovered her crossing Linford's land.'

His shoulders shook with suppressed laughter. 'Lucy, bless her, rounded on Bella like a virago. Never seen the darling in such a passion! Even Papa blinked. Course, the truth came out, then. Papa was furious with Arabella, and with Mama for coming to him with such a farrago of nonsense in the first place.'

'Oh, dear,' Rachel murmured, genuinely perturbed. 'It would seem I have unwittingly caused trouble between the members of your family, sir.'

'No such thing!' he countered bracingly. 'High time Papa put his foot down. And one good thing has come out of all this—Arabella is to be sent away to Aunt Agnes. Lord, what a dragon she is! She'll soon sort the little minx out. And not before time!'

Rachel tried to look disapproving, but failed miserably. 'Arabella must now dislike me more than ever.' She frowned slightly as she looked across at him. 'It wasn't only your sister. Although she said he was acting only under orders, that groom of hers looked to me as though he enjoyed that needless assault on Ben Hughes.'

'He isn't Arabella's servant—he's mine.' Sighing, he shook his head. 'I made a big mistake, there, I know. But what could I do? Renfrew came to my aid a few months back. I was attending a cock-fight a few miles from here, and was set upon by a couple of rogues. After my purse, I suppose.

'He helped me see the blackguards off, and I bought him dinner by way of a thank-you. During the meal, he mentioned he was looking for work in the area. I told him we happened to be in need of a groom, and he jumped at the chance. I've already had words with him, and have told him that if there's a recurrence of that kind, he'll be sent packing.'

Rachel shuddered convulsively, recalling vividly the dreadful confrontation by the home wood. If that groom ever bore someone ill will, his revenge, she felt certain, would be both thorough and merciless.

# *Chapter Eight*

**R**achel watched until the curricle, pulled by those perfectly matched bays, had disappeared from view, then turned away from the library window and sat herself behind her husband's desk.

Taking a sheet of paper from out one of the drawers, she began to reply to a letter she had received the previous week from Lady Barnsdale, but her disordered thoughts made even this simple task impossible, and she threw down the pen in exasperation, splattering ink across the few disjointed sentences.

She had been at the Hall, now, almost two months. One third of her enforced stay in Hampshire was nearing its end. The trouble was, though, she no longer looked upon living in her husband's ancestral home in that light. She was surprisingly enough beginning to enjoy this new, if unlooked-for, change in her lifestyle.

Her husband's attitude towards her, too, seemed to have undergone a subtle, yet definable, change. Since the evening when his cousin and Harry Maitland had dined with them, Linford had been far less restrained; had seemed far less watchful—mistrustful.

Their meals together were no longer those unpleasant interludes when they indulged in small talk for the benefit of the servants, but had become enjoyable occasions when they had discussed a wide variety of topics, sometimes disagreeing, but never nastily so. She no longer found it necessary, either, to seek the sanctuary of her bedchamber once the evening meal had come to an end, and had on several occasions joined Linford in his library, where they had played cards or chess, or had simply read in companionable silence.

Raising her eyes, Rachel gazed across the room to where a picture of her husband—painted, she guessed, shortly before their marriage had taken place—hung above the fireplace. She frowned, perplexed, as she studied that handsome young face. What manner of man had she married?

For years she had considered him as nothing more than a mercenary and callous rake, who had married her for the sole purpose of saving his ancestral home, and then had abandoned her, discarded her like some worn-out shoe. Had her assessment of his character been so very wrong? Had she unjustly maligned him for six long years?

She was still unsure; but she had to own that he had, for the most part, treated her with kind consideration since her return to the Hall—far better than she had, perhaps, deserved to be treated, considering her little subterfuge during the London Season. And as far as his being a rake was concerned. . .? Well, didn't most men in his position keep a mistress? Was he any worse than others of his class?

Her frown grew heavier. When he had informed her at the breakfast table that morning that he would be away for several days, she had accepted his leaving without question.

She had not asked where he intended going, nor had he offered an explanation for his sudden departure; but she could make an educated guess. Unless she was very much mistaken, he would be in London before this day was over, and in the welcoming arms of his light-o'-love.

The thought pained her, and she cursed herself for such weakness. After all, Linford had kept his word, and had not forced his attentions on her at any time, so she ought not to feel hurt and aggrieved if he sought solace in some other woman's arms... She ought not, she knew, but she did.

A knock on the door broke into her disturbing thoughts, and she looked round to see Mrs Litton entering the room. Since the day the housekeeper had made her aware of Alice's continued bouts of coughing, which had been troublesome only at nights, Rachel had viewed the house-keeper in a far different light. She suspected that the housekeeper's attitude towards her had changed, too.

It was only natural that Mrs Litton would have been concerned when she learned that the Hall was to have a mistress at last. After all, she had been given free rein to run the fine Elizabethan residence as she had seen fit, and her conscientious attitude towards her work had obviously found approval in Linford's eyes.

However, once Rachel had made it abundantly clear that she had no intention of interfering in the smooth running of the house, Mrs Litton had visibly thawed towards her, and now even managed a semblance of a smile as she approached the desk.

They had spent most of the morning going through the linen cupboards, an exceedingly boring but necessary task that Rachel's temporary position as mistress of the house behoved her to undertake.

She cast her eyes briefly over the list the housekeeper had placed into her hand. 'That's fine, Mrs Litton. I'll order these items this afternoon.' She looked up to find her still hovering by the desk. 'Was there something else you wished to discuss with me?'

'Yes—no, my lady. Only, perhaps, when you have some

free time, we could go through the china cupboards together.'

'Of course. We'll do it tomorrow.'

Narrow-eyed, Rachel watched the housekeeper leave the room. There had been several occasions during the past two or three weeks when she had felt that Mrs Litton had wanted to say something, had wanted to confide in her, but at the last moment had seemed to change her mind. There was certainly something troubling that woman, she decided, reaching for the pen again.

She spent the remainder of the afternoon writing various letters, including a reply to Lady Barnsdale's, and after dinner that evening retired early to bed. Consequently, she awoke early the following morning.

Her resolve to do something for Ben Hughes had not been forgotten, but an epidemic of measles had kept the young doctor extremely busy during the past weeks, and Rachel had decided to postpone seeking his advice until he was less harassed. Hopefully, there had been no new cases, and she would find the young doctor at home.

Under a cloudless sky, she rode towards the small market town, situated some two miles from Linford Hall, and was fortunate enough to catch Dr Gillis emerging from his small, red-brick house. He looked round at her approach, his expression a mixture of delighted surprise and foreboding.

'Do not worry, Dr Gillis,' she said laughingly, 'I have not succumbed to the epidemic nor, I am glad to say, has any other member of my husband's household.'

'Thank heavens!' he said with feeling. 'No new cases reported this week, so, hopefully, it has run its course.'

'Have I caught you at an awkward moment? Were you about to visit a sick patient?'

'No, ma'am. I was merely going for a ride to enjoy this glorious morning.'

'In that case, can I persuade you to accompany me over to the Hughes' farm? I should like very much for you to take a look at the elder son,' she said, and then went on to divulge her suspicion that Ben Hughes was deaf.

Dr Gillis did not hesitate and when, half an hour later, they arrived at the farmhouse, they were fortunate enough to find Ben sitting in the kitchen with his mother.

Mrs Hughes looked surprised by the unexpected visit, but showed Dr Gillis into the front parlour, where he could carry out his examination in private. She seemed, in fact, more concerned over Rachel's remaining in the kitchen than over the welfare of her son who, she maintained, was as fit as a fiddle.

'I hope the day never dawns when I shall be too proud to sit at a kitchen table, Mrs Hughes,' Rachel told her unequivocally, amused by the kindly woman's fussing and fretting over such an unimportant circumstance. 'When I was a child, I frequently sat at just such a table as this, and still consider the kitchen as one of my favourite rooms in a house.'

Slightly mollified, Mrs Hughes offered her distinguished visitor a glass of home-made wine. Rachel accepted politely, but it took every ounce of self-control she possessed not to grimace at its taste, and her tactful, if far from truthful, praise of the rich red liquid earned her a very warm smile of approval from the hard-working farmer's wife.

The doctor, accompanied by Ben, rejoined them presently, his young forehead furrowed by a deep frown. 'I believe, my lady, your suspicion is correct, but I should like a doctor more experienced than myself in this field to examine Ben, which will mean, of course, a visit to London.'

'Lunnon?' Mrs Hughes echoed, aghast, as though her son were being asked to travel to the other side of the world. 'But—but there's nothing the matter with my Ben. Why, he's never had a day's illness in his life! Not for a good many years, anyhow.'

'It's my belief,' Dr Gillis said gently, 'that Ben is deaf, at least partially so. But I should like to know the full extent of his condition. Have you never suspected as much?'

It was quite evident that she had not. She slumped down on to a chair, her mouth gaping. 'No, Doctor,' she admitted at length. 'I—I thought he was just a little slow, that's all. If you tell him to do a thing two or three times, he does it.'

'Yes, Mrs Hughes, I expect he does,' Rachel put in gently. 'And if you look directly at him and gain his attention before you speak, you would need to say a thing only once. There is nothing wrong with your son's understanding. Let me show you.' She reached out and touched Ben's arm, thereby gaining his attention. 'How is the rabbit you found? Is he well now?'

His reply was a large smile and a vigorous nodding of the head.

'That's good. Ben, would you be kind enough to get Dr Gillis a glass of your mother's excellent wine? I'm sure he'd enjoy it.'

'Well, I'll be damned!' Mrs Hughes exclaimed as she watched her son go directly to the cupboard and pour out her treasured home-made restorative. 'And all these years I thought the lad a slowtop.'

Dr Gillis swallowed a mouthful of wine and, much to Rachel's intense amusement, grimaced at its taste. 'Has he always been as he is now?'

'Oh, no, Doctor. Before the fever he were right enough, excepting he never did talk much. But after, he barely uttered a word, and now just grunts now and then.'

'Fever?' he echoed sharply. 'When was this?'

'A long time ago.' She frowned. 'Let me see. . . He'd o' been seven, or maybe eight. Mortal bad he were. Thought for a time he'd never pull through. But he were different after.' She looked at Rachel. 'But Lunnon, my lady? Course I'd like him to see this other doctor if it would help, but it's going to cost a deal o' brass, and I—'

'Don't you worry on that score, Mrs Hughes,' Rachel interrupted gently. 'I shall see to all that. Your son has helped so many of God's creatures. It's high time someone helped him in return.'

When they rode away from the farmhouse a short while later, Dr Gillis said, 'It's little wonder the poor woman never suspected. I've seen Ben on numerous occasions and the truth never occurred to me. You are to be congratulated, my lady.'

Rachel dismissed this with a wave of her hand. 'I shall be content if this London physician can help.'

'There's no guarantee, but I shall certainly write to my colleague.' He frowned. 'I wish I knew more about Ben's case. He may have been partially deaf from birth, or the fever he contracted might have been the cause. I'll call in to see the family again when I've had a reply to my letter, and question them further. I didn't like to ask too much, because it was quite evident her son's condition had come as a shock to the poor woman.'

'When you do take him to London travel post, and not on the stage. I shall pay all the expenses incurred, including your visit today. It will be daunting enough for poor Ben without the added trauma of travelling on the common coach,' she said, and then, looking ahead, noticed two riders approaching. 'Why, I do believe that's Lucy and Harry Maitland!'

The young doctor raised his eyes heavenwards, experiencing none of Rachel's delight. 'I hope they are not looking for me. Their young brother succumbed to a bad attack of the measles.'

'Yes, so Lucy informed me. I haven't seen much of her during the past couple of weeks. She's been fully occupied with looking after him, so I understand.'

'Yes. And a capital little nurse she is too. Worth ten of that—'

'Pampered sister,' Rachel finished for him, and laughed at his guilty expression. 'I couldn't agree more. Hello, you two.' She had grown very fond of the brother and sister, and smiled warmly at them both. 'Just out for a ride?'

'Yes. Thought I'd put some colour back in poor Lucy's cheeks. She's been cooped up for days looking after young Charles.'

'I trust he hasn't suffered a relapse?' the doctor enquired tentatively.

'Oh, no,' Lucy responded, much to the doctor's relief. 'He's well on the mend.'

'That's good to hear. You'll be able to accompany me out again now that you're free of your nursing duties.' Rachel grimaced. 'It's unfortunate that it cannot be this afternoon, but I'm afraid I'm at my housekeeper's disposal. But I should like very much to ride over to Penley some time, Lucy. I've been informed there's an excellent little shop there that sells the most marvellous selection of fabrics.'

'What a capital idea! You would be able to call in on Linford's brats on your way back, Lucy,' her brother suggested laughingly. 'You know how much you take their welfare to heart.'

'Harry, you ought not to call them that!' she admonished, casting him a disapproving look, and did not notice Rachel stiffen suddenly. 'I should like to go to Penley, my lady. Mama said it's high time I had some new gowns made.'

The trip was arranged for the following week, and they soon afterwards parted company, but Harry's jokingly spoken suggestion rang in Rachel's ears.

The following afternoon, curiosity having by that time got the better of her, she decided to pay a visit to her childhood home.

August had begun cold and wet, but now the month was drawing to a close, the weather had remembered that summer was not quite over and had decided to behave accordingly.

The afternoon was hot and humid; and decidedly thunderous, Rachel thought, as she rode the short distance to her old home. Involuntarily, she shuddered. How she had hated thunderstorms as a child! She vividly remembered hiding under the bedclothes, calling to a father who never came in response to her frightened cries.

More unpleasant memories, almost forgotten, came flooding back with frightening clarity, and she came perilously close to turning back on several occasions, not wishing to go near that house, which had been more like a prison than a home; but a mixture of rampant curiosity and a strong determination not to be cowed by childhood fears forced her to go on.

When at last she arrived at her destination, Rachel drew Firefly to a halt by the wrought-iron gates, which now stood open, welcoming any would-be visitor to enter, but which had been securely padlocked, effectively deterring any callers, when she had been a child.

She gazed about in wonder. What had happened to that 'hayfield' of a lawn which had disgraced the front of the house? What had become of those age-old trees, blown

down over the years in periods of high winds, and left to
decay where they had fallen?

She had given little thought to any changes which might
have occurred during her six-year absence, but never in
her wildest imaginings would she have expected to see
neatly clipped hedges and lawns, and a weed-free drive
lined with young, healthy trees.

Dismounting, she entered the well-tended grounds, still
unable to believe the evidence of her own eyes, and was
halfway along the drive when something small and sharp
hit her in the middle of the back. She turned, scanning the
grounds, wondering what could have hit her, and was
about to continue her walk towards the house when a
further missile was hurled in her direction, this time narrowly missing her shoulder to land a few feet ahead.

Narrow-eyed, Rachel looked down at the small stone,
and then turned her head to scan the line of trees which
edged the driveway. 'All right, come out, whoever you
are, otherwise I shall start throwing a few stones myself!'

She heard the impish chuckle before she saw the small
freckled face peer at her from behind one of the tree trunks.

'Wenches can't frow.'

Wenches? Rachel echoed silently. What an abominable
urchin! She tried her best to adopt a look of indignant
outrage. 'Come here, boy, or else you'll discover just how
wrong you are!'

The child hesitated for a moment, but then noticed the
unmistakable sparkle in a pair of green eyes, which might
possibly indicate a kindred spirit, and came slowly
towards her.

Rachel scanned the mischievous, upturned countenance
but, search as she would, she could detect not a semblance
of her husband's fine aristocratic features in the snub-
nosed, freckled little face, crowned by a riot of unruly
bright red curls. Her frown returned. Linford had a crass

nerve to criticise her colouring when he had produced a child with such carroty-coloured hair! Or was it his child?

'What's your name, boy?'

'Tom—Tom Forpe.'

'Forpe?' Rachel blinked. 'Oh, I see—Thorpe.'

'That's what I said.'

'Well, we shan't argue over that point.' Her lips twitched. 'And how old are you, Tom?'

'Mrs Lucas said as how I were nine.'

'Mrs Lucas?' Rachel echoed. 'Does she look after you up at the house?'

He nodded. 'She and Mr Lucas teaches us to read and write.'

Rachel frowned again as a thought struck her. 'Are you the eldest child here, Tom?'

He shook his head. 'Jack's firteen. And Clem's nearly seventeen. He was the first un 'is lordship brung. But he don't live in the 'ouse no more. He looks after the stables.'

Rachel smiled to herself as she continued her progress towards the house, her very informative companion skipping along beside her. Linford must have begun his lascivious career at a remarkably young age to be the proud father, now, of a sixteen-year-old youth. Linford's brats—as Hetta so charmingly referred to them—were orphans!

The vastly improved condition of the grounds had prepared her for the changes she would see up at the house. There was no sign, now, of the creeping ivy that had covered the front aspect of the red-brick house, making the interior dark and gloomy even on the brightest summer's day.

There were no cracked panes of glass in the windows, allowing bitterly cold winds to infiltrate the gloomy rooms; no peeling paint work and no missing tiles, allowing rain to pour down on to the upper floor. Had she not known it for a fact, she would never have believed that this attractive, well-maintained house was the same gloomy, dilapidated building in which she had grown up.

'I'm sorry, Tom,' she said, realising suddenly that her young companion had spoken. 'What did you say?'

'Do you want me to take yer 'oss round to the stables?'

' 'Oss. . .? Oh, I see! Yes, thank you.'

Rachel handed Firefly's reins over to Tom, and was walking up to the front door when it opened suddenly, and a woman, dressed in a neat grey gown, came out of the house.

'Oh!' The woman looked as surprised as Rachel, but then she smiled. 'I thought I heard one of my charges out here as I was crossing the hall. I sent him out on an errand quite some time ago, and he has not yet returned.'

'You were not mistaken, ma'am. Tom has very kindly taken my mount to the stables.' Rachel returned the smile. 'May I introduce myself? I am Lady Linford. And you, I think, must be Mrs Lucas.'

'Indeed, I am. And may I say how pleased I am, my lady, that you have found the time to pay us a visit.' She moved to one side, allowing Rachel to enter the hall, and noticed the wry smile as her visitor gazed at the white-painted walls and highly polished surfaces. 'Am I right in thinking this is the house you grew up in, my lady?'

Rachel nodded. 'But it bears little resemblance, now, to my childhood home.' She brought her gaze to rest on Mrs Lucas's attractive countenance. 'How many children are in your care?'

'Thirteen. But we expect a new boy any day now.'

'Have you only boys here?'

'Unfortunately, yes. There are just as many destitute girls as boys.' She sighed. 'But it would be impractical to have both sexes here. As you know, my lady, this is by no means a large house, and the children must share the bedchambers.'

Rachel noticed Mrs Lucas glance at the grandfather clock, the only item of furniture in the hall that she recalled from her childhood. 'You are obviously extremely busy, Mrs Lucas. Please don't let me keep you from your duties.'

She received an apologetic smile. 'We do, I'm afraid, need to keep to a strict timetable. My husband takes all the children at this hour, enabling me to help in the dining-room. But if you would care to step into the study, I shall be happy to rejoin you presently?'

'Please do not put yourself out on my account,' Rachel returned politely. 'I have no wish to disrupt your routine, but if you do not object, I should very much like to take a look around before I leave?'

'Please do, my lady. My husband is teaching in the library. I know he would be delighted to make your acquaintance.'

Rachel watched Mrs Lucas disappear down the passage-way leading to the kitchen area, and then looked at the closed library door. She shuddered convulsively. Of all the rooms in the house, she had hated that one most of all. To that gloomy interior had she been summoned when-ever her father had taken the trouble to see her, and then only to berate her for some slight lapse in concentration during her lessons. She would meet Mr Lucas some other time!

Looking about with interest, she mounted the stairs, and went along the passageway to her father's bedchamber. She threw wide the door, and stood on the threshold, staring into that large room where she had exchanged those meaningless vows with a man who had cared not a whit for her. Strangely, though, the knowledge no longer made her feel bitter.

She frowned over this as she gazed about her. Gone

was that four-poster bed with its faded, worn hangings; gone was the paper, mottled with black mould and peeling from the walls; gone was the smell of damp and decay. That depressing room had been transformed into a bright, airy dormitory, sweetly perfumed with lavender, where six small beds stood at intervals against the walls.

Quietly closing the door, she made her way to her old room. Smaller than her father's bedchamber, this room contained just four cots, a wash-stand and a large wardrobe in one corner. Her smile was crooked as she went over to the window. It bore no resemblance whatsoever to her old bedchamber, but, then, none of it bore any resemblance to her childhood home.

She stared out at the back garden to see large, neat beds, filled with brightly coloured flowers, where once only weeds had flourished. Suddenly the irony of it all hit her, and she dissolved into laughter.

'I'm so pleased to discover that my absence has not depressed you unduly, my dear.'

Startled, Rachel swung round to find the Viscount standing beside the door, a mocking glint in his violet eyes. 'Oh, Linford!' she managed before slumping down on to the window-sill and giving way to mirth once more.

Her laughter was infectious, and he was unable to prevent a smile as he came slowly towards her. 'May I be permitted to know the reason for all this hilarity?'

'I'm sorry.' Rachel dabbed at her eyes with her handkerchief. 'It's all this, Linford.' She waved a hand about the room. 'My father never spent a penny on this place that I can recall. He must be turning in his grave, knowing that his money has been used to transform a place he neglected so dreadfully into such a lovely house.'

He smiled down into her laughing eyes. 'I hoped you would approve.'

'How could I not? And to have turned it into a home

for orphans is the ultimate irony. He cared not a whit for his fellow man—children least of all.' She looked up at him, wondering for the second time in the space of a few days what manner of man she had married? 'What made you do this wonderful thing, Linford?'

'I had many reasons, Rachel. I had no need of a second property in the area.' His smile was bitter. 'And there was a child once, my dear, I couldn't help. . .didn't help. A frightened and lonely girl I turned my back on. I started this home in her memory. . .to salve my conscience, if you like.'

Rising to her feet, Rachel placed her hand gently on his arm. 'You were not responsible for my upbringing, Linford,' she said softly. 'Money and possessions have never meant very much to me, but I have to own that had my father left his fortune to me and not to you, I should never have thought of doing such a charitable thing.'

He stared into the depths of her green eyes for endless moments, a frown of puzzlement in his own. 'You have a very generous spirit, my dear. I said I needed to get to know you all over again. I was wrong. I have never truly known you. But I rather think I'm beginning to.'

She moved away, unable to meet that piercing scrutiny; unable to understand why her heart was beating so rapidly at his nearness. 'I think it's time I started to make my way back to the Hall. It will soon be time for dinner.'

The Viscount did not offer to accompany her but, even so, was back at the Hall in good time for dinner.

Afterwards they went into the library, as they had frequently done before his trip away.

She watched him go across to the decanters and pour out two glasses of wine, whilst recalling her visit to her old home earlier. 'Mrs Lucas said she was expecting a new boy any day. Is that why you went away? Did you bring him back with you?

'Yes. I learned of his plight last week. Both his parents died of typhoid, and he was to be sent to the poorhouse.'

'I wish you had told me, Linford,' she said, an unmistakable note of censure creeping into her voice.

'About what?' He handed her her wine before seating himself opposite. 'The reason behind my leaving the Hall? Or the use to which I have put your childhood home?'

'Both.'

He cast her a brief smile. 'Strangely enough, Rachel, I thought you already knew. I felt certain my darling aunt must have told you about my—er—little hobby.'

'She did in a way, I suppose. Only when she referred to the children as your brats, I thought—' She caught herself up on the admission she had been about to make, a guilty flush rising in her cheeks.

'What did you think?' He received no reply, and eyed her narrowly for a moment. 'Rachel, you don't mean to tell me that you thought I housed my—er—by-blows in your old home?' He gave a sudden shout of laughter at the continued guilty silence. 'What a virile man you must think me to have produced such a large progeny! My dear, I'm flattered.'

'I do not consider that in the least amusing, Linford.'

He chuckled at the primness, but suppressed the urge to tease her further. Instead, he delved into the pocket of his coat, drew out a small package and, reaching forward, place it into her hands.

'I had that re-framed, and collected it whilst I was in London.'

'Oh, so you did go to London,' she said, unable to hide the disappointment she was experiencing from creeping into her voice.

'Yes, but I stayed only one night.' Again he looked

thoughtfully at her. 'Why, was there something you wished me to get for you? Or did you wish to accompany me?'

'What. . .? Oh, no.'

She began to undo the small package, feeling not just a little confused. Would he have taken her with him if she had asked? If so, then he had not visited the metropolis with the intention of paying a call on his mistress, she felt sure. He had left Hampshire for the sole purpose of collecting that child. Her tiny smile of satisfaction faded as she stared down at the only likeness of her mother she had ever seen.

She took in every detail of the sweet young face that smiled back at her from the miniature: the small straight nose, the large green eyes and the mass of auburn curls. 'So, this is how you discovered my identity,' she said softly.

'There's certainly some resemblance between you. But I suspected who you really were even before I saw that. The miniature merely confirmed my suspicion.'

'My childhood would have been so very different, I'm certain, had she lived,' she murmured, unable to take her eyes off her mother's lovely face, and did not see the sudden frown crease his lordship's forehead.

'How do you know she's dead, Rachel?'

'My father told me. She died in a carriage accident, not long after she had left him.'

'I see.'

His tone was curt, almost censorious, she thought, and she did not hesitate in coming to her mother's defence.

'I never blamed her for running off with that man, Linford. She was the younger daughter of an impoverished baronet. She must have married my father for security, but it was doomed to failure from the start. She married a man more than twice her age. She, so I've been told, loved company and parties, and pined for gaiety. Lord, what a mismatched pair! You know what a penny-pinching recluse my father was.'

'And do you crave gaiety and parties?' he surprised her by enquiring.

'Not particularly, no.'

'Pity, because I intend holding a dinner-party here in the very near future. And you, my dear, must honour your promise by being the perfect hostess.'

Rachel, surprisingly, was delighted at the prospect. She had by this time dined at the homes of several neighbours, and holding a dinner-party would be a splendid way of repaying their hospitality and the many kindnesses bestowed upon her since her return to the Hall.

She retired to bed in a very contented mood. She had little trouble falling to sleep, but it was an uneasy sleep, plagued by visions of her old home, dark and cold. Then, suddenly, she was back in her old bedchamber, seeing the frightening ghostly shapes against the walls as the lightning flashed, and covering her ears against the deafening claps of thunder.

She screamed out for her father, but he did not come; he never came. Then, unexpectedly, he was there, gathering her into his arms, stroking her hair, comforting her.

'You came, Papa. . .you came to me.'

'Yes, I'm here,' a deep voice responded softly. 'There's nothing to frighten you now. It will soon be over.'

She clung to him, resting her head against his broad chest, marvelling at the strength of him, the comfort of him. She was safe. For the first time in her life she felt completely safe, and sleep came once again to claim her.

She awoke the following morning to see bright sunlight streaming through the bedroom window and Alice standing beside the bed, a concerned look on her young face.

'Did you have a bad night, my lady? I came in earlier,

but you was sound asleep, and I didn't like to wake you.'

'I had a nightmare, Alice,' she replied rubbing the sleep from her eyes. 'I dreamt I was back in my old home, cowering under the covers because of a thunderstorm. How silly!'

'But there was a storm, my lady. Not surprising, really. It was that hot and sticky last night, but it's better now.'

Rachel frowned in puzzlement. So, there had been a storm. How odd! She shrugged as she sat up, and was about to take the cup of chocolate Alice was holding out when she noticed a single strand of black hair, short and slightly waving, on one of the pillows. Her eyes flew to the connecting door. How much of what had happened last night had been dream. . .? And how much reality?

# *Chapter Nine*

**R**achel took one final look at the formal dining-room, her eagle eye searching for any slight fault, but everything looked perfect. And so it should, she reflected, considering how hard she had worked to ensure that the evening would turn out to be a success. And with precious little help from the Viscount, either!

Apart from insisting that the Halhams and Fitzwilliams were invited, he had taken so little interest in the proceedings that Rachel had long since come to the conclusion that he had not been so very enthusiastic over holding a dinner-party in the first place.

The suggestion, probably, had stemmed only from rampant curiosity to see how she would match up to his ideal of a perfect hostess. Well, a temporary Viscountess she might be, but she was determined she would not be found lacking in that department!

Linford might have been of precious little assistance, but Peplow and Mrs Litton could not have done more to help. Nothing had been too much trouble for either of them. They had carried out her orders with such smiling enthusiasm that Rachel suspected they wished the evening to be as big a success as she did herself. Why, even that

148

morning, Mrs Litton had spent over an hour with her, pondering over the seating arrangements.

Rachel had wanted both Lucy and Harry, who would be returning shortly to Oxford, to attend, but felt that she could not possibly have invited them without extending the invitation to include their parents. Like Linford, she found Colonel Maitland, whom she had by this time met on several occasions, a very pleasant, easy going gentleman, but her opinion of his wife had not changed very much, although she was careful not to show her true feelings in front of Lucy.

Inviting the family had made the seating arrangements difficult. Linford had stated flatly that he would not have that 'insufferable woman' placed anywhere near him at the dining-table, and as Lucy was never completely at ease whenever her mother was near, the task had been no easy one, but she believed, as she glanced at the name cards, that they had the placings just about right.

'Yes, Peplow, everything looks very fine.' She cast him one of her lovely smiles, which had made him her devoted slave almost from the moment she had returned to the Hall. 'I don't know how you managed to get Simpkins to part with so many of his prized blooms, but well done. The flower arrangements look lovely.'

'I believe, my lady, that all his lordship's people know what is expected of them on occasions such as these.'

Rachel smiled over this as she made her way up to her rooms. Linford's servants certainly did know what was expected of them, not only on just such an occasion, but at all times. There wasn't one of them, either in the house, or working on the estate, who wasn't devoted to his master. Linford was well respected by all, seemingly; and she had to own that that respect was not misplaced.

Linford was a thoughtful master, and a considerate landlord. It was little wonder that he was so well liked.

Surprisingly enough, she had grown, by almost imperceptible stages, to like the man whom she had vilified for so
many years. A sudden frown replaced the smile. Yes, she
certainly did like him, now. . .perhaps rather *too* well for
her peace of mind.

Brushing this disturbing realisation aside, she concentrated on getting herself ready for the dinner-party. She
had absolutely no intention of stumbling at the first hurdle
by being late to welcome their guests.

She emerged from her bedchamber in good time, dressed
in the dark red gown that she had worn on the occasion
of their visit to the theatre, with an elegant silk shawl
draped over her arms, and with her hair more elaborately
dressed than usual. She descended the stairs and went into
the large salon to find her husband standing by the fireplace, contemplating the huge logs burning brightly on
the hearth.

At the sound of her light tread on the carpet, he turned,
his expression betraying his evident appreciation of her
faultless appearance, his eyes resting for a moment on her
hair, where a bright ribbon was intricately woven through
her shining locks. 'As always, my dear, your appearance
leaves nothing to be desired.'

There was no uneasiness between them these days, and
she accepted the compliment with a gracious smile. 'I
have every intention of living up to your expectations this
evening, Linford, but I think I should warn you that I
have never in my life acted the part of hostess. Although,
through Lady Anne's careful instruction, I believe I know
what is expected of me.'

'You live up to my expectations on all occasions,
Rachel. I have no fears for this evening.'

Although very gratified, and not just a little touched by
this vote of confidence, Rachel found she was unable to

relax completely until all their guests had arrived and were seated in the dining-room, happily conversing and enjoying the delicacies placed before them.

She glanced round the table at the smiling faces before bringing her gaze to rest on the man seated on her right. 'I'm pleased you were able to join us this evening, Dr Gillis. Though I wouldn't have been in the least surprised to receive word that you were unable to attend.'

'A busy social life is a pursuit very few country practitioners are privileged to enjoy. It is one of the disadvantages of our profession, ma'am. But the sick come first. I must always leave word where I am to be found, and am frequently called away from such pleasurable evenings as this.'

He cast her one of his rare smiles. 'I'm sorry I was unable to bring you better news concerning Ben.' He had taken Ben to London the previous week, and the specialist's findings had not been encouraging. 'As I told you, there is little that can be done for Ben, I'm afraid. Although medical science is progressing yearly, knowledge in that particular field is not great. But at least we now know for certain that Ben isn't totally deaf.'

'I cannot in truth say that this has come as any great surprise to me,' she admitted, looking thoughtful. 'How else does he come across those wounded creatures he's forever finding, if he cannot hear their cries?'

She brightened suddenly. 'However, it isn't all gloom, sir. One good thing has come out of our knowing for certain about his condition. I visited the Hughes family yesterday, and was delighted to see how they included Ben in their conversation, attracting his attention first, and then speaking slowly. He understood their every word. Hopefully, his life now will not be quite so solitary.'

After the meal was over, Rachel rose from the table and invited the ladies to join her in the large salon, an elegantly appointed room, but one which had never been frequently used, except on an occasion such as this, when the Carlton family had been entertaining a large number of guests. She invited Mrs Fitzwilliam, a gifted player, to entertain them on the pianoforte, and then joined Lucy and her mother on the sofa.

She smiled warmly at her young friend before turning to the older woman. 'Are you not glad, ma'am, that you decided on the gold colour for Lucy's gown? She looks charming tonight, do you not agree?'

Their trip to Penley two weeks before had begun badly. They had intended to ride, but as the overcast sky had looked decidedly threatening, Rachel had called for Lucy in the carriage, and had been dismayed to discover not only her friend awaiting her, but also Mrs Maitland. However, the trip to the busy market town had, surprisingly, turned out to be enjoyable and quite eventful.

Lucy had lost a considerable amount of weight during the past weeks, and looked a great deal better for having done so, but it was not until that trip to Penley that Rachel had realised that her young friend's character had begun to change also, and had been amazed to discover that Lucy could be quite stubbornly determined when she chose.

The girl had flatly refused to look at any material in white, declaring that it made her look sallow, and had showed little interest, either, in anything in a pastel shade. It had taken a great deal of diplomacy, not to say guile, on Rachel's part to persuade the formidable matron to consider the richer-coloured fabrics for her daughter.

She succeeded so well, in fact, that by the time they had emerged from the shop with three lengths of material, neatly packaged, Mrs Maitland had been firmly convinced that she, herself, had been instrumental in making the choices.

'Personally, I still consider white and pinks more suit-

able for young girls.' Mrs Maitland permitted herself a
thin smile. 'But I must own that, in Lucy's case, richer
shades are more becoming.'

Sarah Halham voiced the same opinion, later, when
Rachel was able to have a quiet word with her favourite of
Linford's neighbours. 'Lucy has improved immeasurably
since your arrival. You've done wonders for the girl's
appearance and self-confidence.'

'It has little to do with me, Sarah,' Rachel countered.
'She has seemed far less restrained since her sister's departure. And Mrs Maitland, too, has taken more interest in
her now that Arabella is not about to pet and fuss over.'
She frowned slightly. 'It must have been no easy thing
for poor Lucy, always to be compared with her far
prettier sister.'

'True,' Mrs Halham agreed. 'There's no denying that
Arabella is the beauty in the family, but I rather think
Lucy is turning into a very pretty girl in her own right.
What is more, the girl possesses charm, which is something
the elder sister decidedly lacks. I don't think there's a soul
in the district who doesn't prefer Lucy to her sister.

'And talking of Arabella,' she went on conspiratorially,
'have you heard the latest? That aunt of hers has taken
her to Paris.'

'If that doesn't beat all!' Rachel exclaimed after a
moment's stunned silence. 'I understood the girl had been
sent to her aunt as a form of punishment. I wish someone
would punish me by taking me to Paris!'

'Well, it most certainly shan't be me,' his lordship
drawled, approaching them unnoticed. 'I should resort to
more tried and tested means to school an unruly female.'

'I do not doubt that for a moment,' Rachel responded,
flashing him such a look from beneath her long, curling
lashes that Mrs Halham gurgled with laughter. 'I hope you
now realise, Sarah, what an overbearing brute my husband

is,' she added, before moving away to mingle with the other guests.

'Your wife is charming, Linford. And a firm favourite with my children. They simply adore her. Young Henry, wretched boy, calls her a great gun. She very nearly beat him at spillikins the other morning when she paid us a visit. In fact, it's my belief she let him win.'

'Yes, she would.' His smile contained a special warmth. 'She's very fond of children. She has spent a deal of time up at the house with the boys during the past two weeks.' He drew out his snuff box and gazed down absently at the delicately painted lid for a few moments before flicking it open with a practised finger. 'I learned earlier that she has also taken a keen interest in Ben Hughes. Did you know he was deaf, Sarah?'

'Ben Hughes. . .? No, I didn't.' She frowned. 'I thought him merely slow-witted.'

'Yes, as did we all, but apparently he isn't. My conversation with our young doctor over the port was most informative. I must remember to speak to my wife later.'

His memory did not fail him. After the last of their guests had reluctantly departed, he asked Rachel if she would accompany him into the library, where a glowing fire still burned brightly on the hearth.

She shivered as she spread her fingers towards the flames. It was now late September, and she had detected a decidedly frosty nip in the night air as she had stood at the front door, seeing the last of the guests safely installed into their carriage.

'I think the evening went very well,' she remarked, shaking her head as he raised a decanter.

'Yes, a most enjoyable evening, Rachel,' he agreed, pouring a glass of brandy before seating himself in his favourite winged-chair. 'I received compliments from every quarter about the very gracious hostess.'

'Your neighbours are charming people, Linford,' she responded, smiling. 'It would be impossible not to like them.'

One dark brow rose. 'What, all of them, Rachel?'

She did not pretend to misunderstand. 'I can tolerate Mrs Maitland, sir. Rather better than you can, I suspect. She was very gratified over the many compliments passed about Lucy. At long last she has taken notice of the girl.' She frowned suddenly. 'I just hope she continues to do so when her elder daughter returns.'

'You have taken a keen interest in young Lucy, Rachel. Not that I blame you—a very sweet, unaffected child.' He paused to sip his brandy, watching her over the rim of his glass. 'Just as you have taken an interest in Ben Hughes.'

She detected the slight note of censure in his voice, and looked at him sharply. 'You do not object, I trust?'

'To your interest, no. But I object most strongly to your laying out money on his behalf.'

She continued to stare at him in a mixture of disbelief and annoyance. Not a cross word had passed between them in a very long time, and this fact held her temper in check.

'I don't believe you mean that, Linford,' she said levelly. 'You said the money left to me by Lady Anne was mine to do with as I choose. I would far rather spend my inheritance on helping people like Ben Hughes than rigging myself out in finery. Why may I not do some good with it if I wish?' The only response was a heavy, prolonged frown. 'Now what have I said to put you out of temper?'

'I am not out of temper,' he assured her, his frown vanishing. 'I applaud your sentiments, my dear. But I'm afraid I cannot condone your laying out blunt on Ben Hughes's behalf. I have asked Dr Gillis to forward an account of his expenses incurred to me. I shall deal with the matter from here on.'

He smiled at the angry flash in her lovely eyes. 'Yes, my dear, I know you feel aggrieved, and think it crass insolence on my part to interfere. But I cannot. . .I simply cannot have everyone discovering the interest you have shown in another man. Think of my reputation! It will be rumoured that you prefer a halfwit to me!'

Rachel gaped across at him in open-mouthed astonishment for a few moments, then burst out laughing. 'Oh, you idiot! And Ben is not halfwitted.'

'So I have been led to infer. I have arranged to ride over to the Hughes' farm with our young doctor tomorrow morning. Something might yet be done for Ben.' He paused to sip his wine, his brow furrowed in thought. 'He'll never make a farmer—that much is certain. He could never bring himself to kill a beast, even for food.'

'Yes, I know.' She sighed. 'His case does seem hopeless.'

'On the contrary, my dear,' he surprised her by responding, 'his love for animals might well prove to be his salvation.'

'What do you mean?'

'I'll see Ben first, and if I think he's capable, I'll ride over to Linfield and have a word with John Trench. Trench could do with some help at that forge of his. He's not getting any younger. And Ben might be just the help he needs. He'd make an ideal farrier.'

'What an excellent notion, sir! I should never have thought of that.'

Rachel climbed into bed that night in a very contented mood, but the Viscount had given her much to ponder over. It had irked her immeasurably, at first, to think that he disapproved of her kind-hearted actions, and although he had made light of it, she had come to the conclusion that perhaps he had had good reason.

She was honest enough to admit that she had given little thought to the consequences of her philanthropic gesture; but if it became common knowledge that she was singling out one particular family, and helping financially by paying a doctor's fees, it might well give rise to ill feeling amongst Linford's other tenants, and that was something which she had absolutely no desire to do.

After all, she thought with a pang of sadness, she was here for a short time only, and resentment was the last thing she wished to leave behind her.

Perhaps it was because she had grown so quickly to enjoy the privileged life of a respected peer of the realm's wife that the weeks sped by, and November, as damp and depressing as the knowledge that her position as Viscountess Linford was only a temporary one, arrived all too quickly. On the first dry afternoon she sent orders to the stables for Firefly to be saddled, and directly after luncheon set off in the direction of Linfield.

On the morning after the dinner-party the Viscount had ridden over to the Hughes' farm; as a consequence of that visit, Ben was now working at the forge. Rachel did not doubt for a moment that it had been through Linford's commendation that the blacksmith had agreed to offer Ben, a young man universally acknowledged to be simple-minded, work at the forge.

She wondered, as the outskirts of the small market town came into view, whether the blacksmith, like Linford, had changed his opinion of the hapless farmer's son?

Even before Rachel had arrived at the smithy, she could hear the clanking sound of hammer on metal, and smiled as she saw Ben through the open doorway, busily repairing a wheel. He did not turn his head as she dismounted and led Firefly into the entrance, but John Trench, a burly man in his late forties, with a mop of grizzled hair and with a big, almost toothless, smile, saw her approach, and went towards her, wiping his hands on a grimy rag.

'Good day to you, Mr Trench. I did not come here with work, I'm afraid, only with rampant curiosity to see how your apprentice goes on.'

'He be doing just fine, my lady,' he beamed, betraying the fact once again that one could count the teeth in his head on one hand. 'I don't deny I were a bit unsure at first, wondering just what I'd be taking on, but there's nought wrong wi' the lad, 'cepting he's a bit deaf.'

'And you don't find that a problem?' she enquired tentatively.

'There's no denying I did at first,' he admitted, 'but that were my own fault. I kept forgetting, you see. But Sally—she be me young niece that keeps house for me now my wife be no longer 'ere—she kept on at me to give 'im a prod afore I speaks, and I remembers now.'

A sudden movement caught Rachel's attention. The next moment a squirrel, a decidedly grubby bandage wrapped around its middle, darted across the rough dirt floor to hide itself in a pile of hay in the corner.

'Oh, dear,' she said ruefully. 'I'd forgotten about that. Are there any more of his injured friends about?'

The blacksmith was amused, his large belly shaking with silent laughter. 'No, only that critter, but I don't mind 'ee.' He moved away, and touched Ben's arm. 'Visitor for you, m'lad. Make haste! Her ladyship don't want to be standing about all day.'

Ben, his young face wreathed in smiles, came towards Rachel. Firefly whinnied at his approach, and nuzzled his outstretched hand affectionately.

'There ain't a creature don't like 'im, m'lady,' the blacksmith said, giving Ben a hearty slap on the back, which would have sent a less robust individual sprawling to the ground. 'Why, only last week Farmer Dent brought that evil beast of 'is to be shod. Nasty brute of a roan it be, ma'am. A real kicker! But wi' young Ben 'ere, it were as gentle as a lamb. Wouldn't 'ave believed it ifen I 'adn't seen it wi' me own eyes. The lad's a wonder!'

'Yes.' She smiled softly. 'He certainly does have a way with animals.'

She turned as a customer arrived at the forge, her smile vanishing as her eyes met those of Harry Maitland's hard-featured groom.

Although Renfrew always accompanied Lucy whenever she rode over to the Hall, Rachel, thankfully, had seen little of him since that disgraceful incident near the home wood. Whenever they had arranged to ride out together, she had always arrived at Lucy's home accompanied by one of Linford's grooms, thereby cunningly avoiding the necessity of bringing Renfrew along.

The groom turned his malevolent gaze on to the blacksmith. 'Old Maitland wants this nag seen to—loose shoe.' He tossed the reins at John Trench. 'And be quick about it. I don't want to be 'anging round 'ere all day!'

'Your manners certainly do not improve, Renfrew.' Rachel looked him up and down in disgust. 'How very glad I am that you're not one of my husband's servants.'

'Huh!' His eyes, if possible, seemed to grow harder. 'I'd never work for the likes of 'im.'

'Believe me, Renfrew,' she responded, her smile far from sweet, 'you'd never be offered the opportunity.' She turned to the blacksmith. 'I think I shall ride home by way of Bluebell Ridge, Mr Trench, so I'll bid you good day.'

'Don't you be a-dawdling along, my lady,' he warned. 'There'll be rain afore long.'

By the time Rachel had arrived at the ridge, the sky had grown considerably darker, the clouds threatening to release their moisture at any moment, and she wished she had paid more heed to Mr Trench and had taken the shorter ride home. She urged Firefly on, and was halfway along the bridal path which skirted the ridge when she distinctly heard the sounds of another rider behind her.

Drawing Firefly to a halt, she looked round, hoping to see a neighbour, Lucy or even Linford come trotting round the bend in the path, but now there was only silence, a cold, eerie silence. How strange! She could have sworn she had heard hoof beats.

She looked about her at the wooded landscape. How sadly depressing the trees looked now, bared of their leaves. To her right the land rose sharply; to her left it sloped down gently to a sparkling stream, which rippled its way along the shallow valley.

Kicking her foot free of the stirrup, she slipped to the ground and, after securely tethering her mount to the branch of a tree, she went to the edge of the path to stare down at the stream, which had swelled considerably in the past days of heavy rain. Only thorn bushes and brambles covered the slope.

Everywhere looked so depressing, so unfriendly; but Lucy had assured her that in the spring it was a wonderful sight, covered with its blanket of blue. But she would never see that. Long before the bluebells had broken through the ground to transform the landscape with their delicately perfumed flowers, she would be gone.

The realisation was like being dealt a physical blow, knotting painfully at her insides and bringing tears to her eyes. How quickly she had grown to love this life she led! How quickly she had adapted to being a Viscountess, carrying out her duties just as though she had been born to the life. Which was quite remarkable in itself, she reflected sombrely, considering she was nothing more than a rich merchant's daughter.

Therein lay the crux of the matter, she knew. Linford had married her to save his ancestral home. Strangely, even this cruel fact no longer grieved her as it once had. How she had grown to love that stone-built Elizabethan house—not large in comparison to other ancestral homes, but far more comfortable than many of the grander houses.

What torment Linford must have suffered, knowing that he might easily lose that lovely house through no fault of his own. Little wonder he had grasped the opportunity her father had offered without a second thought. Had circumstances been different; had he married her for love, she felt sure their marriage would have been a successful one. They had so much in common: they seemed to laugh at the same things; seemed to like the same people; seemed to enjoy the same pastimes.

Some detached part of her brain registered that Firefly had whinnied, had been disturbed by something, but so deep was she in her depressing reverie that she did not even turn her head to see what had troubled the filly; and it was only when spots of rain began to fall that she gave herself a mental shake and came back to the present.

Sighing deeply, she turned and walked back to where she had tethered Firefly. Untying the reins, she climbed on to a conveniently fallen tree trunk and hoisted herself into the saddle. Then it happened, taking her completely by surprise.

Firefly, normally the gentlest of creatures, reared wildly like an animal possessed. Rachel's foot slipped out of the stirrup, she lost her grip on the reins, and was thrown through the air to land heavily amongst the damp, decaying leaves.

For a few moments she lay there, winded, her heart thumping against her ribs. Then, very slowly, she eased herself into a sitting position and turned her head in time to see Firefly galloping round a bend in the track. What on earth had come over the animal? she wondered. Skittish Firefly frequently was, but she had never behaved that way before.

Perplexed, she felt her shoulder. It ached abominably, but she did not think it was broken. Apart from still feeling badly shaken, she believed she had sustained no real injury, until she tried to stand. The pain in her right ankle was excruciating, and she fell down amongst the rotting leaves once again. Now what on earth was she going to do? Should she stay where she was and hope that someone would come along soon, or try to make it to the Hughes' farmhouse, less than a mile away?

She was still debating on which course of action to take when she heard a noise, like that of a twig breaking, and out of the corner of her eye saw a movement. Suddenly, there was a searing pain at the back of her head. She slumped forward, and felt the wet leaves against her face.

What was happening. . .? Was she moving. . .? What was that noise. . .? Laughter—such an evil, malicious sound! Another searing pain, in her side this time. Now she was rolling, falling. . .It was growing darker, ever darker. . .

# Chapter Ten

**P**eplow, a frown of concern creasing his brow, went quietly into the library, where his lordship was to be found most days at this time busily dealing with estate matters.

'I am sorry to disturb you, my lord, but Alice has just informed me that her ladyship has not as yet returned from her ride.'

Raising his eyes, the Viscount peered at the ormolu clock on the mantelshelf, and then turned his head to glance out of the window. It was not particularly late, but it was getting decidedly gloomy, and it had been raining steadily for the past half-hour.

'Her ladyship is usually back by this time, my lord,' the butler continued. 'She is very considerate to the feelings of Cook, and always returns in plenty of time for dinner.'

'Have you any idea where she went?'

'I believe she said she was riding over to Linfield, sir.'

'Very well.' Putting the papers aside, the Viscount rose to his feet. 'Send a message to the stables to have Ramon saddled. And tell Jem he had better accompany me.'

A short while later, when they set out towards Linfield, the rain, thankfully, had ceased. Linford was, naturally, a little concerned that Rachel still had not returned, but was certainly far from anxious, as several reasons for her having not done so had occurred to him.

She might well have sought shelter from the rain, or she might have called in briefly on one of the neighbours; more than likely the Halhams, who lived within a mile of the small market town. He expected to see her coming trotting towards them at any moment, but by the time they had reached Linfield, they still had not caught sight of their quarry.

His lordship had a fairly shrewd notion where Rachel had intended going that afternoon, and headed straight for the smithy, where John Trench stood at the closed wooden doors, a sturdy padlock in his large hand.

'Why, m'lord! I were just about to lock up for the day. Was there something I can do for you?'

'Have you seen my wife this afternoon, Trench?'

'That I 'ave, sir.' He cast one of his near-toothless smiles up at the Viscount. 'She came along earlier, asking after young Ben.'

'What time was this?'

'Must be two hours or more ago.' His smile faded. 'Be there aught amiss, m'lord?'

'She hadn't arrived home when we left, and we didn't catch sight of her along the road.'

'That be strange.' The blacksmith scratched his grizzled head. 'Ah! I mind, now. Her ladyship said as how she were going 'ome by way o' Bluebell Ridge.' His kindly face betrayed concern. 'But she ought to 'ave been back at the Hall long since, m'lord.'

'No doubt she has arrived by now,' he responded lightly. 'Thank you for your help, Trench.'

The young groom cast his master a quick sideways glance as they rode back along the main street. The Viscount had sounded quite unconcerned, indifferent, almost, but Jem was not fooled. He had worked up at the

Hall since he was twelve years old, and knew his master well. He sensed the Viscount's growing uneasiness, and was not surprised in the least when his lordship turned Ramon down the track leading to the ridge.

'Do you think her ladyship has met with an accident, sir?' he enquired tentatively.

'It's certainly a possibility, Jem. As a horsewoman your mistress is competent enough, but accidents happen even to the best riders. Added to which, I feel certain she would have sent a message if she had visited one of the neighbours and had known she would be home late, but from what Trench said, she had intended riding back to the Hall. So, keep a sharp look-out.'

By the time they had arrived at the ridge, the light was fading fast. Like all the other servants at the Hall, Jem had grown fond of his thoughtful mistress, and strained his young eyes to pierce the gloom. They were halfway along the ridge when his vigilance was rewarded, and he caught sight of something lying on the ground.

'What be that, sir?'

Dismounting, he bent to pick up the article, and knew, even before he handed it up to his master, to whom the green velvet hat belonged.

For several moments the Viscount stared down at the mud-coated hat in silence, his countenance ashen, then, 'Rachel! Rachel!' but only an ominous silence answered his frantic shouts.

He joined his groom on the ground, and looked about the track. He quickly noticed that in one place the thick covering of leaves had been recently disturbed, as though something, or someone, had been dragged along the ground. He traced the furrows to the path's edge, his keen eyes searching the sloping ground, but it was Jem who spotted what appeared to be a bundle of rags by the edge of the stream.

'What be that, sir?'

Tossing Ramon's reins to his young groom, the Viscount began his descent. Thorn bushes and brambles snared at his greatcoat, and his boots slipped on the leaf-covered ground, made even more treacherous by the recent downpour, but he forged his way on with little thought to his own safety, for the closer he drew to that recumbent form, the greater became his conviction that he had found his wife. Pray God she was alive!

The pounding of his heart had little to do with his exertions, he knew, as he knelt down beside her. Placing his hands on her shoulders, he gently turned her over. She did not stir, and beneath the streaks of dirt he saw the lovely face was deathly pale and the lips were tinged with blue.

Removing his glove, he slipped his hand beneath her jacket, and then sighed with relief as he felt the gentle rise and fall of her chest and detected the faint, but steady beating of her heart. Her face was scratched, and her torn and mud-splattered habit was sodden, but this was neither the time nor the place to try to discover the full extent of her injuries.

The climb down had been difficult; the climb back was both lengthy and exhausting. On numerous occasions he found himself sliding back down the slope, but held firm to his precious burden. When at last he reached the summit, breathless and arms aching painfully, he laid Rachel down and, removing her gloves, began to chafe her hands.

'She's alive, Jem,' he said in response to his groom's anxious expression, 'but as cold as ice.'

'Look, sir! She be coming round.'

His lordship, too, had heard the faint moan, and saw the movement beneath the eyelids before they briefly fluttered open. Delving into the pocket of his greatcoat, he drew out a silver flask, gently raised Rachel's head on to his lap and placed the flask to her lips. A trickle of liquid ran down her chin, but he did succeed in getting a little down her throat, for she coughed and spluttered and grimaced at its taste.

'That's better.' He could see the bluish tinge leaving her lips. 'Rachel, Rachel, can you hear me? Come, open your eyes! Look at me!'

The anxious voice broke through the veil of darkness drawing her back—back towards the light. Surely she recognised that voice? She opened her eyes, but the face that loomed above hers seemed featureless, distorted.

'Rachel, come back to me. Do you not know who I am?'

'Linford?' she murmured questioningly.

'Yes, it is I.' Smiling faintly, he placed the flask once again to her lips. 'Come, take some more of this. It will make you feel better.'

She meekly obeyed, and the fiery liquid, which burned its way down her throat, slowly began to spread its warmth, restoring a semblance of feeling to her frozen limbs. She made a feeble attempt to raise herself, but was pressed gently back.

'No, do not try to get up,' ordered that familiar, deep masculine voice. 'You've had a nasty fall. Lie still for a while longer.'

A fall? Rachel closed her eyes in an effort to remember, but her head ached so abominably that she abandoned the attempt. Not only her head, but her whole body felt battered and bruised, and there was an excruciating pain in her right ankle when she tried to move her leg.

Linford noted the spasm of pain flit across her face. 'Where are you hurt?'

'Everywhere.'

'Can you be a little more specific, my love? Anywhere in particular?'

This time when she opened her eyes, it was not like

trying to peer through a thick, swirling mist, and she could see his handsome features clearly, and his voice no longer seemed to come from far off. Her wits at least seemed to have been restored.

'My right ankle pains me dreadfully, it hurts to breathe, and my head is throbbing.'

'Not surprising, my darling. You have a lump the size of an egg. I felt it when I placed your head on my lap.'

'How charming! Now all I need to be told is that I have a black eye and my injuries are complete.'

He chuckled at the dry tone. 'I cannot be sure of that as your face is streaked with dirt, but I can discern at least two scratches.'

She managed to raise her hand in an arresting gesture. 'Pray, tell me no more, otherwise I shall undoubtedly go into a decline.'

The Viscount smiled down at her tenderly. His young wife had the heart of a lion. She was putting a brave face on it all, but he knew she must be in considerable discomfort from her numerous injuries. He needed to get her back to the Hall as quickly as possible, but dared not risk taking her the five-mile journey on horseback.

Furthermore, it was too risky to bring the carriage along this narrow track. If it did not get stuck in the mud, there was every chance that it would topple over the edge. Most pressing of all was the need to get her somewhere warm, and out of those wet clothes.

He turned to his groom. 'Jem, I want you to ride back to the Hall. Tell Peplow what has occurred. He'll know what to do. Then bring the carriage to the Hughes' farm. I'll take her there. But before you leave, help me get your mistress to her feet.'

This was accomplished easily enough, but Rachel swiftly discovered that her right ankle would bear no weight. She swayed slightly as she tried to balance on one foot, and clung to Jem for support, whilst his lordship removed his greatcoat and placed it round her shoulders.

She was now more than ever painfully aware of her many injuries, but made no protest when Linford picked her up once more and placed her very gently on Ramon's back. Her head swam and she was grateful when he eased himself in to the saddle behind her, and she could lean back against that broad expanse of chest.

'I'm sorry there's no easier way to get you home.' His voice for the first time betrayed anxiety. 'But it won't be long before we reach the Hughes' farmhouse.'

'I'm fine,' she lied, desperately trying to fight the sudden feeling of nausea. She watched Jem galloping down the track ahead of them until he disappeared from view, and then closed her eyes.

After some minutes the feeling, thankfully, began to subside, and she risked opening her eyes again to find they were now traversing a large field. Where on earth were they? More importantly, how had she managed to get herself into such a state?

Her riding habit was damp, very damp. It was too dark to see clearly, but she suspected that it was covered in mud. Which would be in no way remarkable, considering she had woken to find herself lying on the ground. But what had she been doing there in the first place?

She frowned in puzzlement. Everything was so hazy. A fall—Linford had mentioned a fall. She was dressed in her habit, so she must have been thrown from her horse, common sense told her. . . But if that was the case, where, then, was Firefly?

'What happened to me, Linford? I cannot remember a dratted thing. It is most disconcerting.'

'Don't attempt to, my darling,' he adjured her softly. 'No doubt it will all come back to you in time.'

'But you told me I'd had a fall,' she persisted. 'Obviously I was riding. So where is Firefly?'

'I haven't a clue,' he replied frankly. 'She would never find her way back to the Hall, so no doubt she's wandering the countryside somewhere. I'll send men out at first light to search.' He caught the faint sigh. 'Don't worry. We'll find her.'

Yes, just as you found me, she thought, smiling softly. 'How did you manage to find me, Linford? Did you know where I was going?'

'No, but you told Peplow you were riding over to Linfield. You called in at the smithy.'

'Did I?' She frowned. She could not even remember that.

'Yes,' he reiterated. 'And it was John Trench who told me you had ridden back by way of Bluebell Ridge.'

'Bluebell Ridge,' she echoed as a sudden flash of memory returned. Yes, she had been standing on the path, gazing down at the stream. Again she frowned. She had been perfectly all right then, she felt certain. She had walked back to Firefly, and. . .what? It was all a blank. She recalled nothing whatsoever until Linford had forced that fiery liquid down her throat.

'Look, over there!' he said suddenly, breaking into her perplexing thoughts. 'Can you see that faint light? It's the Hughes' farmhouse. We'll soon be there, my darling.'

By the time they had arrived at the rambling stone-built house, Rachel was trembling with cold, or maybe delayed shock, or perhaps a combination of both; Linford did not know, but the need to get her into the warm was pressing. As they entered the yard, he shouted at the top of his voice for assistance. Almost at once the kitchen door was thrown wide, and the industrious farmer, a lantern in his hand, peered out into the gloom.

'Who be that a-calling?'

'It is I, Linford. Her ladyship's been hurt.'

Moving aside, Hughes allowed Lord Linford to carry the Viscountess into the warm kitchen, and quickly closed the door against the cold, damp air. The only other occupant of the room was Ben who, the Viscount would have noticed had he not been so concerned over his wife, seemed strangely agitated over something, and there were the remains of a meal on the wooden table.

'Is your wife about, Sam?'

'No, sir. Young Clem took her over in the cart to the Stokes' place. The babe be on the way.' He cast a worried glance over the trembling Viscountess. 'Do you take your good lady into the parlour, sir? There be a fire in there. No, no, Ben, not now!' he snapped at his elder son, who was grasping his arm frantically. 'Can't you see 'er ladyship's hurt bad? Been thrown from 'er 'orse, I'll warrant.'

'Yes, and if that filly were here now,' the Viscount said grimly, having seen his wife's terrible condition clearly for the first time, 'I would be very tempted to put a ball through its brain.'

He followed Hughes down the narrow passageway and into a small room, where a mound of logs burned brightly on the hearth, and set her down on the wooden settle by the grate.

'I'll fetch 'ee a blanket, my lord,' the farmer offered, going about the room with a taper, lighting candles. 'And do you think 'er ladyship would like some broth? There be some made. Won't take but a few minutes to warm up.'

'That will serve admirably. But the blanket first, I think.'

Rachel, staring blindly down at the burning logs, was only vaguely aware of the conversation which passed between her husband and Sam Hughes. She paid little heed to the steam rising steadily from that part of her skirt nearest to the fire, or to Linford when he suddenly knelt on the floor in front of her and began to remove her left half-boot.

It was only when he gently raised her other foot on to his knee and began to loosen the ties on the right boot that she came out of her brown study as a spasm of pain ran through her.

'I'm sorry, my darling, but it must be removed,' he said softly, coaxingly, and she nodded, catching her bottom lip between her teeth to stop herself crying out.

When at last the terrible ordeal was over, she lay back against the settle and closed her eyes, only to sit bolt upright again a few moments later as she felt her skirts being raised.

'What on earth do you think you are doing, sir?' she demanded, indignation bringing colour back to her cheeks, as she tried, ineffectually, to push his hand away and lower her skirts.

'Don't be silly, Rachel,' he told her, in a voice he might have used when dealing with a recalcitrant child. 'Your stockings are soaked. They must be removed.'

His tone brooked no argument, and as she was hardly in a fit state to put up any worthwhile resistance, she had no choice but to submit, with as much grace as she could muster, to the indignity.

'Your ankle isn't broken, thank goodness, but it's badly sprained and very swollen,' he informed her after a gentle examination of the bared limb. 'Now, where's Hughes got to?'

As if on cue the door opened and the farmer re-entered, and handed the Viscount a thick woollen blanket.

'Don't know where our Ben's loped off to,' he informed them testily. 'Never about when he's needed. Came in earlier a-fussing and a-fretting. Reckon he found another of 'is injured critters on 'is way 'ome from the smithy. Wanted me to come out to the barn to take a look at 'im, but I wanted me dinner fust. Reckon 'ee be out there now. P'raps just as well, otherwise he'd be a-fretting you, my lady.'

He smiled down at Rachel. 'You be looking a mite better, now. I'll put the broth on to warm. That'll set you up a treat.'

'Don't worry about bringing it in here, Sam. I'll fetch it.' Linford watched the farmer leave the room, and then turned his attention back to Rachel, who was, indeed, looking a great deal better. He could clearly discern that beneath the dirt a semblance of colour had returned to her cheeks, she was no longer trembling and her eyes, now, were brightly alert.

'Come, let us get you out of those wet things.' He reached for the top button on her jacket, only to have his hand slapped away none too gently.

'I am quite capable of removing my own garments, thank you!' she informed him tartly, but quickly discovered that even this small task was beyond her. Her right shoulder reacted painfully to the slightest movement, and it was left to Linford to ease the jacket down her arms.

'Right, now let's have the skirt.' His tone was so mundane that he might have been asking nothing more than for her to hand him a cup of coffee.

She looked up at him dispassionately. 'You do not, surely, expect me to sit here in just my petticoats?'

'No, of course not. Everything's coming off.'

'What!' she exclaimed in astonished outrage. He couldn't possibly be serious. . .? Dear God, he was! Her chin jutted forward stubbornly. 'If you think I shall permit you to—'

'Rachel, this is no time for maidenly modesty,' he interrupted, his expression a strange combination of gentle amusement, exasperation and determination. 'You have been in those wet garments far too long already, and I'm not risking your taking a chill on top of everything else. For once in your life, my girl, you're going to do as you're told!' and before she could give voice to further protest, he had released the ties on her skirt.

Hooks, buttons and more ties were undone. His nimble fingers worked as rapidly and as efficiently as those of the most skilled abigail, and she seriously suspected that he had had much practice in removing female attire. He gently raised her from the settle, allowing the garments to fall down one by one about her feet.

She could feel the heat, which had little to do with the glowing fire, slowly rising from her heels to the top of her head during those final humiliating seconds before he covered her nakedness with the blanket, and lowered her with infinite gentleness back down on to the settle.

She watched in disbelief as he began, quite calmly, to gather together her soiled clothes. Just as though nothing untoward had occurred! She clasped the blanket tightly about her, and shuddered, doubting she would ever forget what she had been forced to endure at his hands.

'I'll fetch that broth now, Rachel.'

How matter of fact he sounded, too! She cast him a malevolent glance as he left the room, but was grateful when he returned a few minutes later and handed her the bowl of wholesome, warming broth.

When she had swallowed the last spoonful, he put the bowl to one side. 'Feeling better now, my darling?'

'No, I am not!' she snapped, with a return of spirit. 'And if you ever dare to refer to this humiliating episode again, Linford, I shall take the greatest pleasure in murdering you!'

She could see his body shaking with suppressed laughter, and could not repress a smile, her own lively sense of humour coming to the fore. The one and only time her husband had ever seen her naked and she had been covered in mud, scratches and bruises and had had, perforce, to stand on one leg like a stork. What a sight!

But she had to own, albeit reluctantly, that he had been right. Rough though the blanket most certainly was, she felt far more comfortable than she had when dressed in those wet things, and a warm feeling of complete safety washed over her as she nestled against Linford's tall, powerful frame.

Her contentment was destined not to last very long, however. The carriage soon afterwards arrived, and Alice entered the room, carrying a fur-lined cloak and a pile of clean clothes over her arm. Linford, scarcely giving the young abigail opportunity to take stock of her mistress's appalling condition, immediately took charge again, adopting the high-handed tone which he had used to such good effect earlier.

Dismissing a change of raiment as unnecessary, he wrapped the heavy cloak about Rachel and, before she could insist upon being properly attired, picked her up in his arms once more and carried her out to the waiting carriage.

Swaddled in warm fur with a hot brick at her feet, and with the supporting comfort of Linford's powerful frame on the seat beside her, Rachel found the swift journey back to the Hall no hardship, and before she knew it she was in his strong arms again and being carried into the house, a very concerned Alice hurrying behind, trying to keep up with his lordship's long-striding gait.

'A footman has been despatched for the doctor, my lord,' Peplow informed him, his countenance betraying none of the concern he was experiencing at sight of his young mistress's sorry state.

'Good. Show him into the library when he arrives. I wish to speak to him before he sees her ladyship.'

Sweeping up the staircase, Linford carried Rachel to

her room, and there left her in the capable hands of Mrs Litton and Alice. Lethargy was beginning to take a firm hold, and Rachel was quite content to have everything done for her. Neither Mrs Litton nor Alice plagued her with questions, for which she was very thankful. Both worked swiftly, but with gentle consideration to her condition.

Lowering her carefully into the hip-bath, filled in readiness and placed in front of the fire, they quickly washed the mud from her hair and from her poor bruised and scratched body. By the time Dr Gillis entered the bedchamber, Rachel was feeling slightly better. She had had the worst of her cuts smeared with a soothing ointment, and was tucked up in her warm, comfortable bed.

The Viscount awaited the doctor's return, occupying himself by mixing a bowl of warming rum punch. It was some little time before the young physician, his forehead creased by a heavy, worried frown, rejoined him in the library.

'From your expression, I gather my wife's condition is more serious than I had supposed.'

'Not at all, my lord,' Dr Gillis hurriedly assured him, accepting a glass of warming liquor before seating himself in a chair by the fire. 'Your assessment was very accurate. As you said, her ankle is badly sprained, and she will need to rest it for several days.'

A boyish smile erased the frown. 'I feel I ought to warn you that her ladyship didn't take too kindly to the idea of spending a week in bed. I fear she will make a difficult patient, my lord.'

'You may safely leave that side of things to me.' There was a thread of determination in the Viscount's voice, but a decided twinkle in his eyes as he joined the doctor by the fire. 'And what of her other injuries?'

'Most are only slight. Painful, certainly, but not serious.

As you are aware, she received a nasty blow to the head, but I don't envisage any serious complications arising from that.'

For the first time the Viscount betrayed his deep concern as he asked, 'Is that a possibility?'

'In your wife's case, no. Although she remembers nothing about the accident itself, on all other matters she is quite lucid. She may sometime in the future recall in detail what befell her; she may never do so. Only time will tell.'

Linford eyed him steadily over the rim of his glass. 'Then what precisely is it that troubles you?'

'Your wife is young and healthy. She will heal quickly enough. It isn't the injuries themselves that cause me some disquiet, but their location most certainly does.'

His heavy frown returned. 'You tell me your wife fell from her horse. This may well be what occurred. The greater part of the bruising is down her right side. If she was thrown from her filly, then she fell on that side. But the injury to her head is situated at the back and slightly left of centre. Also, several ribs on her left side are badly bruised.

'Although—' he shrugged '—if one of the filly's hooves happened to have caught her, it might account for that.'

'Well?' his lordship prompted.

The young doctor gazed fixedly into those violet eyes. 'It may well have been an accident, sir. But don't rule out the possibility that your wife might have been attacked.' Without even waiting for a response, he tossed the contents of his glass down his throat and rose to his feet. 'I shall call in to see Lady Linford again tomorrow. I have given her laudanum, so she should sleep until morning.'

Soon after the doctor had left, the Viscount made his way upstairs to his bedchamber, his mind's eye conjuring up a clear vision of the two furrows he had noticed in that narrow track. Could the doctor's suspicion possibly be right? he wondered. But who on earth would want to harm Rachel?

He paused outside her room and, noticing the light beneath the door, quietly entered to find Alice sitting in a chair by the bed, sewing by the light of an oil lamp, turned down low.

He gestured her to remain seated as he came slowly towards the bed, and stared down at his sleeping wife. The bruise on her cheek and the two long scratches were more noticeable now the mud had been washed from her face. Instinctively, he reached out a hand and traced his finger gently down her cheek.

Could the doctor's suspicion possibly be right? he asked himself again. A footpad, surely, would never choose such a place to lie in wait for an unwary traveller. He could be there all day and never catch sight of a soul. It just didn't make sense.

'The doctor has given her something to make her sleep, sir,' Alice said softly, 'but Mrs Litton said as how it would be best if I remain here tonight just in case she does wake.' She could easily discern the troubled look in his eyes, and suddenly came to a decision. 'Sir, do you think it was an accident?'

Linford turned his attention on to the young abigail. 'Has her ladyship given you any reason to suppose that it was not?'

She shook her head. 'Miss Em—her ladyship said as how she fell from Firefly, only—only. . .'

'What is it, Alice?' he urged softly. 'What is it that troubles you?'

'She's never taken a fall before, sir. Her ladyship's a good rider, and Firefly's a gentle creature and wouldn't throw her unless. . .'

'Unless, perhaps, she had been frightened by something, or someone,' he finished for her, eyes intent. 'Do you suspect that someone was lying in wait for your mistress, Alice?'

'It wouldn't be the first time, sir,' she astounded him by divulging. 'Miss Em told me weeks back that someone had tried to kill her when she was in the home wood.'

'Why was I not informed of this before?' His tone was severe, but then he caught the stricken look in her young eyes before she lowered them. 'It's all right, Alice. I'm not angry with you,' he went on gently. 'When did this happen?'

'I'm not sure, my lord. Maybe two or three weeks after you brought us here.'

'Is there anything else about the incident that you can tell me?'

Her slender shoulders rose in a shrug. 'All I remember, sir, is that my mistress came in here one afternoon looking very pale and frightened, saying that someone had fired a shot at her. I said as how she ought to tell you, my lord, but she wouldn't. Said she wasn't sure, and didn't want to cause a stir.'

'You were quite right to inform me of this, Alice, and I thank you. No doubt we shall learn more in the days to come, when your mistress is more herself.' He patted her slim shoulder. 'But, in the meantime, we shan't plague her ladyship with questions.'

Deeply troubled, now, the Viscount retired to bed, but it was a long time before sleep claimed him. Alice was young, but certainly not fanciful, and he did not doubt the truth of what she had divulged. The doctor, too, was young, but a dedicated and intelligent man. Rachel's injuries had aroused sufficient doubt in his mind to question whether it had been an accident.

Now he, too, was beginning to think there was more to

it than a mere fall from a horse. First thing in the morning, he decided, he would ride back to the ridge and inspect the area where they had found Rachel more closely.

Whilst residing in the country his lordship was an early riser, but the following morning he awoke rather later than usual. He had only just finished dressing when there was a light tap on his door and Peplow, looking decidedly nettled, entered the room, and informed him that the blacksmith awaited him below.

'Trench? What the deuce brings him here?'

'I tried to ascertain that information myself, sir.' Peplow sniffed. 'The response I received is unrepeatable. Suffice it to say that he wishes, nay, demands speech with you at once. Shall I have the person removed, sir?'

His lordship's lips twitched. 'It would take you and several footmen to remove John Trench, if he didn't wish to go. No, I'll see him. Show him into the library. I'll be down directly.'

Whatever attitude John Trench may have adopted when dealing with Peplow, he looked far from belligerent when the Viscount entered his library. The blacksmith jumped to his feet, twisting his misshapen hat nervously in his large hands.

'I'm sorry to 'ave disturbed you, m'lord. But the matter be urgent.'

'I never doubted that for a moment, Trench.' The Viscount invited his ill-at-ease visitor to resume his seat, and then asked what had brought him to the Hall at such an early hour.

'Ben, and 'er ladyship's filly, m'lord,' he surprised Linford by replying. 'I gets up this morning to find Ben at the kitchen door. As fidgety as a colt he were. But our Sally, that be my niece, sir, she seems to understand the boy better than most. Get on real well they do. She managed to calm 'im down, and he takes us out to the stable, sir. And there, as large as life, be her ladyship's horse!'

His expression turned grave. 'Hurt bad, the poor beast be, sir. Think you ought to take a look. Ifen Ben'll let you, that is. He were in a reet state when I left, knowing I were coming 'ere.'

'We'll go at once.' The Viscount went to the bell-pull. 'Did you ride here?' Trench nodded. 'Then we'll ride back together.'

The blacksmith's large roan was no fiery steed, and it took some time before they arrived at the smithy. They discovered Ben sitting outside the stable. As soon as he saw the Viscount approaching, he was on his feet in an instant, his huge frame barring the stable door.

'Now come on wi' 'ee, Ben,' the blacksmith said sternly. 'Enough of this! His lordship wants to take a look at the filly. It be 'is right.'

The sound of her uncle's raised voice brought Sally from the kitchen. She was a small, plump young woman in her early twenties who, the Viscount quickly discovered, was quite capable of dealing with a man twice her size.

'Now, Ben,' she said, wagging her finger at him like some irate school-ma'am. 'I've told you to stop this nonsense! You know his lordship would never hurt the beast.' She turned her homely, but kindly face up to the Viscount. 'For some reason, my lord, he's taken it into his head that you mean to do the filly harm. Did you say you would shoot her?'

For a few moments Linford stared down at her, nonplussed, then he recalled his hasty and empty threat, uttered in a moment of deep concern at the farmhouse the evening before. 'Yes, Miss Trench, I did, and it was a stupid thing for me to have said.' He turned to Ben. 'I shall not hurt Firefly, I promise. May I see her?'

Ben looked directly into the Viscount's eyes for endless

moments, then, seemingly satisfied with what he saw there, moved to one side.

Firefly whinnied softly as Linford approached. He rubbed his hand down her sleek neck and down her foreleg. Then he noticed the deep, weeping gash on her back. 'God in heaven!' he murmured. 'How the devil did she come by that?' He turned to Ben. 'Where did you find her?'

'I think I can tell you that,' Sally informed him, coming to stand by Ben. 'He discovered her in a field when he was walking home, late yesterday afternoon. That much I've managed to discover from him already.'

The Viscount nodded, recalling Sam Hughes' words. He said that Ben had discovered an injured animal, but, of course, the farmer had not known that it was her ladyship's mount. He looked directly at Ben. 'So you took Firefly home with you, and then, later, brought her here. Was she saddled when you found her?'

He received a nod in response. Then the young man delved into the pocket of his rough homespun jacket, and placed an evil, twisted piece of metal into the Viscount's hand. Linford stared down at it, and could see traces of dried blood on its sharp edges.

'You dug this out of her back?'

Again Ben nodded.

'God in heaven! No wonder she threw her ladyship. The poor animal must have been in agony.' He looked up at Ben again. 'Will you take care of Firefly for me? Keep her here until the wound has healed?'

'If anyone can get her right, it's Ben,' Sally put in, patting the big man's arm. 'It'll mean him staying here, Uncle John. Which I won't mind a bit. I don't like him walking all that way back to the farm in the dark, as you very well know.'

'Aye, you've been hankering for a reason to keep 'im

'ere, ain't you, gel?' The blacksmith's big shoulders shook. 'Well, it do make sense, I s'pose.'

'I shall pay all the expenses incurred for both Ben and the horse.'

'No need for that, m'lord. Ben do work 'ard enough for 'is keep. And what's a bit o' straw and hay for the beast?' John Trench stared down at the twisted piece of metal again, and frowned. 'I learned up at the Hall that 'er ladyship 'ad an accident, m'lord. What beats me, sir, is 'ow the poor beast bore 'er ladyship's weight for so long with that beneath the saddle. The filly seemed fine when I seen 'er yesterday.'

'The answer to that is simple—it couldn't possibly have been there then. At some point, after she had left here, this was, with malicious intent, placed beneath that saddle.' He looked keenly at the blacksmith. 'When I came here yesterday you told me that Lady Linford was riding back to the Hall by way of Bluebell Ridge. When she told you this, was there anyone else here who might have overheard your conversation?'

'There be always folk about, m'lord.' The blacksmith scratched his head. 'I can't rightly remember.'

'Bad man,' Ben said clearly.

'Yes, Ben,' his lordship responded, his voice deceptively soft. 'Whoever did this is a bad man, and I mean to discover who it was.' His violet eyes glinted ominously. 'And when I do. . .God help him. . .because I won't!'

# *Chapter Eleven*

**R**achel surveyed the room with a jaundiced eye. After more than three full days in bed, she found her lovely bedchamber was rapidly beginning to pall. She glanced across the room to where Alice stood busily putting away freshly laundered clothes, and frowned. Of course, she would never dream of hurting the girl's feelings by admitting to it, but even her maid's gentle ministrations were becoming irksome.

Neither Alice nor Mrs Litton could do enough for her, attentive to her every need; but the fact remained that she was not accustomed to being petted and fussed over. From a very early age she had been used to doing most everything for herself.

Self-reliance was something that she valued highly, and something that she was not prepared to relinquish for longer than was absolutely necessary. Perhaps the time had come for her to regain a little of that highly prized independence.

'Is there something wrong, my lady?' Alice said, turning suddenly and catching the pensive expression on her mistress's face.

'No, there's nothing wrong.'

'Perhaps Miss Lucy's visit earlier has tired you,' the

young abigail suggested, going over to the bed. 'I thought it too soon for you to be receiving visitors.'

'You did, did you?' Rachel looked up at her steadily. 'Well, let me assure you that far from tiring me, I found Lucy Maitland's visit both enjoyable and invigorating. Nothing would have given me more pleasure than to have dressed in my habit, and joined her for a ride.'

'You couldn't have done that, my lady,' Alice returned in all seriousness. 'You're not well enough. Besides, your habit was ruined and has been burnt. Don't you remember me telling you?'

'Of course I remember!' Rachel snapped pettishly. 'My wits aren't addled. A minor inconvenience! I shall have a new one made.'

'No need for you to fret yourself over that, Miss Em,' the maid informed her, smoothing down the bedcovers with a loving hand. 'I think his lordship's already ordered the making of a new one.'

'Has he? How very thoughtful!' Her delighted smile faded as she glanced across the room at the clock. 'Where is his lordship? He usually pays me a visit at this time.'

'He left word that he would be in to see you later, my lady. He's ridden out with the steward, I think.'

Has he, indeed? Rachel thought, looking for all the world so innocently angelic as she contemplated the fingernails on her left hand. Then, suddenly, she threw back the bedcovers and swung her feet to the floor.

'Do you have need of the chamber-pot, my lady?'

'No, I do not! But I do have need of a change of scenery. And a change of scenery I mean to have!' she replied determinedly, thrusting her slender feet into her slippers. 'And don't you dare to argue with me!' she ordered when Alice opened her mouth to do just that. 'Go fetch my robe!'

Alice, looking decidedly ruffled and not just a little concerned, helped her mistress on with her dressing-gown.

'But what will his lordship say, Miss Em?' she uttered, in a vain attempt to reason with her suddenly difficult and surprisingly headstrong mistress. 'You was supposed to keep off that ankle for a week. You know what the doctor said. And his lordship gave instructions that you wasn't to—'

'The devil take his lordship's instructions! I'll not remain imprisoned in this room a moment longer!' she declared with such steely resolution that Alice dared not argue further, and thoughtfully offered a supporting arm.

The distance from her bedchamber to the head of the staircase seemed to have lengthened considerably, but, by alternately hopping, and then gingerly bearing her weight on her, still painful, though slightly less swollen, right ankle for a few paces, she at last reached the highly polished bannister rail. Panting from her exertions, she leaned against it for support. Having made it thus far, she was stubbornly determined to reach her destination.

Ignoring the smug 'I told you it would be too much for you' look on Alice's face, she eyed the bannister rail measuringly, and then glanced down into the hall below. It appeared deserted. But best be certain and check first, she decided, turning to her maid.

'Go down into the hall and see if anyone is about.'

Alice obeyed without hesitation, and confirmed that there was no one lurking. Smiling with satisfaction, Rachel tucked her clothes beneath her and, before Alice realised her intention, raised her right leg to straddle the rail, and glided effortlessly down the highly polished wood.

'I've always wanted to do that,' she confessed, looking for all the world like some mischievous urchin who had just indulged in some wicked prank. 'What fun children have!'

Alice tried to look disapproving, but failed miserably,

and once again offered her mistress a supporting arm to achieve the distance across the hall to the library.

A short while later Rachel was as contented as could be. Lying on the comfortable sofa, which had been positioned so that she could look out of the window on to the park, with several cushions supporting her back, a warm cover over her legs and with a glass of lemonade on the table by her elbow, she settled down to enjoy the book Lucy had brought for her to read that morning.

Her contentment was destined not to last very long, however. Not ten minutes had elapsed before the door opened, and she raised her eyes to see the housekeeper, looking decidedly solemn, quietly enter the room.

'No doubt Alice apprised you of my little venture downstairs.' She smiled wickedly up at the woman of whom she had, surprisingly, grown very fond, but this time won no answering smile. 'Come, Mrs Litton. Surely, having acquired a fair knowledge of my character, you didn't expect me to remain tamely incarcerated in my bedchamber for very much longer?'

'No, madam, I did not,' the housekeeper replied, still looking grave. 'I admire your fortitude at being kept abed for so long. No, that isn't why I wished to speak to you. It is over an entirely different matter.' She paused for a moment, clasping her hands together nervously. 'I know this isn't, perhaps, the right time to seek an audience with you, but—but I fear I must look for a new position, and came to ask if you would be kind enough to give me a reference?'

'But why?' Rachel was stunned. Apart from those first few weeks of cool formality, whilst they had been assessing each other, their dealings had always been very amicable. 'I—I thought you were happy here. If it is something I have said or—'

'No, no, my lady! Never that,' she hurriedly assured

her, tears welling in her grey eyes. 'No one could have a kinder, or more. . .'

Rachel watched in dismay as the poor woman, unable to control herself further, gave way to her emotions. None of Lady Anne Norton's painstaking instruction had prepared her for dealing with a situation such as this. For a few moments she was at a loss to know how to proceed, and then decided to adopt the kind, but firm, attitude she would have taken had it been Alice standing before her.

'Come, Mrs Litton, sit down, and calm yourself. Something, evidently, has distressed you greatly, but I am at a loss to understand what it could possibly be. Has it something to do with his lordship? Or one of the servants, perhaps?'

Dabbing at her eyes, the housekeeper shook her head. 'No, my lady, nothing like that.' She hesitated for a moment, then, as though coming to a decision, delved into the pocket of her starched white apron and drew out a folded sheet of paper. 'It is because of this,' she said, handing the note to Rachel before seating herself on the very edge of a nearby chair.

Unfolding the letter, Rachel frowned as she ran her eyes across what could only be described as an uneducated scrawl. Puzzled, she read a second time: *Running short again Madam Sharpe. If you wants me to still keep me mouth shut, bring fifty this time. The same place on Friday.*

Totally at a loss, she raised her eyes to look at the housekeeper, who thankfully had regained control of herself, and stared gravely back at her. 'I'm afraid I must be slow-witted, for I can make head nor tail of this nonsense. Fifty what must be brought to the same place?'

'Sovereigns, my lady.'

'Ah! I begin to see the light. At least,' Rachel amended, frowning again as she cast her eyes over the note, 'I believe

I do. Evidently it has been written for the sole purpose of extorting money. But who is this Mrs Sharpe?'

'That is my name, my lady. I reverted to my maiden name after my husband's death.'

Rachel regarded the housekeeper in silence for a few moments. It was not uncommon for higher female servants to adopt the status of a married woman, but it was unusual for a female who had a legal right to the title to link it with her maiden name. 'Was there a particular reason for resorting to the use of your former name?'

'Yes, my lady, there was.' Her eyes held those of her mistress steadily. 'It was rumoured in some quarters that I had murdered my husband, and I thought it wisest, when I was forced to seek a position, to change my name.'

'And did you murder him?' Rachel enquired so matter of factly that the housekeeper could not forbear a smile.

'No, my lady, I did not. But I must admit, if I'm honest, there were many times when I wished to do so.'

'Mmmm. Yes, very understandable,' Rachel responded meditatively. 'I've experienced the selfsame desire myself on numerous occasions.' This drew a surprising chortle of laughter from the normally strictly serious housekeeper, and Rachel smiled across at her approvingly. 'That's better. Now, I think you had better explain everything from the beginning.'

Relaxing slightly, the housekeeper sat further back in the comfortable chair. 'I will begin by telling you, my lady, that I was reared by a very dear aunt. She owned a comfortable house in a quiet, but unfashionable, part of London. She took in lodgers, and when I was old enough I paid for my keep by undertaking the duties of housekeeper. She left me the house when she died, and I continued to take in boarders.

'One day Thomas Sharpe came enquiring after a room. We enjoyed each other's company and, foolishly, when he asked me, I married him. . .and everything I owned became his.'

Rachel experienced a pang of sadness as she instinctively gazed down at the band of gold on her left hand. 'Yes, Mrs Litton. Life can deal some harsh blows.' She raised her eyes to find the housekeeper regarding her intently, and went on hurriedly, 'No doubt you discovered your husband's true character soon after the nuptials had taken place?'

She nodded. 'I knew he enjoyed a drink, my lady, but I didn't realise to what extent he indulged himself. He was pleasant enough when sober, but when he'd been drinking. . .'

Her eyes hardened. 'About a year after we were married, he lost his job as a clerk in a shipping office, and my savings soon afterwards dwindled. He began to sell the furniture to pay for his gambling and other pleasures. The only income came from my lodgers, but as time passed, and the house became shabby, I could no longer be so choosy over the people I took in.'

Lowering her eyes, she fixed them on an imaginary spot on the carpet. 'He came home one evening the worse for wear, demanding money as usual. When I told him I had none, not even for food, he grew violent. I ran from the room across the landing. He followed, reeling drunkenly. He must have caught his toe in the threadbare carpet. He fell down the stairs and broke his neck.'

'But surely no one blamed you for that?' Rachel enquired after a moment's stunned silence, and watched the housekeeper's lips twist into a bitter smile.

'My lady, I was never blessed with any degree of beauty, but I once had a deal of spirit. I was almost thirty when I married Thomas Sharpe. Before that I was independent and hard-working. I didn't submit tamely to my husband's demands. There were many heated arguments during our five-year marriage, and many wagging tongues eager to testify to that. I was taken off to Bow Street, and no one, not even those lodging with me at the time, spoke up in my defence, but I was eventually released through lack of evidence.'

'And mud sticks,' Rachel said softly.

'Quite so, my lady. After the inquest, I returned to my home to discover my lodgers gone, taking with them nearly all the furniture I had left.' Her soft laughter was bitter. 'A charming family they were. A man and his wife, and their obnoxious son. Renfield was the name, if my memory serves me correctly.'

'Did you not set the authorities on to them?'

'No, my lady. I had had more than enough of Bow Street by that time.' She shook her head. 'No, I made the best of it. I sold the house, and after settling my husband's debts was left with very little.'

She smiled at the sympathetic look in Rachel's eyes. 'It wasn't so bad, my lady. A friend of my aunt's, who had married well, took me on as housekeeper. She was a kindly soul, but I found I couldn't put the past behind me. Whenever I accompanied her out, I was forever bumping into someone who recognised me.

'In the end, I decided it would be best if I moved right away from London. I reverted to my maiden name, and was fortunate enough to attain the position of housekeeper in the home of Lady Fitznorton, where I remained for ten years until her death. Her son, Sir Lionel, wrote me a glowing reference, and with it I was able to attain the position here.'

She looked across at her mistress, who sat silently regarding the letter in her hand. 'My past has caught up with me, my lady. I never thought I would need to relate all that I have, but—but. . .I shall leave immediately if you wish it. If you would be so kind as to furnish me with a reference, I can—'

'No, Mrs Litton, I find myself unable to comply with your request,' Rachel cut in abruptly. Raising her eyes from the letter, she gazed fixedly at the suddenly crestfallen servant. 'Unless, of course, you are unhappy here, and truly wish to leave?'

'Oh, no, my lady,' she assured her, brightening. 'I have always been happy here, more so since your arrival. I know at first I must have seemed a little remote, but that was only because—well, because I didn't know quite. . . Oh, dear,' she finished in some confusion, igniting that wicked twinkle in her mistress's lovely eyes once again.

'Because you didn't know what to expect from the redhaired, flashing-eyed termagant who swept into the hall that day, and wondered how God in his goodness could have dealt you yet another such thundering blow.'

Rachel gurgled with laughter at the guilty flush mounting the older woman's cheeks as she tried to stutter her way through a staunch denial, but then became serious.

'You do not wish to leave, Mrs Litton, and for my part I see no reason why you should. I am duty bound, however, to speak to my husband. I do not believe for one moment that he will ask you to find a position elsewhere, but should this be the outcome of my disclosures, then I am in a position to offer you employment in my house in Somerset.'

'Oh, my lady, th-thank you! I would be more than happy to go there and—'

'Not so fast,' Rachel cut in. 'You have given me every reason to believe you wish to remain here, but you must have given some thought to the outcome of not meeting this infamous person's demands.'

Mrs Litton paled visibly. 'Yes, my lady, and that is why

I thought it best to leave. This isn't the first letter I've received, and I simply have no money left.'

'When did you receive the first demand?'

'About two months before you came, my lady.'

'And how many such demands have you been forced to meet?'

'That is the third. One of the footmen gave it to me earlier. Like all the others, it was found pushed under the front door.'

'I see. And you have no idea who's behind it?' She received a shake of the head in response, and was silent for a moment, then said, 'Assuming his lordship has no objection, and you do decide to stay, if you take my advice you could do no better than to take Peplow into your confidence. In him you would have a staunch ally. If and when rumours begin to circulate, he will know how to quash any below-stairs tittle-tattle.'

When Mrs Litton, looking completely relaxed, and far happier than she had ever appeared before, left the room a short while later, Rachel returned to her novel. So absorbed did she become in the book's intricate plot that she did not even hear the opening of the door, and was sublimely unaware that a pair of violet eyes were regarding her with blatant disapproval, until,

'And what the devil do you think you are doing down here, madam?'

Rachel started visibly, spilling some of the lemonade down the front of her robe. 'Confound you, Linford! Must you creep up on a body like that?' Placing the glass back on to the table, she began to dab at the spillage with her handkerchief. 'Now see what you've made me do!'

He came slowly towards her, his expression, if anything, darkening. 'Well?'

She peered up at him through her long, curling lashes.

He had never known her resort to any feminine wiles, and could not help but be amused by it.

'There, I knew you were not really angry,' she said, triumphantly, catching the betraying twitch of those shapely lips. 'You know I cannot bear to be confined, Linford. I would have gone distracted had I remained in my bedchamber a moment longer.'

'Dr Gillis does not keep you abed for his own pleasure, my dear, and neither do I. That ankle of yours won't heal unless you rest it.'

'I know. And I promise I shan't do it again, so do not scold.'

'She calls that a scold,' he muttered, raising his eyes heavenwards as he moved across to the decanters. 'It is perhaps as well for you, my girl,' he went on, with an unmistakable threatening edge to his voice, as he came back towards the couch with two glasses of wine, 'that I do know the full extent of your injuries. Here, and do not spill this one.'

She flashed him a look from beneath her lashes, but refused to be drawn, and watched as he placed a low stool beside the couch and sat down, stretching his long legs out in front of him, his eyes almost on a level with her own.

'What's that you're reading?'

'Oh, just a book Lucy has loaned me.' Picking it up off her lap, she placed it next to her wine on the table, and her eyes fell on the letter which she had retained for his perusal. 'Great heavens! I'd all but forgotten. Here, Linford, read this!'

He took one glance at it, and felt for his quizzing glass. 'And who, pray, is Madam Sharpe?'

'Mrs Litton, would you believe!' She then went on to divulge all that had passed between the housekeeper and herself. When at last she had related all, she looked at her silent husband imploringly. 'I told her that I would need to apprise you, but—but you're not going to turn her off, surely?'

'That certainly wouldn't be my first choice, no.' He glanced down at the letter again. 'Friday is the day after tomorrow. I shall speak to her myself later, and see how much she can tell me. With luck, we just might catch this blackguard. There are few crimes more despicable than blackmail.'

'I knew you would feel that way.' Her glowing smile of approval was quickly erased by a puzzled frown as she looked at the letter in his hand. 'The person who wrote that is certainly not well educated, but the paper is good quality. Why, it could be your own!'

'The paper, perhaps, my dear, but you'll most certainly never find a wafer of that colour polluting any of my drawers.' He looked down at the virulent green-coloured strip in distaste. 'In fact, I know of only one household to use such garish colours—the Maitlands.'

'Surely you don't think anyone there sent it?'

'Of course, I don't think it came from any member of the family. But one of the servants, perhaps?' He shrugged. 'It is fruitless to speculate. I shall discover, first, where she has been leaving the money.'

'That poor woman has parted with all her savings, Linford.' She shook her head sadly. 'I sensed weeks ago there was something troubling her. I wish she had confided in me before.'

'And, no doubt, you would have been more than willing to pay the demands yourself.'

'No, I would not!' she answered vehemently, but then smiled. 'Though I must confess, I came perilously close to reimbursing Mrs Litton earlier. I have more than enough money, Linford, and that poor woman, now, has nothing. It's so unfair. But I don't think she would accept it, even if I offered.'

He looked at her searchingly. 'Money means nothing at all to you, does it, Rachel?'

'I shouldn't go as far as to say that. It is a great comfort knowing one has sufficient for one's needs, but. . .' she shrugged '. . .I have never coveted great wealth, no.'

'Nor do you resent those who acquire great wealth.'

'Of course not. Why should I?'

He held her eyes by the sheer intensity of his own. 'No, I came to that conclusion several weeks ago, when we stood in the bedchamber of your old home. You lied to me, didn't you, Rachel? You didn't run away from me all those years ago because your father left his fortune to me.'

Cursing herself silently for the trap into which she had so blindly walked, she managed to draw her gaze away from those all-too-perceptive violet eyes. It was useless even to try to deny it, now. Linford was far too astute.

'No,' she admitted, breaking the silence which had grown between them.

'Then why did you leave me, Rachel?' He stilled the slender white fingers, nervously plucking at the coverlet, by the simple expedient of capturing her hand in his own. 'Why did you hide from me for six long years? What did I do to give you such a disgust of me?'

'I didn't—I never. . . Oh, it does not matter!' Confusion and agitation added an edge to her voice. 'I was so young, scarcely more than a child. What did I know of such things?'

'What things, Rachel?' he persisted, determined to get to the truth. 'I do not believe that you, now, hold me in abhorrence. I believe we have become. . .friends. If through some thoughtless action, I hurt you, then I can only say I'm sorry, but, believe me, it wasn't intentionally done. During our six years apart, Rachel, I was made to suffer.

'Do you not think I have the right to know why I was

forced to endure years of malicious innuendoes and furtive, censorious glances? Why, during those years, I was never allowed to lead a normal life, wondering whether you were alive or dead—never permitting myself to form an attachment with any virtuous female, knowing it could only end in heartache? Do you think me unreasonable to demand an explanation?'

Until that moment Rachel had never given a thought to the consequences of her actions. She gazed down at the shapely hand still holding hers firmly, yet so very gently. 'No,' she said softly, 'I do not think you unreasonable. You do have a right. I owe you that much, at least. But you, too, must believe me when I tell you that there was no malice aforethought. I never ran away from you, and stayed away, to extract some childish, petty revenge.'

'Having come to know you, my dear, that likelihood would never enter my head.'

He caught the wan smile before she lay back against the cushions, and watched as those lovely eyes clouded over, adopting a faraway, almost entranced look.

'It seems so long ago; seems to have happened in a different time, to a different person. That child wasn't me, Linford. How could she have been? She was lonely, unloved. Her only companions were servants, but she did grow fond of one governess, a kindly woman who would give her story-books to read. What wicked delights!

'On fine days, whenever the master of the house was away from home, the girl would take one of these illicit treats with her into the garden, and read of knights in shining armour, of fair damsels with flowing hair, of dragons and of castles. From time to time she would glance up to watch a traveller pass by the gates.

'One day she saw a tall youth on, shall we say, in keeping with our story, a fiery charger. He looked in as he passed, saw the girl and, doffing his hat, smiled at her.

How handsome was that knight in shining armour! What bliss to be swept up before him on that fiery steed and taken to his castle!

'The years passed, but our heroine never forgot her handsome knight. On rare occasions, if she was lucky, she would glimpse him riding past, sometimes alone; sometimes accompanied by friends.

'Then one day, miraculously, he was there, standing in the master's bedchamber. But what was he doing there? Why had he come? Her heart hammered so loudly that she felt sure he must hear it. . . What was that. . .? Marriage? Did the man of her dreams wish to marry her? No, it couldn't possibly be true! But it was—it was true!'

Her shout of laughter was mirthless. Linford looked at her gravely. 'Rachel, I—'

'No, do not interrupt.' She pulled her hand from beneath his to raise it arrestingly. 'Our heroine's story becomes far more interesting from here on. To continue: the handsome knight installed his young bride in his sumptuously furnished castle, but didn't remain with her for long. Soon after the old master had died, he went away, leaving her in the care of a cousin.

'His distant relation was a kindly soul, but sadly obtuse. She had an unfortunate propensity for indulging in gossip, especially with her maid. Our young heroine was passing the lady's bedchamber one day. The door was ajar, and she clearly heard,

'". . .of course, he only married her for the money. Anyone can see that. She's a sweet enough child, but not in Linford's style. His tastes have always veered towards sophisticated ladies of ample charms and few morals. You mark my words, he's back at Grosvenor Square right now indulging in his wicked ways. . ."'

Rachel's lips curled into a far from pleasant smile. 'Poor, poor little heroine. She didn't want to believe it.

No, none of what she had overheard could possibly be true. Money? What money? Her father had had no money. Her old home and her shabby, worn clothes were proof of that.

'And her husband did love her. Of course he did! Hadn't he given her the most beautiful bedchamber, warm and richly furnished? Hadn't he promised her lovely new gowns? Surely he must love her, mustn't he?

'Sadly unworldly our young heroine might have been, but she was most certainly not halfwitted. The evil seed of doubt had been well and truly sown, and she was determined to discover the truth. She would seek out her knight in shining armour. . .her saviour. . .the great love of her young life. She would hear him deny that wicked slander.'

Linford's sigh was audible. 'So, you did come to London for the sole purpose of searching me out?'

Rachel drew her eyes away from the imaginary spot on the wall, where they had remained from the beginning of her sorry tale, and fixed them on the Viscount's grave countenance. 'You discovered that much, then?'

'Yes.' His voice matched his expression. 'Whilst we were in London in the spring, I enlisted the aid of a man to try to discover your whereabouts. He learned of a young girl knocked down by a carriage. That girl was you, wasn't it?'

'Yes.'

'Were you badly injured?'

'I received a blow to the head, which rendered me unconscious.' She laughed this time in genuine amusement. 'I seem to have acquired a propensity for that sort of thing.'

There was no semblance of a smile round his lordship's mouth, however, as he said, 'And the person in the carriage was, I assume, Lady Anne Norton?' She nodded, and his heavy frown descended. 'Why did she not inform me of what had befallen you?'

'Initially, because she didn't know that I was your wife. Then, later, when she knew my true identity, I told her that if she ever tried to contact you, I would disappear from her life for ever.'

'Why?' he demanded angrily. 'Because of some silly middle-aged woman's gossip-mongering?'

'Dare you deny the truth of it?' Her voice had adopted a hard steel-like quality. 'Very wise, Linford,' she continued, when he did not attempt to speak. 'No, not because of that, but because I couldn't ignore the evidence of my own eyes.'

She stared at him in silence for a few moments, easily detecting puzzlement and a certain guarded look.

'I did eventually reach Grosvenor Square. Somewhere in the distance I heard a church clock begin to strike the hour. Before it had finished its chiming, a door opened and a man emerged from one of the fine houses. You walked right past me, Linford. You were so close I could have reached out and touched the silken lining of your cloak. To this day I still don't know why I didn't call out to you, but I didn't.'

She shook her head. 'Perhaps Fate had ordained it so. Instead, I followed you. I was so tired, and you seemed to walk for such a long time, but eventually you reached your destination—a small, but fashionable, dwelling at the end of. . .' she waved her hand, dismissively '. . .I don't recall the street. I waited for you, but you didn't emerge.

'After a time, cold and decidedly weary, I walked round to the back of the house. Why I didn't merely knock on the front door, and ask to see you, I'll never know.' She shrugged. 'But I was very timid in those days and, maybe, I feared your reaction. . . Perhaps, though, once again, Fate had ordained it so.

'There was a small garden. In it grew a sturdy tree whose branches reached out to a narrow balcony. I climbed that tree on to that balcony.' Her voice, now, was cold, emotionless. 'Through the chink in the curtains I saw you—saw you sitting on a sofa, kissing and fondling the voluptuous body of your naked mistress.'

He did not attempt to speak; did not try to deny the truth of it. Never before had Rachel seen such a look of utter desolation on anyone's face, and prayed she would never do so again.

'Now you know the truth, Dominic,' she said softly, and he was to realise much later that that was the first time she had ever called him by his given name. 'I suppose you could say the girl died that night. But she was reborn, and so vastly changed that you would never have recognised her—did not, in fact, recognise her when you saw her again.'

'Did you come to London the second time for the sole purpose of seeing me, Rachel?' he asked, his voice, unlike his expression, betraying no emotion.

'Yes,' she responded without preamble.

'What would you have done had I not discovered your true identity?'

'I would have returned to Somerset, where I had every intention of writing to you to suggest the very thing that you yourself have proposed—an annulment to a marriage which should never have taken place.'

Wretchedness was still mirrored in his eyes before he lowered them. She wished she could have offer some words of comfort. But what could she say? He had demanded an explanation, and had been given one; and that, as far as she was concerned, ought to be an end to the matter.

When she retired that night, she felt as if a great weight had been lifted from her mind. She refused to dwell on her painful, humiliating confessions, and forced herself, for perhaps the umpteenth time, to try to remember details of her recent accident.

It was, now, four days since the incident occurred. She had by this time recalled riding over to the smithy on that particular afternoon; had recalled riding along the ridge and dismounting to look down at the stream. She remembered, with humiliating clarity, everything after Linford had forced that brandy down her throat.

But the accident, itself, continued to remain a complete blank. Dr Gillis had assured her that it would all come back to her in time. Linford, however, had never referred to the incident at all, which was strange.

Her efforts, frustratingly, were once again in vain, and after a while she abandoned the attempt, giving herself up to the healing powers of sleep. She began to dream of her Somerset home; of the elderly groom who had taught her to ride; of her first setting eyes on Firefly, presented by her beloved benefactress on the day her protégé had attained her majority.

What a lovely creature the filly was! So gentle, yet so playful! Smiling delightedly, she moved towards Firefly. Then, suddenly, everything changed. Swirling grey mists surrounded her, and the sound of hoof beats echoed through the fog.

She moved closer to the filly, and mounted her. The horse reared, eyes wildly rolling. . . The pain! Her ankle— was it broken? There was someone there—a menacing, evil shadow drawing ever closer. . . 'Don't let him hurt me, Dominic! Don't let him touch me. . .!'

'Rachel! Rachel, wake up! I'm here! You're safe!'

He was there. She could feel the comforting strength of those strong arms as he rocked her gently to and fro. She clung to him, like a frightened child, afraid to let him go lest her attacker return.

'It was only a dream, my darling. Nothing more than a bad dream.'

'No, Dominic, it wasn't a dream.' She was wide awake, now, in full possession of her faculties. She raised her head from the warm comfort of his broad chest to peer up at him. 'It wasn't an accident, Dominic. There was someone there. I've remembered. I glimpsed a pair of stout workman's boots before the brute rendered me unconscious.' He made no response, and even in the darkened room she could discern a guarded look in his eyes. 'You knew, didn't you?'

'Yes, I knew,' he admitted. 'I thought it best not to tell you so soon after the attack. Nor to tell you that Firefly was also hurt.'

'What. . .? Badly?'

'No,' he hurriedly assured her. 'She has a deep cut on her back. It's healing nicely, but I'm afraid it will leave a scar.'

She laid her head against his chest once more, frowning, perplexed. 'How did she come by that?'

'A sharp piece of metal had been placed under the saddle. That was why she threw you.'

Her eyes narrowed. 'I think I know when that must have happened. I thought someone was following me, Dominic. I left Firefly tethered to a tree. I heard her whinny, as though disturbed by something.' She sighed deeply. 'But who would want to hurt me? And why?'

'I don't know, Rachel. But I mean to find out.' He began to stroke those long, dark auburn tresses gently. 'Do not think about it any more. Go to sleep. There's nothing to frighten you now.'

No, not whilst you're here, she thought, a fond memory returning. 'This isn't the first time you've come to me. You came to my room on the night of the storm, didn't you?'

'I heard you calling out. You were frightened. I couldn't leave you so.'

Her eyes grew misty. 'You have been so very good to me, Dominic. So—so very kind.'

'A veritable paragon of all the virtues, am I not?'

She did not see the self-deprecating sneer, but the bitterness in his voice was all too evident. 'You're thinking of what I told you earlier. You must not dwell on it. The past cannot be altered, so you must put it from your mind.'

'That, my darling,' he murmured softly, 'is something I can never do.'

# Chapter Twelve

**A** week later Viscount Linford was sitting at his desk in the library, reading through the letter he had just penned. The past days had been cursed by frustrations and disappointments.

His attempts to discover the identity of the miscreant who had been blackmailing his housekeeper had been in vain. Sadly benighted the villain might be, but he certainly did not lack guile. Cunningly, he had chosen an open stretch of land on the road to Linfield for the deposit and collection of his ill-gotten gains.

His lordship had ordered Jem and another groom to take it in turns keeping watch throughout the day from the nearest vantage point, a small copse, situated some five hundred yards from the milestone behind which the money was to be placed. They had reported that many travellers had passed along the road that day, but not one had stopped at the milestone to investigate the pile of stones secreted behind.

Linford himself had ridden out early the following morning to discover the pile of stones disturbed and the purse, containing only pebbles this time, gone. He would have dearly loved to catch the villain, but it was not to be, and satisfied himself with the knowledge that Mrs

Litton was, at least, free from the blackmailer's evil clutches. Those whom she had feared knowing of her sorry past did know, and all stood firmly behind her. She had nothing now to fear.

He gained no satisfaction whatsoever from his investigations into the attack on his wife. A thorough search along that area of track where the incident had taken place had brought no new evidence to light.

News of the assault on the Viscountess had quickly spread, and many people had come forward, eagerly confirming that they had seen her ladyship on the afternoon in question riding through Linfield, but none could say with any degree of certainty whether or not she had been followed.

His lordship's shapely lips curled into a rueful smile. History certainly had a habit of repeating itself, he mused. His attempts to gain information concerning Rachel had met with as little success as they had six years before. This time, however, he was not prepared to sit back and leave things to chance. It was time to enlist the aid of another, and he knew of only one tenacious enough to root out the truth.

Reaching for his pen once again, he began to write out the direction on his carefully worded letter, when he became aware of the sounds of an arrival. He heard the deep tones of a jovial and familiar masculine voice raised in the hall. The next instant the library door was thrown wide, and Mr Charles Cheffingham, sporting one of his dazzling waistcoats, came slowly into the room.

'By all that's wonderful!' Linford moved round his desk to shake the older man's hand warmly. 'Needless to say it is delightful to see you, old fellow, but what brings you here?' His warm smile of greeting faded. 'Nothing wrong with Hetta, I trust?'

'No, no. She's as fit as a fiddle,' Cheffy hurriedly

assured him, easing his large bulk into one of the comfortable chairs placed by the hearth. 'Well, yes. She's fine, I suppose. Just spent two weeks with her in Bath. That was enough. Never could stand the place myself.'

Having poured out two glasses of Madeira, his lordship handed one to his unexpected visitor before seating himself in the chair opposite. 'How long will you be staying with us?'

'Just for the night, m'boy. Must be in London tomorrow. Wouldn't have imposed on you at all, but I promised Hetta I'd call. She's still all of a twitter over the gel, you know. Told her you were quite capable of looking after your own, but. . .well, you know what your aunt is. She's very fond of that little wife of yours. Worries needlessly.'

'She has good reason to be concerned. I make a very poor protector,' his lordship responded, his expression grave, and then went on to disclose what had befallen Rachel.

As far as Linford was concerned, one of Mr Cheffingham's most endearing qualities was his easygoing complacency. When, however, after hearing an account of the appalling incident, his visitor just sat there, benignly, savouring his wine, just as though he had been informed of nothing more important than the latest vogue in tying a cravat, it took all his self-control not to reach out and box the older man's ears soundly.

Cheffy was saved from a possible attack upon his person, and the colourful diatribe which rose in his lordship's throat, by the sudden opening of the door. He turned his head to see the Viscountess, dressed in a very becoming burgundy carriage-dress, enter the room, walking with the aid of a stout stick. Cheffy was on his feet with remarkable speed for a man of his size, and surprised both the Viscount and the lady herself by placing a fatherly kiss on her cheek.

'How lovely to see you, Cheffy! I hope this isn't to be a flying visit.'

'Afraid so, m'dear. Been with Hetta in Bath, but I'm off to London in the morning.'

Rachel caught the brief look of concern in his eyes as she limped across to the sofa. 'No doubt Linford has informed you of my—er—little accident. Yes, I can see he has,' she went on, after a quick glance in her husband's direction. 'Most unfortunate, but I do not wish to dwell on that. Tell me how you found Hetta.'

She frowned slightly as she watched him ease himself down into the chair again. 'It might be my imagination, but when reading her last letter, I gained the impression she was not at all happy.'

'Ah! You're a clever little puss, and no mistake. No, m'dear, I don't think she is happy,' he admitted. 'She tried to put a brave face on it whilst I was there, but she didn't fool me. She's regretting leaving Surrey, but won't admit to it.'

'Yes, I thought she would.' Rachel looked across at him consideringly. 'It's a great pity, Cheffy, that you're a confirmed bachelor. If you married Hetta, she would have the perfect excuse for returning to her favourite county.'

Linford, unable to sit idly by and see a member of his own sex so sadly discomposed, quickly came to his amiable friend's rescue by changing the subject and asking Rachel where she had been that afternoon.

'Visiting the Halhams.' She cast him one of her quick, mischievous smiles. 'It is very comfortable travelling everywhere in your carriage, and I don't want you to think I'm ungrateful, Dominic, but since Firefly's return, I can hardly wait to ride again.'

'And so you shall, my dear. Firefly's injury is healing nicely, but it wouldn't hurt to leave it another week before

we risk putting a saddle on her again. By which time, of
course, if you do as the doctor suggests and rest frequently,
that ankle of yours ought to be fully recovered.'

Rachel longed to respond with a teasing rejoinder, but
refrained. Linford was right. Although she had made light
of her many injuries, she was, even now, still in some
discomfort, and could not walk very far without the aid
of a stick. She also wearied easily; consequently, she
retired that evening as soon as they had dined, leaving the
gentlemen to their own devices.

Linford took his guest into the library, where they
whiled away the late evening hours by chatting away
pleasantly on a number of topics, whilst playing several
hands of piquet, but Mr Cheffingham became increasingly
aware of the many times his host had recourse to the
brandy decanter.

'Damnable thing to have happened to your wife,
Linford,' he said unexpectedly. 'Beats me how anyone
could bring himself to hurt such a sweet gel. I sincerely
hope you find the villain.' He shook his head. 'Wish there
was something I could do.'

'You can, Cheffy,' the Viscount responded without a
moment's hesitation. 'When you go to London tomorrow,
you can deliver a letter for me personally. I've asked for
help again from that ex-Runner I engaged earlier in the
year. Stubbs is a good man, and won't delay in coming
here longer than necessary, but I should feel easier in my
mind if I knew for a fact that he had received my letter.'

'Consider it done, m'boy. I shouldn't like to think that
anything else was going to happen to that little wife of
yours.' His large stomach shook with silent laughter.

'Wasn't always so kindly disposed towards her, don't
you know. It wasn't until she spent that time with Hetta
that I really got to know her. Could see, then, that her
fondness for your aunt was genuine. Mind, I admit, m'boy,

she gave me a nasty turn, earlier, when she mentioned marriage. Dear me, yes.'

The Viscount's lips twitched. 'I saw that she had.'

'Yes, well.' Mr Cheffingham tugged at his cravat, which seemed to have grown uncomfortably tight quite suddenly. 'It ain't marriage Hetta craves, just companionship. She was hoping to persuade Rachel to live with her, if I'm not very much mistaken.'

'She may well still do so,' Linford responded, and then smiled faintly at the look of astonishment on the older man's face. 'Rachel didn't return here, my friend, of her own free will. You might say I—er—abducted her; then persuaded her to remain by offering an annulment—by offering her a way to be free of a man she found utterly contemptible.'

As had happened earlier, Cheffy did not respond to his lordship's startling disclosures. He merely sat there, his kindly eyes seemingly glued to a spot on the richly coloured carpet. This time, however, Linford felt no animosity towards his old friend.

Leaning back in his chair, he stared down at the dregs in his glass for several moments, and then apprised his silent companion of the reason why, six years before, the young Viscountess Linford had felt herself unable to remain under the protection of her husband's roof.

'It is ironic, is it not,' he continued, reaching for the decanter yet again, 'that the one woman I could happily spend the rest of my life with happens to be the girl I married? Never would I have believed it possible to take unto me someone so much after my own heart. I could search the world and never find her equal.'

He released his breath in a heartfelt sigh. 'I married to save my ancestral home, and yet, now, I would part with it all, if I could but truly make her my own. . .my wife.'

'Eh?' Cheffy blinked. 'Do you mean you haven't— you've never—?'

'No, our marriage has never been consummated,' his lordship admitted, once again smiling faintly at the older man's look of astonishment. 'Surely you remember what she was like when we married? She seemed so young for her years. It would have felt as though I were molesting a child. But that is a poor excuse for my behaviour.

'Had I taken my duties as a husband seriously, I might, then, not have sought my pleasures in the arms of a woman whose name I cannot even remember. But I chose not to do so, and have paid dearly for that inattention to my young bride. . .and shall continue to do so until the end of my days.'

'Not if you're the man I think you are,' Cheffy countered bracingly, a heartening look dispelling the sympathy in his kindly eyes.

'Quite understandable why the gel left you, Linford. Dear me, yes. Can't say I blame her for doing so, either. But she's here now, no matter the reason, and she's very fond of you, m'boy. Any fool can see that. Don't let some demmed antiquated sense of chivalry prevent you from keeping what you hold most dear. If you allow her to leave, you may never again be offered another chance.'

Nothing would have given Linford more pleasure than to take the older man's advice, but in the days that followed he searched in vain for a sign that Rachel might be agreeable to a closer relationship developing between them.

Her lovely smile was ever present, but not once did he glimpse a provocative look, or an encouraging gesture, to give him reason to hope that she might be willing to undertake every wifely duty. No, friendship was all Rachel sought from him, he felt certain. And a good friend he was determined to be, and a better protector than he had been before!

Rachel submitted tamely to the many rules imposed upon her by her, suddenly, very domineering husband. Henceforward, he ruled that she was not permitted to ride out in the carriage without her maid, or some other female companion; she was allowed to walk in the gardens, but not out across the park; and she was strictly forbidden, when the time came, to ride anywhere without the Viscount or a groom as escort.

This, she knew, would be the hardest regulation to obey, for she prized her freedom highly, but meekly agreed even to this; and, almost a week after Mr Cheffingham's visit, was rewarded for her acquiescence by the arrival of a large box containing a very stylish black riding habit and a lovely evening gown in deep green velvet.

After quickly donning her new habit, she went down to the breakfast room to find the Viscount, as usual, already seated at the table, reading his correspondence. He looked up as she entered, and just for an instant she thought she could detected signs of strain in the depths of his eyes before she received that customary smile of greeting.

'The habit fits perfectly, Dominic. Thank you. I can hardly wait to ride again.'

'So I see.' His smile, now, was indulgent. 'And what of your other gown? Does that please you?'

'It's beautiful, but you ought not to have gone to such expense.'

One black brow rose. 'Have you forgotten the Maitland ball takes place the day after tomorrow? I cannot—I simply cannot have my wife attending such a grand occasion looking anyhow. Think of my reputation!'

Her eyes twinkled in response. 'And here I was proposing to wear that faded muslin I don when going through the linen cupboards. I cannot imagine how I managed before I had you to instruct me on how to go on.'

'Baggage!' he retorted good-humouredly just as the door opened; Peplow entered, carrying a letter brought by a servant from the Green Man at Linfield.

'I'm afraid, my dear, you'll think me a bore, but I must insist you forgo your ride,' his lordship informed her, after casting his eyes over the missive. 'There's someone I'm wishful for you to meet.'

She betrayed interest. 'Oh?'

Placing the letter into his pocket, the Viscount looked across the table at her, a wickedly twitching smile hovering about his mouth.

'Several months ago I enlisted the aid of a man to help me retrieve a certain—er—valuable piece of property of mine, which disappeared from this house some six years before. He was successful in his endeavours, and so I have enlisted his aid once again as the aforementioned piece of property is causing me yet more concern.'

'Really?' Rachel bit into her slice of bread and butter. 'I cannot help but feel, Dominic,' she went on, meditatively, 'that it might have been wiser not to look for the—er—property in the first place. It seems to have caused you many problems.'

'Far more than it realises, my dear,' he said softly, coming to stand beside her chair. He took her chin in his long fingers, and she raised her eyes to his. 'But this acquisition is so very, very special. . .would be irreplaceable, in fact. I should not be best pleased if it suffered any further damage.'

Rachel lowered her eyes in some confusion, unsure of how to respond, and felt untold relief when he turned and left the room without another word.

\* \* \*

Thankfully, she had completely regained her composure when, an hour later, they entered the inn at Linfield. So in control of herself was she, in fact, that she did not betray her slight feeling of resentment towards the individual who had been instrumental in restoring her to her husband's ancestral home.

She greeted Mr Stubbs with just the correct amount of warmth, and then proceeded, under his lordship's direct instructions, to relate all the details she could recall about the recent attack upon her.

'I'm afraid I can give you so very little to go on, sir. The only part of him I saw clearly was his boots—rough workman's boots.'

Stubbs made a note of this, then said, 'When you decided to take that route home, my lady, was there anyone else about who might have overheard your conversation with the blacksmith?'

'No—yes. Yes, there was!' Rachel glanced up at the Viscount, who was warming his coat-tails by the roaring fire. 'How strange, Linford, that I had forgotten. But Renfrew, Harry Maitland's groom, was there.'

Again the ex-Runner made a note of this in his book. 'I'll have a word with this fellow.'

'Do be careful, Mr Stubbs,' Rachel enjoined him. 'He's a most unpleasant individual.'

'Is he, now? Unpleasant enough to attack a helpless female, maybe?'

'I wouldn't put anything past him. But—but—' she shrugged '—what motive could he have had? I've done nothing to him, after all.'

'And you can think of no one who bears you a grudge?'

'No, I cannot,' she responded without a moment's hesitation. 'But certain other possibilities have occurred to me. My father was not well liked. Perhaps someone bore him a grudge, and thought to attain some petty form of revenge by injuring his offspring. Unlikely, I know, but certainly a possibility.

'More probable, of course,' she went on matter-of-factly, but with a decided twinkle in her eyes, which the Viscount would have recognised instantly had she been looking in his direction, 'is that Linford, here, has been abominable to some poor unfortunate, and the fellow extracted retribution by harming me.'

Rachel refrained from looking in his lordship's direction, but Mr Stubbs did not hesitate, and glimpsed astonished outrage before violet eyes narrowed suspiciously, and fixed themselves on the Viscountess's lovely profile.

'My wife, no doubt, would be only too eager to confirm my reprehensible twice-weekly practice of going about the locale in search of some hapless individual with whom I might come to cuffs,' he remarked blandly, and watched slender shoulders shaking with suppressed laughter.

'And now, madam, do you think we could possibly continue this interview with Mr Stubbs with slightly less flippancy? And you may begin by informing him of the first attempt made upon your life, which I am reliably informed occurred some months ago.'

Giving a visible start, Rachel's eyes flew to his face. 'How on earth did you know——? Of course, Alice must have told you.'

'She did, indeed. And I should like to know why you found yourself unable to inform me of it yourself?'

'Well, I——I. . .' Feeling decidedly uncomfortable, Rachel began to twist the strings of her reticule nervously round her fingers, whilst her eyes darted between the uncompromising expression on her husband's face and the enquiring one on the ex-Runner's. Deciding Mr Stubbs would be more sympathetic, she turned to him. 'I know I must seem a pea-goose, sir, but the truth of the matter is I simply forgot all about it.'

'Forgot that someone had tried to shoot you?' Linford's tone was scornful. 'Come, madam. You must do better than that!'

'But it's true, I tell you!'

'Perhaps it would be better, my lady,' Mr Stubbs put in gently, before his lordship could counter with a further reproof, 'if you explained to me exactly what happened.'

She cast him a look of gratitude before relating, as best she could, the few details she recalled about the incident.

'You see, Mr Stubbs, there isn't much I can tell you, and it happened so long ago. I had been back at the Hall less than a month. No, wait a moment.' She frowned suddenly. 'I can be more accurate than that. It happened on the afternoon I visited the ruined monastery at Trinsham. You remember, Linford. The day I had that little confrontation with Arabella Maitland.'

The Viscount's eyes narrowed. 'Their groom was present, was he not?'

'Yes, he was, but he rode off with the girls.'

'But you didn't come straight home, if my memory serves me correctly. Did you not go with Ben Hughes to visit that barn of his?' She nodded, and his lordship turned to the ex-Runner. 'There would have been time enough for that groom to have escorted the Maitland sisters home, and to have gone back to the wood. Arabella Maitland has recently returned from a visit abroad.'

He frowned slightly. 'No, I think we'll have a talk with the younger sister, and see if she can recall if the groom did, indeed, escort them home.'

'Even if he didn't, I still don't see what it would prove.' Perplexed, Rachel shook her head. 'What grudge can he possibly have against me? I'd never set eyes on the fellow in my life before I met him that day.'

'And you suspected no one at the time?' Mr Stubbs asked suddenly, and watched a guilty blush add extra colour to the Viscountess's flawless complexion.

'Er—well, no, not really.' she responded, not very convincingly.

'Come, Rachel, out with it!' The Viscount, too, had noticed his wife's heightened colour. 'Who did you suspect of having taken a pot shot at you?'

'Oh, very well!' she snapped, annoyed at the constant barrage of prying questions. 'If you must have it, Linford, I thought it was you!'

'What. . .? What?' He stared down at her, his expression a combination of incredulity and outrage. 'Why the devil should you suppose that I'd want. . .? I need a drink!'

Rachel watched him storm across the room to call to the tapster. 'There, you see! I knew he wouldn't be best pleased if I told him.'

'Hardly surprising, ma'am, if you'll forgive me saying so,' Mr Stubbs responded, doing his level best to suppress a quivering lip. 'Might I be permitted to know why you suspected your husband of doing such a dastardly thing?'

'Yes, I'd like to know that, too!' his lordship snapped, having overheard the question as he stalked back into the room.

'It was only that I saw you, on the day in question, walking from the direction of the home wood with a gun over your arm.'

'*Mea culpa!*' He raised his eyes heavenwards. 'No doubt I'd been out shooting at rabbits. . .not at vixens!'

His lordship's good humour had not been restored half an hour later when they left the inn. His far from gentle helping hand as he assisted Rachel into the carriage left her in little doubt as to his frame of mind. She was content to sit quietly in the corner, gazing through the window at the rolling landscape, until they suddenly passed a sturdy farm cart.

'Oh, I do believe that was Mrs Hughes and her son! On their way to market, no doubt.'

There was no response.

'I never did thank Sam Hughes for his help that evening, Dominic. I think I'll ride over to the farm this afternoon.'

'There's no need,' was the brusque response. 'I've already done so on your behalf.'

'Nevertheless, I should still like to see him myself.'

'Just as you wish.'

'How long have they been tenants of yours?' she asked, in an attempt to draw him out of his ill-humour.

'About fifteen years.'

'Sam Hughes is a good, hard-working man, is he not?'

'Very. The complete opposite of the boorish, good-for-nothing oaf who had the farm before him.' Momentarily, he forgot his grievances as his mind went back over the years. 'I was at Eton when my father finally sent him and his family packing. He came upon him one day beating a horse unmercifully. Renfield was a cruel, bullying rogue, given to bouts of almost insane temper. What became of them, I do not know.'

'Renfield,' she echoed, frowning. 'Now, why does that name sound familiar, I wonder?'

'A common enough handle, I should have thought,' he responded, his offhand tone betraying a return to his former humour.

'Oh, for heaven's sake!' Rachel exclaimed in a mixture of exasperation and amusement. 'What on earth is the matter with you, Dominic? You are behaving like a sulky schoolboy!'

'And with good reason!' he countered sharply. 'How could you. . .? How could you think that I'd wish to harm you?'

'I've already explained about that.' Suppressing the urge to tease him further, she stared into his hurt and angry eyes. 'You must realise, Dominic, that I hadn't been at the Hall very long when it happened. I didn't know you as well as I do now. At the time, it occurred to me that it would be a very convenient way to be rid of an unwanted wife.'

'Such is the working of the female mind!' he muttered, raising his eyes heavenwards. 'Why the deuce, madam, would I have brought you back to the Hall if I had wanted to put a period to your existence? Surely it must have occurred even to you, pea-goose that you are,' he went on rudely, 'that had that been my intention, I would hardly perpetrate the act on my own doorstep, where I'd undoubtedly become the prime suspect, considering the history of our marriage?'

'Of course it occurred to me, Dominic. And that is precisely why I didn't retain the suspicion for very long. But, pea-goose that I may be,' she went on with emphasis on the slur which she had found insulting, 'it was also quite evident to me that the reason you gave for my remaining at the Hall for a period of time was not your main one.

'I seriously suspected that revenge was part of your motive. After all, I could quite easily have made my true identity known in Somerset, or even London, had I chosen to return there in the autumn. Then, any suspicions that remained in people's minds that you had done away with me years ago would have been quashed once and for all.'

'Don't be ridiculous!' he snapped, turning his head to stare out of the window. 'That course of action would not have served the purpose at all.'

'You are being deliberately provoking!' she returned, her patience wearing thin. 'And I cannot bear with you in this mood. In fact, I shall ask Jem to accompany me over to the Hughes' farmhouse this afternoon. He will be far better company.' She cast a frowning glance at his averted face. 'And do not sulk!'

# *Chapter Thirteen*

**R**achel awoke the next morning and was astounded, when she looked out of her bedroom window, to see the park covered in a soft blanket of white. The weather the day before had been dry, and quite mild for the time of year; there had been nothing to indicate that there would be a fine covering of snow before morning.

Involuntarily, her mind went back to her childhood, when she had woken, elated, to discover just such scenes. She had never been allowed to go out of doors and play as other children had done. Building snowmen and enjoying tumbles on sledges were treats forbidden to her.

Now, she supposed, she was too old to indulge in such escapades. But nothing and no one was going to stop her from venturing out of doors and hearing the crisp snow crunching beneath her boots, and seeing the shrubs in the garden adorned with their lacy covering of white.

Forgoing breakfast, she donned a pair of stout half-boots and a thick woollen cloak. She left the house by way of the door leading to the stable yard, and was surprised to see Jem leading Ramon back into his stall. Her eyes narrowed. Linford must have been up and about very early to have been out on some errand and to have returned already.

What on earth could have taken him out at such an early

hour? she wondered. Or had he, perhaps, done so with the intention of deliberately avoiding her company at breakfast? She shook her head. Surely not. True—he had been far from his usual convivial self the evening before, but she felt certain that he had been over his sulks of the morning.

Although, she reminded herself, there had been numerous occasions during these past days when she had found him staring at her—almost assessingly, she had thought.

She shrugged, dismissing it from her mind as she set off along the path leading to the shrubbery. She rounded the corner of the fine Elizabethan mansion, and then stopped dead in her tracks. There, standing on the edge of the south lawn, was the master of the house, his back towards her, gazing out across the park.

For a few moments she remained perfectly still, watching him as he surveyed the snow-covered landscape, which glistened in the bright morning sunlight like some enchanted fairytale land. She noticed the folds of his cloak moving slightly in the light, but bitingly cold, wind, and clinging to his shapely, muscular legs; but it was the beaver hat, set at a rakish angle on his thick black locks, which eventually captured her attention.

Very slowly she edged her way towards him. He still did not turn. He was either so wrapped in thought that he did not hear her footsteps, or deliberately ignoring her.

Prompted by some imp of mischief, she bent to scoop up a mound of snow. Carefully secreting a small stone in the centre, she compacted it into a tight ball. The many hours she had spent as a child, sat at her bedroom window, throwing pebbles at the branches of a dead tree had not been in vain. Taking careful aim, she hurled her missile. It caught the fine beaver hat just above the brim, sending it toppling to the ground.

'What the devil!' Not surprisingly startled, his lordship

swung round to see his wife convulsed in silent laughter.
'Why, you little—!' His lips twitched, but his eyes
narrowed dangerously. 'I warned you about throwing
things at me, my girl. Wait until I get hold of you!'

Uttering an unmaidenly shriek, Rachel set off down the
path. Young and slender, she was as swift as a fawn but,
hampered by petticoats, she was no match for her husband,
who in a few strides had shortened the distance
between them.

He made a dive for the billowing folds of her woollen
cloak, and his foot slipped in the snow, sending him
cannoning into her. They both fell to the ground, and
tumbled over and over down the gentle slope to the south
lawn, laughing uproariously like two boisterous children.

The Viscount ended up lying half on top of his, still,
highly amused wife. He pinioned her shoulders to the
ground, effectively preventing her from rising, and gazed
down into eyes filled with mischievous laughter.

'And now, madam wife, I'll teach you to hurl things at
your husband,' he growled before his gaze became fixed
on her softly parted lips.

Rachel saw his smile fade before his head lowered. She
felt herself tremble, but neither from cold, nor fear, as
those firm, dry lips were placed over hers so gently, almost
tentatively. Fleetingly, her mind went back to the only
other time he had ever kissed her. Then, she had made at
least a token attempt not to respond to the warm pressure
of that shapely mouth; now she experienced not the least
desire to do so.

All sensible considerations for the consequences of her
actions were thrust aside by a novel and uncontrollable
longing coursing through her veins, and she abandoned
herself, willingly, to his expertise, revelling in the feel of
him, the strength of him, the manliness of him.

Then quite suddenly, unexpectedly, he wrenched his

mouth away. She heard him muttering something under his breath before opening her eyes in time to see him, scowling heavily, turn his head. Then she heard it, too, and followed the direction of his frowning gaze to see an elegant and very familiar carriage sweeping down the curve of the drive.

Prudence returned with a vengeance. 'Great heavens, Linford! It's the Maitlands!' Rachel squealed, hot with embarrassment, as she allowed him to pull her to her feet. 'Supposing they saw us!'

'And what if they did? I am accountable to no one for my actions, my dear, with perhaps one exception.' Smiling crookedly, he watched her making a great play of brushing the snow from her skirts. 'Surely you don't expect me to apologise?'

'What. . .? I—er—no, of course not,' she answered, still in some confusion. Then she noticed the wicked amusement in his eyes, and realised he was deriving a good deal of perverse pleasure out of her acute embarrassment. 'Don't just stand there, Linford!' she snapped, in an attempt to mask her continued discomfiture. 'Go and meet them, whilst I change my dress.'

With cheeks flaming, and with his lordship's teasing laughter echoing tauntingly in her ears, Rachel sped along the path and into the house. By the time she had arrived at her bedchamber she was, understandably enough, breathing heavily, but the erratic pulse throbbing in her temple and the thunderous pounding of her heart had little to do with exertion, she knew.

Alice quickly arrived in response to the summons and, after helping her mistress don a dry, clean dress, repinned the lustrous mahogany tresses. Rachel did not delay in returning downstairs, but succeeded masterfully in avoiding the Viscount's eyes as she entered the small salon, and moved across the room to greet the visitors, all seated together on the sofa.

Instinctively, she recalled the very first time the Maitland ladies had called to see her. How different Lucy was now! Gone was the shy, diffident girl who had sat, head bent, twisting hands nervously in her lap. In her place sat a demure young lady whose young brown eyes glov. ed with self-confidence, and whose smile of greeting betrayed deep affection.

Mrs Maitland, too, had altered, Rachel realised suddenly. Although her greeting held only a modicum of warmth, there was no mistaking the respectful tone in her voice. Only Arabella seemed unchanged: calculating, mistrustful and, Rachel suspected, still deeply resentful.

This was the first time she had seen the elder girl since her return from Paris the previous week, and politely enquired how she had enjoyed her sojourn abroad.

'It was wonderful!' she enthused, animosity forgotten for the moment. 'London is nothing to it! Frenchmen are so droll. And the fashions are far superior to anything you can find here.'

'I am afraid I cannot agree, Arabella.' The response came, surprisingly, from her mother, who sniffed loudly as she cast her eyes over her elder daughter's fussily adorned Parisian carriage dress, and then glanced briefly at Lucy's plain, but elegant, attire. 'I'm very pleased with the way that bronze velvet made up,' she went on, turning to Rachel. 'It suits Lucy very well, do you not agree?'

'Yes, I do, ma'am. That visit we made to Penley was certainly very worth while.'

'It was indeed. I am wishful to make a return trip in the near future, and was wondering whether I might persuade you to accompany us, my lady? I have decided, you see,' Mrs Maitland continued without giving Rachel an opportunity to reply, 'to take Lucy to London for the

Season next year. I am one of those people who deem it quite unnecessary to see an elder daughter suitably settled before bringing out a younger. Lucy will be eighteen in a few weeks. I see no reason why she should await Arabella's convenience.'

Rachel, naturally, was delighted to discover that Mrs Maitland was retaining an interest in her younger daughter, but wondered how Lucy felt about the prospect of sharing a London Season with her vivacious elder sister. Her young friend's expression gave nothing away, and she did not quite know how to respond, but was saved the necessity of doing so by Linford, who said,

'No doubt, Miss Maitland, after the heady delights of Paris, you will find it quite dull until you leave for London in the spring.'

Arabella pouted prettily across at him. 'You must think me a very poor creature to suppose that I cannot find enough to keep me occupied. Besides, there are many treats to look forward to. Our ball tomorrow evening, for one. You will be attending, won't you, my lord?'

'I wouldn't miss it for the world, Miss Maitland,' he assured her. 'My wife is particularly looking forward to going. It will be the first large gathering she has attended since leaving London.'

As Rachel had given him no reason to suppose that she was looking forward to the occasion with any degree of enthusiasm, she was at a loss to understand from where he had gleaned such information, but swept the puzzling thought aside as she noticed Arabella's lips curling suddenly into a satisfied smile, like that of a cat's which had just been given a rare treat.

'Oh, yes. You above all others must attend, my lady,' Arabella said, that unpleasant curl on her lips still very much in evidence. 'Whilst I was in Paris, I met some very interesting people, one of whom is wishful to make your acquaintance again. They will be arriving tomorrow.'

Rachel frowned in puzzlement. 'I do not think I number among my acquaintances anyone who has recently visited Paris. Who is it, I wonder?'

'I shan't tell you. It is to be a surprise. Mama and Lucy don't even know, so it's of no use your asking them.'

Linford, eyes narrowing, fixed his gaze on Arabella for a moment, and then turned his attention to the younger sister. 'I understand that you have recently acquired a grey mare. My wife informs me that she is a darling creature. Would it be too much to ask, I wonder, for me to come over this afternoon and see you put her through her paces?'

Lucy smiled delightedly. She had long since lost all shyness when in the Viscount's presence. 'I should be happy to, my lord! Since I have known Lady Linford, I have been riding much more than I was used to do, and Papa thought it time I had a more suitable mount.'

Linford was a very shrewd judge of horseflesh, Rachel knew, but she doubted, as she watched him tool his curricle up the sweeping drive some time later, that it was a desire to see the new mare which took him over to the Maitland house—more likely a desire to speak to Lucy in private.

He mentioned nothing of his visit when he joined her at dinner that evening, nor did he inform her that he would be out for much of the following day; and when she saw him briefly just before it was time to dress for the ball, he offered no explanation whatsoever for his long absence from home.

She puzzled over this, as she sat before her dressing table, allowing Alice to add the finishing touches to her hair. That Linford was very worried over the attack upon her was obvious—he was doing everything humanly possible to uncover the identity of the miscreant.

She felt certain he had spent the day in the company of

Mr Stubbs with this very end in mind; but she could not rid herself of the lowering feeling that he was, now, for some reason best known to himself, deliberately avoiding her.

No, she wasn't being fanciful, she told herself, automatically rising from the dressing-table to enable Alice to help her into the new dark green velvet evening gown. Linford's attitude had definitely changed towards her. Almost from the day of Cheffy's visit there had been—yes—a restraint about him. He was not unfriendly—far from it, in fact—but he did seem ill at ease when alone with her, and had certainly kept himself at a distance whenever possible.

Instinctively, she began to dwell, as she had so many times, on the incident in the garden, when Linford had kissed her. She held herself entirely to blame. Unwittingly, through her playfulness, she had initiated what had taken place between them. The mere thought made her cheeks flame with embarrassment, and yet honesty prompted her to admit that she didn't regret what had happened.

More importantly, though, did he regret it? He had certainly made light of it at the time, laughing it off as though it had meant nothing to him. But then, she reminded herself bitterly, kissing members of the opposite sex was hardly a new experience for him. Yet, since then, his avoidance of her company had been more marked. Had her willing response given him a disgust of her? she wondered. Or had it, merely, put him on his guard?

Her eyes narrowed. Was he, perhaps, afraid that she might renege on their agreement; that she might try by any feminine wile to remain Viscountess Linford?

Anger welled at the mere thought. If that was, indeed, the case, then she would swiftly disabuse him. She might be only a merchant's daughter, but she was an honourable woman. She would keep to her side of the bargain. And he had better ensure that he kept to his during her final three weeks at the Hall!

At her young maid's eager prompting, Rachel automatically walked across the room to the full-length mirror, but gained little satisfaction from her reflection. With its square neckline, cut low across the bosom, and its tight, full-length sleeves, the soft dark green velvet seemed to cling to her like a second skin.

She would never have dreamt of choosing such an alluring gown herself, but she could not deny that Linford's taste was impeccable, and that it suited her very well.

'Are you not pleased, my lady?' Alice asked tentatively, noticing the almost indifferent expression on her mistress's face.

'Very! I particularly like the way you have arranged my hair,' she assured her, gazing at the riot of dark red curls that crowned her head. Alice had trimmed the front and sides, so that tiny curls, now, feathered across her forehead and down her cheeks, leaving only three large ringlets to hang caressingly over one white shoulder. 'Yes, that is a nice new touch. I think I prefer it a little shorter at the front.'

Gratification glinted in the young maid's eyes. 'You look beautiful, my lady. Every inch a Viscountess!'

'Do I, indeed?' A wry smile curled her lips. 'But then, Alice, you must remember that looks can often be very deceptive.'

Rachel sat herself once again at the dressing-table, and was looking through her jewel case for some suitable adornment, when there was a knock on the door, and a moment later the Viscount entered, elegantly attired in formal evening wear and carrying a flat square box.

'Ah, Linford! The very person to help me choose a necklace to wear with this dress,' she said, bestowing a cursory glance over him as he came towards her.

'I have already done so, my dear,' he responded, opening the box to reveal the most beautiful necklace of emeralds and diamonds, with a pair of matching ear-rings. 'At the risk of a further assault upon my person, dare I ask you to accept these as a token of my sincere regard for you?'

Rachel, experiencing combined sadness and anger, gazed down at the beautiful adornments glinting on their bed of velvet. Much to Linford's annoyance, she had flatly refused to wear any of the family jewels, deeming it unseemly for her to don the gifts of love bestowed upon her predecessors. She had no right to wear them, nor could she bring herself to do so; but this set, she felt certain, did not belong to the collection.

No, Linford had purchased this especially for her, and she might have been deeply moved by such a touching gesture, had not some malicious demon reminded her that most men in his position presented a farewell token to certain females when they were about to dispense with their services.

Again a wry smile curled her lips. She had not been his mistress, it was true, but she did not doubt that this was his very tactful way of saying that she was about to receive her *congé*, nonetheless.

'What is wrong, Rachel?' He gazed down at her searchingly. 'Are they not to your taste?'

'They are exquisite.' Her smile, he noticed, nowhere near reached her eyes. 'And I shall be honoured to wear them.'

'May I be of assistance?' he offered, after watching her struggling in vain for several moments with the clasp on the necklace, and noticed, too, the way she seemed to flinch at the light touch of his fingers on the nape of her neck.

'Ooh, Miss Em,' Alice husked, forgetting formality in

her rapt admiration of her lovely mistress's stunning appearance. 'You look like a queen.'

'It would seem I rise ever higher in the world! A private joke, Linford,' she told him as he placed the fur-lined cloak about her shoulders. 'Tidy up here, Alice, but on no account are you to wait up for me! I am quite capable of getting myself ready for bed.'

As they descended the staircase, Rachel noticed that there seemed to be an inordinately large number of servants busily occupied in the hall, and remarked on this as the carriage swept through the gateway and out on to the open road.

'They were certainly not hovering to catch a glimpse of me in formal evening attire, my dear. They've seen that spectacle often enough.' The carriage lamps enabled him to see an unmistakable flush of colour rise in her cheeks. 'They're very fond, and very proud, of their beautiful mistress. It's only natural that they would wish to see her dressed for such an occasion as this.'

'They—they are good and loyal servants, Dominic,' she said softly, trying to force back the lump which threatened to lodge itself in her throat. 'You're fortunate to have such people about you.'

He heard the faint sigh as she leaned back against the squabs, and watched her turn her head to stare resolutely out of the window. 'What is it, my dear? What's wrong?'

'Why, nothing!' She turned her head to look at him again. 'Why should there be anything wrong?'

He regarded her for a moment under half-closed lids. 'You make a very poor liar, my darling. That is, of course, possibly to your credit. But I have come to know you too well during these months we have been together, and am very well aware that, since our brief meeting this afternoon, something has occurred to disturb your peace of mind.'

Hovering on the brink of indecision for a moment, Rachel gave him back look for look, and then decided that only frankness would serve.

'Nothing has occurred to upset me, Dominic,' she reiterated, 'except I feel that your attitude towards me has changed. As you say, we have come to know each other very well, and I have noticed that you have been strangely withdrawn these past two weeks. Furthermore, I have increasingly felt that you are deliberately trying to avoid my company. Am I being fanciful?'

He lowered his eyes, but not before she noticed a certain guarded look flickering in their violet depths. 'I have had much on my mind, Rachel, it is true. But I have not been deliberately avoiding you. As you may have guessed, I have spent most of today with Stubbs.'

'To any purpose?' curiosity prompted her to enquire.

'Yes, and no.' Linford leaned his broad back against the velvet squabs. 'I took him to the ridge, and then we called in at the forge. Trench could not remember whether the Maitlands' groom had been there or not, but Ben certainly remembered. Bad man, he said quite clearly. He had said that to me before, the day after you were attacked, but of course I hadn't a notion to whom he was referring. More importantly, though, when Stubbs asked him if he saw which way Renfrew went after he left the forge, Ben said "Yes" very distinctly, and pointed in the direction you had taken.'

Rachel shrugged. 'I don't see what that proves. He may have had another call to make.'

'Just what he told us himself when we questioned him later. Said he had called at the inn for a tankard of ale.'

'And don't you believe him?' she asked as he frowned heavily.

'It cannot be proved one way or the other. The inn-keeper, of course, doesn't remember whether he came in on that particular afternoon, or not. Which is in no way remarkable. One cannot expect him to recall his every customer. But what is remarkable is that Stubbs recognised that groom. Seems to think Renfrew lived in London for a time. He denied it. In fact, he became quite belligerent when Stubbs endeavoured to question him further.'

'You think he was lying?'

'He's certainly hiding something, yes.' Again he frowned. 'Most puzzling of all, though, is that I thought there was something oddly familiar about him. It's the first time I've ever seen him up close, and he put me in mind of someone, but for the life of me I cannot think who it can be.'

Rachel was silent for a moment, digesting these snippets of information, then said, 'I have never made any secret of the fact that I dislike Renfrew intensely. And it would come as no great surprise to learn that he had been in trouble with the authorities, but I still cannot understand why he should wish to harm me, if indeed he was the one.'

She sighed. 'I shouldn't like to think you were hounding an innocent man, Linford. And please do not think I'm ungrateful, but—but, I cannot help but feel that all this is a complete waste of your time *and* money. In a little over three weeks I shall be gone from here. And that will be an end to the matter.'

The opportunity had been there for her to set his mind at rest, to assure him that he need have no fear that she would not be gone by the end of the year, but his reaction was hardly what she would have expected. He said nothing, merely turning his head to stare out of the window. An almost oppressive silence lengthened between them, and she experienced untold relief when the coach finally arrived at the Maitlands' large, red-brick house.

Jem, resplendent in black and gold livery, had pulled the door open and had the steps down almost before the carriage had come to a halt. Smiling her thanks, as he assisted her to alight, Rachel walked up the shallow stone steps, and could clearly hear the strains of music and voices raised in cheerful discourse even before she entered the hall, where a footman relieved her of her cloak.

Through the open doorway leading to a large, brightly-lit salon, she could see the master and mistress of the house, standing side by side in readiness to greet their guests, and only hoped, as she led the way across the hall, that Linford had come out of his strangely solitary mood.

He greeted his host and hostess cordially enough, but Rachel was hardly given the opportunity to assess his mood, for no sooner had he guided her further into the room than Harry Maitland claimed her hand for a dance.

For the next half hour Rachel had a succession of partners, one of whom was Linford's cousin, Cedric, who had come down from Oxford with Harry Maitland the day before, and who, surprisingly, turned out to be a very graceful dancer. She was not so fortunate in her next partner, and as soon as the set came to an end, she hurriedly left the floor before her poor bruised feet were forced to endure further punishment.

Making a bee-line for Lucy, who had just been escorted to a vacant chair by Dr Gillis, Rachel sat herself in the seat beside her young friend, and sighed with relief.

'I flatly refuse to dance again, unless you can assure me that my prospective partner possesses a sense of direction and has at least a modicum of control over his feet.'

Lucy chuckled. 'I'm afraid Mr Witherington is not the most graceful dancer. I've been forced to endure the experience myself. But if you will insist on attending a ball looking so beautiful, Rachel, you've only yourself to blame. It's only natural that most men would want to dance with you.'

'Sycophant!' Rachel scolded gently. 'Your own appearance leaves nothing to be desired. That amber silk is very becoming on you, Lucy. I wonder, though, whether you will be permitted to wear such colours when you go to London?'

'Mama is coming round to my way of thinking. I have no fears that she would try to make me wear anything that did not become me.'

'You sound as though you are looking forward to a Season.'

Lucy's shoulders rose in an almost indifferent shrug. 'I wouldn't go as far as to say that, but I am no longer terrified at the prospect, as I once was. And going with Arabella does have its advantages. She, of course, will be the centre of attention, which will leave me free to do what I want.'

'I wouldn't be too sure of that, if I were you,' Rachel countered. 'At the risk of giving you a swollen head, I think you should know that there are several gentlemen here tonight who much prefer you to your sister. And talking of Arabella—where is she this evening? I do not recall seeing her.'

'Oh, she's about somewhere. Possibly with those people who arrived, unbeknownst to Mama, this afternoon.' Lucy chuckled. 'Mama is not best pleased. Poor Cedric and Harry have been forced to put up at the inn in Linfield to make room for Arabella's strange assortment of guests.'

Rachel glanced about the large room. With the odd exception, she knew most everyone present. She caught sight of the Viscount standing down the far end of the room. He was conversing with a lady wearing a purple turban, and beside her stood a very pretty girl with bright gold ringlets.

'Who is that talking with Linford, Lucy? They are not from round these parts, surely?'

'Madame and Mademoiselle de Sonnebrune. Two of those guests whom Mama is not best pleased at having to put up. Arabella became friendly with the daughter in Paris, and took it upon herself to invite them here for a few weeks.' Lucy laughed suddenly. 'There's Arabella, now, with that man who arrived with his wife this afternoon. Oh, no! She's bringing him over. Heavens, Rachel! Did you ever see such a quiz?'

Casting her young friend a reproving glance, Rachel tried to school her features, for Arabella was, indeed, heading in their direction.

The man's size was not conducive to rapid movement; consequently, Rachel had ample time to take stock of the portly gentleman, whose many chins found some support in the intricate folds of his snowy-white cravat, and whose dazzling green-and-yellow-striped waistcoat drew more than one pair of fascinated eyes to follow his slow progress across the floor.

Arabella, that unpleasant cat-like smile hovering about her mouth once again, at last stood before them. 'Lady Linford, may I present Sir Henry Fotheringale?'

Rachel found her fingers clasped in a large, sweaty hand, and felt certain she detected a creaking sound as the Baronet executed a far from graceful bow.

'I should have known you anywhere, m'dear,' he said, patting her hand fondly. 'May I say what a pleasure it is to make your acquaintance after all these years?'

Rachel, disliking the over-familiar fondling, drew her hand away as she stared up at his florid countenance, wondering why this gentleman should wish to meet her. 'Are you acquainted with my husband, sir?'

'Our paths have crossed from time to time, don't you know. Bumped into him in Paris last year, as a matter of fact. Is he here tonight?'

'Yes, he's over there.' Rachel gestured towards the far

end of the room, where her husband stood, staring back in their direction, a decidedly forbidding frown creasing his brow. If Linford was, indeed, acquainted with the Baronet, one could only assume from his expression that they were not upon the best of terms.

'Why not take Lady Linford up to your wife, Sir Henry?' Arabella suggested, that unpleasant smile still very much in evidence. 'You know how eager Lady Fotheringale is to renew her acquaintance.'

Slightly bemused, but politely agreeing to accompany the Baronet, Rachel walked back with him towards the door. As she drew close to where Linford stood, she saw a look in his violet eyes which was hard to interpret. Not a warning, precisely, more that of foreboding. She saw him move, as though he were about to approach her, then he seemed to check himself, and set off across the room in the direction of the Maitland sisters.

'From what Miss Maitland said, Sir Henry, I gather that I have met your wife before,' Rachel remarked, trying to ignore his heavy wheezing, as they began to mount the staircase, and praying he would not expire before they had reached the top.

'Eh?' His round, insipid blue eyes betrayed astonishment; then he rumbled with laughter. 'A little joke, eh, you naughty puss?'

For one dreadful moment Rachel thought he was going to reach out and pinch her chin, and took evasive action by hurrying up the last few steps ahead of him. Could it possibly have been that about which Linford had been trying to put her on her guard? Had he been endeavouring to warn her that she was venturing off with an ageing roué?

Dear Lord! She sincerely hoped not. But one thing was certain—there was absolutely no way the obese Baronet could possibly catch her if she was forced to flee from him.

With this comforting thought at the forefront of her

mind, she walked slowly along the passageway beside him. He came to a halt outside one of the bedchambers, and took a moment or two to catch his breath before throwing wide the door.

'Here she is, my pet,' he said jovially. 'I've brought her to you, just as I promised I would.'

Rachel walked a few paces into the room, and then stopped dead in her tracks as her eyes met those of the woman reclining gracefully on the chaise longue.

# Chapter Fourteen

'Oh, Henry, she is just too, too lovely! She reminds me of me at that age.' A wisp of lace was raised very affectingly to the corner of one eye. 'I do wish, now, I hadn't asked you to bring her up to see me. It's so very lowering to be reminded of what one was like in one's youth.'

The Baronet moved across to the sofa, and took a hold of one slender white hand. 'You are still a beauty, my pet. Am I not forever telling you so?' He looked back at Rachel and winked conspiratorially. 'And, my dear, there's not a doubt about it—at that age you were most certainly the prettier.'

The woman gave a trill of delighted laughter. 'Oh, Henry, you do say the sweetest things!' Disengaging her hand, she held it out. 'Come, my child. Come, give your mama a kiss.'

Rachel remained where she had stood from the beginning of this bizarre interchange between the Baronet and his wife, her eyes glued to the woman's finely boned face, noting the green eyes and the dark red curls peeking from beneath the frivolous cap... Mama? The word reverberated in her ears like some thunderous peal of bells.

Was this some kind of cruel, malicious hoax? Who was this person? Certainly not her mother—her mother had been dead for years. . . And yet, she could certainly discern a resemblance between them herself.

'I am sorry, ma'am, but I do not perfectly understand you,' she responded at last, her voice sounding strange, stilted, even to her own ears. 'Are we related in some way?'

Lady Fotheringale blinked across the room at her. 'But of course we are, silly child! I am your mother. Why should you doubt it?'

'Because my mother is dead, ma'am,' Rachel responded without a moment's hesitation this time, a surge of animosity towards this unknown female restoring her composure. 'If you knew anything about my family at all, you would know my mother died when I was four years old.'

'Died?' she echoed, and then tinkled with laughter once again. 'Your father, no doubt, told you that. The wretch!' Swinging her satin-shod feet to the floor, she held out both hands this time. 'Come here, my child. At least grant me the opportunity to try and explain.'

Still very sceptical, but intrigued, nonetheless, Rachel moved slowly forward. Ignoring the outstretched hands, she sat on the very edge of the couch, and cast a suspicious glance up at the Baronet, who smiled benignly back down at her like some indulgent uncle.

'Little wonder, my child, that you are bewildered. But how typical of your father to have told you such a wicked untruth!'

'Forgive me, ma'am, but I cannot help but ask myself why he should have done so, if it were not true?'

One slender shoulder rose in a graceful shrug. 'I could never understand the workings of Roderick's mind, my dear. But I suspect it was some petty form of revenge. What a miserable purse-pinch the wretch was! I was most wickedly deceived.'

There was certainly more than a grain of truth in what

the Baronet's wife had just said. The lady, at least, seemed to have acquired a fair knowledge of Roderick Weston's character, and Rachel began to have the uneasy feeling that this might not be a hoax, after all.

Sighing, Lady Fotheringale lay back against the couch. 'It all seems so long ago, now, but I'll do my best to explain.' She was silent for a few moments, absently plucking the frothily laced neckline of her pale green negligée, then continued.

'I had only just turned seventeen when I married your father. Sir Percival, your grandfather, was a darling man, but sadly inept where money matters were concerned. Neither my sister nor I had any kind of dowry to speak of, so we could hardly be over-particular when it came to choosing a prospective partner. Although, I must say, your Aunt Augusta did rather better than I.'

'Aunt?' Rachel made no attempt to hide her astonishment. 'I was unaware that I had an aunt.'

'Sadly, you no longer do. My sister died three years ago. She was very fond of you, Rachel, though I suppose you were too young to remember her. After I left, she wrote to your father many times, begging him to let you stay with her. He always refused. In the end she gave up, knowing he would never permit any contact between you. He was a most unnatural man!

'Why, the very day after our marriage took place he brought me into Hampshire, and here I remained, incarcerated, for five long years. The house was well enough, I suppose, but the furnishings were so dreary and old-fashioned, and he refused to purchase so much as a pair of new curtains. Miserly creature!

'You were born within a twelvemonth, and things just seemed to get progressively worse after that. The only decent society was to be found at Linford Hall, but the wretch quarrelled with your husband's father over an unimportant piece of land, and we were never afterwards invited back to the Hall.' She threw her hands up in an exaggerated gesture. 'The tedium, my dear! You would not believe it.'

'Oh, but I should, ma'am,' Rachel countered, her lips curling into a far-from-pleasant smile. 'I was made to endure more than five years there.'

For the first time Lady Fotheringale betrayed signs of unease as she scrutinised her daughter's features. 'Yes, no doubt you do blame me for abandoning you, but indeed at the time it was not my intention to do so,' she confessed— almost indifferently, it seemed to Rachel. 'Shortly after your fourth birthday, my sister invited me to stay with her in London for a few weeks, and it was then that I met dear Sir Henry.'

She reached out her hand to him, and he automatically took it in his fleshy fingers, and began to fondle the soft white skin. 'So very different from your father—so kind and understanding, so generous.'

Rachel cast her eyes over the obese Baronet, whose florid countenance seemed to adopt a foolishly doting expression whenever he looked in his wife's direction. Yes, he was far different from her father—she couldn't but agree with that. The only similarity between them was one of age. Unless she was very much mistaken, the Baronet would never see sixty again. Lady Fotheringale, evidently, was attracted to men old enough to be her father.

'Your dear mama would have gone into a decline, my dear, had she returned to Hampshire,' Sir Henry explained, his face now seemingly transfixed in that nauseatingly lovesick expression. 'Wouldn't have had that happen for the world. So I gave orders for my best team to be har-nessed to my travelling carriage, and whisked her off to my estates in Ireland.'

Rachel, wicked amusement glinting in her eyes, stared from one to the other. It was like taking part in some ludicrous theatrical farce: hugely diverting, but highly improbable; with Sir Henry, the most miscast actor imaginable, valiantly trying to portray the hero. 'How very dashing of you, Sir Henry!' she remarked, only just managing to control a quivering lip.

'And so it was!' his lady concurred. 'Though it was most unpleasant afterwards. Unless I agreed to have no further contact with you, your father refused to consent to a divorce. And people were so very beastly, especially to me. We were ostracised—positively shunned by London Society! I have never been back there since.'

She released her breath on a tiny sigh. 'Those years until Sir Henry and I could legalise our union were most trying. We divided our time between our home in Ireland, and Henry's plantation in the West Indies.

'Now, of course,' she went on, brightening, 'we live for the most part in Paris. Life there is so very gay. But we do return to Ireland from time to time, which we are in the process of doing at the moment. We are only staying here for one night, and then we're off again in the morning.'

Rachel sat calmly assessing what she had been told, whilst staring levelly at the stranger seated beside her. Lady Fotheringale put her in mind of nothing more than an over-indulged child, whose good behaviour was almost guaranteed providing she was given her way in all things. There was little doubt that the compliant Sir Henry made the ideal spouse for such a spoilt and selfish faded beauty.

'I am happy that things have turned out so well for you, ma'am,' she managed in an even tone.

'Why, thank you, my dear!' She gave a little crow of delight. 'As they have for you, too. Naturally, I did eventually learn of your marriage to young Dominic, and of your subsequent disappearance.' Another trill of laughter filled the air. 'I said to Henry, at the time, that it was like history repeating itself. But I have since learned from that sweet friend of yours, Arabella Maitland, that you are now reunited with your husband.'

Rachel's eyes narrowed. 'I was not aware, ma'am, that you were well acquainted with the Maitlands?'

'I'm not, my dear. Nor do I wish to be. From what I have learned, the mother sounds a positive dragon. Poor Arabella! I met the child for the first time a few weeks ago when her aunt brought her to Paris. She told me she hailed from Hampshire, and we fell in to talking—you know how it is. When she discovered that I was your mother, she positively insisted that I pay a visit.'

'How very thoughtful of her,' Rachel said woodenly.

'And so it was! But what with that abominable Channel crossing, and the journey here in the draughtiest carriage I have ever had the misfortune to travel in. . .then to discover we had arrived on the day of a tedious country ball, without so much as a welcome from either the master or mistress of the house, leaving it all to sweet Arabella to make us comfortable. . . Well, it has all been too much! And I now have the headache.'

'I am very sorry to hear that,' drawled a voice from the doorway. 'It is perhaps as well, ma'am, that I am come to relieve you of my wife's company.'

Rebecca's eyes flew across the room to see the Viscount moving slowly towards them. She was on her feet and by his side in an instant. Instinctively, her hand sought his for comfort and support, and his fingers curled round hers, warm and reassuring.

'Oh, Henry, would you just look at them! What a handsome couple they make!' Her smile vanished to be replaced by a childish pout. 'Though why I am speaking to you at all, Linford, I do not know. Allowing the poor child to believe her mama was dead was quite wicked of you.'

His lordship's eyes grew flint-like as he held those of the Baronet's wife. 'Forgive me, ma'am, for my sad lack of judgement. But I believed, you see, that had you wished your daughter to be apprised of your existence, you would have taken the trouble of informing her yourself.'

A most uncomfortable silence followed whilst Lady Fotheringale regained her composure, then she said, one slender shoulder rising in what can only be described as an indifferent shrug, 'Well, you know how it is. The years passed and there were times when I forgot I had a daughter. But we are reunited again, now, and I should like to see something of her. We leave in the morning for Ireland. But why not bring her to Paris in the spring?'

'It shall be as Rachel wishes, of course, but for my part I see no reason why that cannot be arranged.' He executed an elegant bow. 'And now, ma'am, I am afraid I must deprive you of your daughter's charming company. It is nearly time for supper, and they await us downstairs. Sir Henry, your servant,' and with that he turned, still retaining a hold on his wife's hand.

Rachel could do no more than smile weakly at Lord and Lady Fotheringale before she allowed Linford to lead her from the room. She felt so strange, bewildered. Before the Viscount's entry she had been mistress of her emotions, conversing with Lady Fotheringale quite dispassionately, as though she were of no more consequence than any other mere stranger whom one might meet at a party.

Linford's unexpected appearance, however, had changed all that. At sight of him, the full magnitude of what she had discovered began to permeate her brain. Her mother was alive! She ought, she knew, to feel overjoyed. Why, then, did she feel so strangely hollow inside, bereft of feeling?

'It has, naturally, been a shock, Rachel,' his lordship said gently. 'I could have wished that you might have discovered the truth in a different way—at a more suitable time and place.'

'It is so strange. I just don't know how I'm supposed to feel.' She checked at the head of the stairs, the sounds of music and laughter seeming suddenly quite deafening. 'Oh, God, Linford, I cannot go back in there! Take me home, please!'

'If that is what you wish, then of course we shall go. As long as you realise that by so doing you will be giving Arabella Maitland the satisfaction of knowing that she has come out the victor.'

She looked at him keenly. 'What do you mean?'

'You do not imagine, surely, that she invited your estimable parent here as an act of kindness?' He smiled crookedly as he saw her stiffen. 'Quite so, my dear. No, Miss Maitland, unless I'm very much mistaken, is hoping to see you skulk away like a whipped pup, cowed and with your tail between your legs.'

Rachel was silent for a few moments, digesting fully what he had said. She recalled vividly a certain conversation with Lucy months before when she had divulged that Roderick Weston's young wife had run away with another man, and shortly afterwards had died.

It would have been the most natural thing in the world for her young friend to recount that conversation to her mother and sister, but if Mrs Maitland had known the true state of affairs, Rachel would have sworn that she had not divulged it to her daughters.

No, Arabella Maitland had discovered the truth when in Paris—Rachel felt certain of that. And what better revenge could anyone who disliked her so much have taken than to humiliate her publicly by making her mother's scandal-

ous past common knowledge? Worse, even than that—
she was being made to look a liar.

Iron resolve restored her courage, and she requested the
Viscount to escort her back down to the salon. He seemed
more than willing to do so, but the instant she entered the
room, she found her courage waning once more, as all
eyes seemed to turn in her direction.

'Oh, God, Linford!' she murmured, reaching automatically for the comfort of that shapely hand once again.
'Everyone is staring at me.'

'So?' One dark brow rose. 'You ought to be accustomed
to that, my darling,' he drawled. 'It is a rare man, indeed,
who will not turn to admire a beautiful woman when she
enters a room. And the ladies, of course, are probably
assessing the possible cost of your gown, and wondering
if it would suit them half so well. It wouldn't, of course,
but they're welcome to dream.'

She chuckled at this sally, but then became serious
again. 'You know full well why they are staring. If I know
anything about Arabella Maitland, all have been apprised
by now.'

'And if I know anything about that heartless minx, they
have not,' he countered. 'I have never made any secret of
the fact that our esteemed hostess is not a person with
whom I have a great deal in common, but she has certainly
risen in my estimation this night.

'She has made it abundantly clear to her elder daughter
that if and when you choose to acknowledge your mother
is entirely a matter for you and you alone, and that she
would be excessively displeased if your close relationship
to Lady Fotheringale was made public by any member of
her family. I doubt that even Arabella would dare to flout
her mother's particular wishes.'

He smiled down at her reassuringly. 'And now, madam

wife, it is high time you danced with your husband. Then I shall escort you in to supper.'

For a few blissful minutes, whilst Linford's hand lay gently on her waist, and they swirled about the room together, Rachel was able, almost, to forget her shocking discovery. She detected no surreptitious glances cast in her direction; heard no whispered mutterings behind raised fans. Only from Lucy did she receive a sympathetic look, but even her young friend did not attempt to approach her to offer words of comfort.

Linford's judgement had been correct: she doubted that more than half a dozen people present knew of her relationship to Sir Henry Fotheringale's wife; but even so she found herself unable to relax and was not sorry when, shortly after supper had ended, Linford suggested that it was time for them to leave.

As far as Rachel was concerned the evening had been memorable, but hardly an enjoyable occasion. It might, however, have been a complete disaster, but for the intervention of one person, and she did not hesitate, whilst Linford went to order the carriage to be brought to the door, to seek out their hostess.

'I do not think, Mrs Maitland, that I have ever attended such a grand country affair. You put the rest of us to shame by the splendour of your winter ball.'

Mrs Maitland permitted herself a thin smile of satisfaction. 'I believe it is an event much enjoyed by everyone.' She was silent for a moment, and Rachel thought she could detect a flicker of sympathy in her neighbour's hard, dark eyes.

'I owe you an apology, Lady Linford. When Lucy informed me that you had mentioned your mother was dead, I believed that you simply chose not to recognise her. Which, of course, is entirely your own affair, and I did not enlighten my daughters. Linford, however, informed me this night that you truly believed your mother to be dead. And I can only say that I admire you greatly for remaining here after discovering the truth yourself.'

Again she fell silent for a moment, then said unexpectedly, 'A child cannot be held responsible for the actions of a parent.'

Her eyes moved in the direction of her elder daughter, who was surrounded, as usual, by several gentlemen admirers. 'It is rather unfair, therefore, that a parent must be held responsible for the thoughtless, not to say spiteful, conduct of an offspring. But so it is. And I can only apologise on my daughter's behalf for any distress she may have caused.'

Rachel felt greatly moved by the surprising show of compassion from this, normally, dictatorial and forthright woman. It was quite evident that she held herself to blame for her daughter's conduct, and Rachel would have liked to offer some words of comfort in response, but doubted whether such a gesture on her part would be well received.

She was saved the necessity of putting it to the test, however, by the sudden return of his lordship who, with remarkable perspicacity, summed up the situation in an instant and, with a few well-chosen phrases, thanked their hostess for the evening's entertainment before whisking Rachel outside to the waiting carriage.

She smiled to herself as the carriage turned out of the drive and they headed homewards. 'That was well done of you, sir. I was about to make the grave error of commiserating with Mrs Maitland on her elder daughter's unfortunate nature. She holds herself entirely to blame, but indeed she should not, for it's my belief she had no idea as to the identity of the people who had arrived earlier in the day.'

'No, she hadn't,' he confirmed. 'She was as astounded as I to see you leave the room on Sir Henry's arm. No sooner had I joined the Maitland girls, enquiring whether the Baronet's wife was also ensconced under their roof, than Mrs Maitland came over, demanding to know the very same thing. Domineering and assuming Mrs Maitland may be, but there's little amiss with her understanding. She summed up the situation in a trice.'

His lips curled into a wicked, reminiscent smile. 'I'll never forget the conclusion of that monumental diatribe she bestowed upon her elder daughter. "Arabella," said she, "there is a side to your character that distresses me greatly. For reasons best known to yourself, you have contrived to discompose a guest under my roof, which is something not easy to forgive.

'"Unlike yourself, Lady Linford was denied the many privileges normally bestowed upon females of breeding, and yet I have never once seen her behave with less dignity than that of a gracious lady. You would do well to set aside whatever petty grievances you may be harbouring, and follow your sister's lead by modelling your behaviour in the future on that of Viscountess Linford."'

Rachel felt she did not deserve such praise, but was human enough to find it very gratifying. Her few brief moments of satisfaction were soon thrust aside, however, when a very important particular occurred to her, and she asked, unable to keep a note of censure from creeping into her voice, 'Why didn't you tell me my mother was alive, Dominic?'

'Initially, because I thought you knew,' he replied softly. 'And when I eventually realised that you had been misinformed, I suppose I was waiting for the right opportunity to set you straight.'

A knowing little smile hovered about her mouth. Yes, she thought, he had recoiled at being the one to disillusion her. And little wonder! Furthermore, she doubted she would have believed him.

From an early age she had created a mythical being, bestowing upon it the epithet 'Mother', and accrediting it with every possible virtue. Her father had always featured as the villain of the piece; her mother the saintly heroine whose only slight fall from grace had been her love for another man.

What a crass little fool she had been all these years! But she had certainly had her eyes opened this night. Her mother was a frivolous, selfish creature with little to commend her. Perhaps there had been some justification for the way her father had behaved, and maybe one day she might find it in her heart to forgive him.

A tiny sigh escaped her. 'I know I ought to feel overjoyed at being reunited with my mother, Dominic, but I do not. Shame is what I feel. What parents to have been blessed with!'

'You are your own person, Rachel,' he countered. 'You take after neither of them. And do not be too hard on your mother. She made a grave mistake in marrying your father. Oil and water do not mix. Would you have had her pay for that mistake for the rest of her life?'

She did not reply; could not reply. She was filled with conflicting emotions, her mind a whirl of discordant thoughts. Resolutely she stared out of the window into the darkness, and said not another word until they had reached home, where she bade him good-night at the foot of the stairs, and then went slowly up to her room.

After carefully hanging her new dress in the wardrobe and donning her nightgown, she sat at the dressing-table and began to unpin her hair. Taking up the silver-backed brush, she pulled it through her glossy auburn tresses, which glinted beneath the candles' glow no less brightly than the dancing flames still flickering on the hearth.

She stared into the mirror, but it was not her reflection which stared back at her from the glass, but a fading beauty's, whose green eyes seemed dulled by selfish indifference—such soulless, emotionless eyes.

She closed her own, successfully blocking out the image, but the truth could not be so easily erased. Lady Emily Fotheringale was her mother. But did that woman honestly suppose she could just reappear after an absence of more than eighteen years and gain her daughter's affection? Rachel's lips curled into a wry smile. She doubted whether the lady in question cared very much one way or the other.

Strangely, this realisation pained her, but she refused to wallow in self-pity, for her life had been blessed with wonderful, loving people who had truly cared about her. Never could she have found a better surrogate mother than Lady Anne Norton. Her life, too, had been enriched by true and loyal friends: dear Lady Barnsdale, little Lucy. . .and Dominic.

Raising her eyes, she stared across the room at that closed door which connected their respective apartments. A little earlier some detached part of her brain had registered that he had entered his bedchamber. Now she could hear him quite clearly moving about his room.

How comforting, how reassuring the knowledge that he was there, a matter of yards from her; ever vigilant, ever ready to come to her if she should call, if she should need him. And how she had needed him, how she had turned to him time and again for reassurance and support, as though to do so were the most natural act in the world!

Yes. . .therein lay the simple truth of it all, she realised suddenly with frightening clarity: she *did* turn to him; she *did* trust him; she *did* need him. Now, she could no longer ignore the bittersweet judgment of her own heart. By almost imperceptible stages, she had fallen deeply in love with the man whom she had so wickedly maligned.

Had the realisation not been so cruelly painful, she

might have laughed at the irony of it all. She had loved him as a girl. But the love she now felt bore no comparison to those idolatrous feelings she had experienced years ago. Oh, no, she was no longer blind to his faults. Viscount Linford was no knight in shining armour: he was just a man, with a man's qualities and failings. But a most honourable man withal.

And would such a man wish her to remain at the Hall? The answer came hard on the heels of the question. Of course he would! That, in all probability, had been his real motive for bringing her back to Hampshire. Perhaps, through some misguided sense of chivalry, because she had been the means by which he had retained his ancestral home, he was offering her the opportunity of remaining his wife.

What a first-rate dunderhead she had been not to realise that long ago! He had been all kindness and consideration during these past months; and she felt certain he had grown genuinely fond of her. But fondness and obligation were poor substitutes for what she most craved: his love.

No, she could not remain here under such terms. Her lips curled into a wry little smile. As he had so rightly pointed out: she was not like her mother—she could never seek to attain her own happiness at the expense of someone else's. And there would be precious little happiness, she reminded herself, in a marriage where the love was only on one side.

Feeling suddenly so very weary, she leaned forward, about to blow out the candles, when something sparkling in the mirror caught her attention. Raising her hand, she touched, almost reverently, the precious glinting stones which still encircled her neck. She had even misjudged him over that kind gesture. . . A token of his sincere regard, he had said. But not a token of his love.

Tears blurred her vision, but she held them in check.

Iron resolve was all important, now. The next three weeks were going to be painfully hard to live through; harder than any she had endured in childhood; she was under no illusions about that. But from somewhere she must find the strength to conceal her true feelings, and to give the man she loved what he most desired: the freedom to marry the woman of his choice.

After struggling in vain with the clasp for several minutes, she glanced frowningly across at the bell-pull. Alice would have retired long since. Instinctively, her eyes went to that connecting door and, without a second thought, she rose to her feet and ventured quietly into the only suite of rooms in the house that she had never entered before.

Dressed only in a strikingly patterned brocade robe, the Viscount stood beside his dressing-table. Then, as though sensing he was no longer alone, he swung round to see Rachel hovering by the door, her gaze riveted on the large four-poster bed.

'Why, Rachel! Is there something wrong?'

'N-no, there's nothing wrong,' she responded nervously, drawing her eyes away from the room's most imposing feature, and feeling suddenly very shy and unaccountably vulnerable. 'It's just that I cannot seem to undo the clasp on my necklace. Would you mind?'

He came slowly towards her, his eyes roaming with a slow intimacy over her pretty, yet modest nightgown. Then he was behind her, raising the swathe of dark auburn hair and placing it over one slender shoulder.

It took every ounce of self-control she possessed to remain perfectly still, to try to ignore the feather-light touch of those warm fingers on her neck, and to try to suppress the urge to flee to the sanctuary of her own room. She groaned inwardly. She must have been mad to come here in the first place! What must he be thinking?

'There,' he said softly, after what seemed an interminable length of time. Reaching out, he set the necklace down on to a nearby table before placing his hands on her shoulders and turning her round to face him squarely. 'You're trembling, my dear.' His voice sounded so strangely husky. 'You're not afraid of me, I trust?'

She raised her head, forcing herself to look into eyes which glinted with an emotion she could not interpret. 'Of course not,' she responded, sounding totally unconvincing even to her own ears. 'I—I had better return to my own room,' but his hands only tightened about her arms, forcing her to remain where she stood.

'Oh, no, my darling. I have been remarkably patient, but you have kept me at arm's length long enough, I think.' His voice, now, seemed dangerously soft and as frightening as the depth of feeling smouldering in his eyes. 'At long last you have come to me. And, by God, I'll take you! This night you shall be mine!' and before Rachel knew what was happening, she was in his arms and being carried across the room.

Panic welled as he lay her down in that huge four-poster bed, which seemed to enclose her like a cage. Never before had she seen him in this strangely intense mood. Impassioned, his hands easily captured her wildly flailing arms, and his mouth effectively silenced her requests for release and her pleas for reason. Like an animal caught in a trap, escape was impossible.

Yet some detached part of her brain registered that the hands which held her captive were not cruelly painful, merely adequately restraining, and the lips on hers were not hard and punishing, but gently coaxing. Slowly the fear began to subside as something deep within stirred.

He was instantly aware of the tension in her ebbing away, and released his hold. Burning a trail of feather-light kisses across her cheek and down her throat, he ran his fingers up the length of her arm to the ties of her night-gown. Then, freed of encumbrance at last, he explored her softly pliant body, arousing, awakening, drawing forth little moans of pleasure which he had waited so long to hear.

Intoxicated by a powerfully exquisite longing never experienced before, Rachel was lost to everything except the delicious ecstasy his skilled lips and hands evoked. Any thought of denying him had long since passed and she gave herself up willingly to his gentle expertise, know-ing only a moment's pain before he finally made her his own.

Only later as she lay, still naked, in the circle of his arms, her cheek resting on the soft mat of dark hair covering his chest, did she begin to question the wisdom of what had taken place between them. Yet, in her heart of hearts, she could not find it within herself to regret it.

'What are you thinking about?' he startled her by asking suddenly, unexpectedly, and she raised her head to look at him.

'I thought you were asleep.'

'No, I've not been asleep, my love.' His fingers moved beneath the swathe of hair, caressing the soft white skin. 'Now, tell me what you were thinking about.'

Only the candle on the bedside table had not guttered, and it offered sufficient light for her to see his features clearly. She lowered her eyes lest he should glimpse the uncertainty in her own.

'I was thinking about what has taken place between us,' she responded truthfully.

'I hope for your sake, my little love, that you've no regrets, because, of course, it changes everything.'

'It does?' she responded, still uncertain.

'Naturally it does.' His tone was almost matter-of-fact.

'The agreement we made six months ago is null and void. There's no question of your leaving now.'

'There isn't?' She risked looking at him again, and what she saw in his eyes made her heart pound with elation. But she had to be sure; had to be certain that he was not acting out of some misguided sense of obligation. 'Is that what—what you really want, Dominic? Do you truly want me to remain your wife?'

In one swift movement he flicked her over on to her back and, raising himself on one elbow, stared down into green depths which mirrored continued uncertainty.

'My beautiful pea-goose.' His body shook with silent laughter. 'Why on earth do you imagine I brought you back here in the first place?'

This was no time for prevarication, she knew. 'I suspect you felt obligated.'

'Obligated, be damned!' he snapped before a rueful smile curled his lips. 'Yes, I suppose I should have been honest with you from the start. But I felt certain you would never have believed me.' He ran his finger gently along the soft curve of her jaw. 'When I went to see you that day, shortly before you left London, there was no thought in my mind of making you my mistress. I had fallen in love with you. . .wanted to spend the rest of my life with you.'

Her eyes grew misty. 'You loved me then?'

'Yes, I loved you then.' Again, his smile was rueful. 'But, for all that I've changed in these past years, I'm still an arrogant, selfish creature, Rachel. I believed, given time, I could make you come to view me in a different light; could make you come to care for me. But tonight, when you stood there looking so lovely, so utterly desirable, no matter what your feelings were, I knew I couldn't give you up. . .wouldn't give you up.'

She looked at him in wonder, her eyes devouring the

strong contours of his handsome face. He loved her, and nothing else mattered.

'I honestly don't know at what precise moment my feelings for you began to change,' she reflected, her attention focused on the curling black hairs at the base of his throat. 'My love grew slowly over the weeks—so slowly, in fact, that I, stupidly, didn't even realise what was happening to me. It wasn't until tonight that I knew just how much you had come to mean to me.'

She raised her eyes shyly to his. 'But I hope you don't think that I came in here with the intention of—of seducing you?'

His deep rumble of laughter echoed round the large room. 'With my experience of the fair sex, my love, I think I can safely say that that possibility never entered my head.' He saw a shadow flit across her face, and looked gravely down at her, understanding perfectly the niggling doubt which disturbed her peace of mind.

'Since that day in London, Rachel, there has been no other woman in my life. Nor shall there ever be. You need have no fears on that score,' he assured her. 'I would never ever risk losing you again. My life would be empty, meaningless without you.'

All doubts, all fears dispelled, she wound her arms round his neck, drawing his mouth down to hers. They had been lawfully joined in matrimony for more than six years, but their marriage, she knew, had only just begun.

# Chapter Fifteen

**A** little over three weeks later Rachel awoke to the joyful chiming of church bells welcoming in the New Year. Luxuriatingly, she stretched her arms above her head, sheer contentment drawing her lips into a smile as she gazed absently about her bedchamber. Today, of course, was the day she was to have left the Hall, but there was no question of her doing so now. Or of her ever doing so for that matter, she thought, her smile widening.

Not once since that first wonderful night had she slept alone; and last night, instead of sweeping her up in his arms and carrying her into his own bedchamber, Linford had slipped into her bed beside her, briefly stigmatising the abundance of frothy white lace adorning the pillows, but quickly forgetting his grievances in the untold joys of lovemaking.

Yes, the past three weeks had been wonderful, she mused, and quite eventful, too. The very day after the ball they had received a visit from Lucy, who had ridden over to inform them that Lord and Lady Fotheringale had, indeed, left that morning for Ireland and, like her mother the night before, had apologised for any distress their unexpected presence may have caused.

She had then gone on to inform Linford of Renfrew's

mysterious disappearance. There had been neither sight nor sound of the groom since the Viscount and Mr Stubbs had spoken to him on the morning of the ball. This intelligence had had the effect of sending Mr Stubbs hotfoot back to London, and they had neither seen anything of him, nor received word from him, during the intervening weeks.

Rachel could not say in all honesty that she had been disappointed by the unexpected turn of events. Of course, she no longer bore Mr Stubbs any ill-will. In fact, after that first and only meeting with him at the inn, she had come away with a very favourable impression.

His presence in the neighbourhood, however, had tended to remind her of the unfortunate incident which she would far rather forget. So, if Renfrew had, indeed, been her attacker—she still entertained grave doubts over this—his disappearance must surely put an end to the matter once and for all.

Only one circumstance had caused her some disquiet during these past blissfully happy weeks, and that was the singular lack of communication from Lady Barnsdale. A frown of concern marred the perfect symmetry of her brow. Since Cheffy's visit in November, she hadn't received one letter from Hetta, which was strange, considering her friend had been a regular correspondent before that.

Linford, himself, had written to his aunt the previous week, but seemed sublimely unconcerned that he had received no reply, putting it down to the fact that Hetta, in all likelihood, was staying with friends.

He was, probably, absolutely right; but if no letter had arrived from Lady Barnsdale by the end of next week, Rachel was determined to pay a visit to Bath, which would be highly convenient, as she would need to visit her house in Somerset in the very near future, anyway.

It seemed a shocking waste, leaving such a lovely property unoccupied except for a handful of servants, but she had little use for a house in Somerset now. No, her life was most definitely here, in Hampshire, at her husband's side; but she felt duty-bound to visit those loyal servants, most of whom had been with Lady Anne for many years, and to inform them in person that she had no intention of returning to Somerset and would be selling the house.

If she could find a buyer who was willing to retain the staff, all well and good; if not, she would not abandon them to their fate. She would either try to find them a position in the locale, or offer them the opportunity of working here at Linford Hall or in the surrounding area.

The door opening broke into her thoughts, and she turned her head, surprised to see Mrs Litton enter the room, carrying a cup of chocolate.

'Where's Alice this morning, Litty?' she enquired, resorting to the pet name which she now always used whenever they were alone together.

'She's contracted another chill, my lady, so I took it upon myself to order her back to bed.' Twinkling amusement, which was frequently glimpsed nowadays, sparkled in the housekeeper's grey eyes. 'His lordship would not be best pleased, I'm sure, if she passed the malady on to you.'

'Very true,' Rachel agreed, propping herself up against the mound of pillows and taking the cup which Mrs Litton held out. 'And I have decided, Litty, that I very much enjoy being a married lady, and having a husband who's attentive to my every need.'

'Quite so, my lady. And that is precisely why I have instructed Rose to attend you until Alice has recovered.'

Sipping her chocolate, Rachel gazed up at the housekeeper thoughtfully for a moment, then asked, 'Litty, how would you like a trip to Bath in the near future?'

'I would like it very much, my lady. I never have visited that part of the country.'

'That's good, because I intend paying a visit to my house in Somerset, and shall pay a call on Lady Barnsdale on the way.' Again she cast her a thoughtful glance, frowning this time over the housekeeper's severe black dress. 'And do not forget you are to accompany me on that shopping expedition with the Maitland ladies to Penley on Friday. It will give us the opportunity to select some materials for new dresses for you.

'And do not dare to argue with me, Mrs Litton!' she ordered when the housekeeper opened her mouth to do just that. 'If you imagine I'm travelling all the way to Somerset and back with you dressed in widow's weeds, you're very much mistaken. I should find the whole trip utterly depressing.'

The housekeeper could not help chuckling at her lovely young mistress's pained expression, but she was not fooled, and knew that the kind-hearted Viscountess was trying to reimburse her for the money which she had foolishly given to that villainous blackmailer.

'I would not dare to argue with you, my lady,' she responded. 'His lordship would not be best pleased if I did.'

Rachel cast her a smile of approval before glancing over at the clock. 'Great heavens, Litty! Look at the time! I'm turning into a real slug-a-bed.'

'His lordship gave instructions, before he went off with the steward, that you were not to be disturbed.'

Drat the interfering wretch! Rachel thought silently with a complete turnabout of her former high opinion of her doting spouse. Flinging the covers aside, she rose from the bed. 'Since it's so late, I'll forgo breakfast and take an early luncheon. Then I think I'll ride in the park for an hour. But I'd like to talk to you again about our trip to Somerset, so come to the small salon at two o'clock.'

\* \* \*

Later, when she collected Firefly from the stables, Rachel was pleased to see that the weather, too, was doing its best to welcome in the New Year. A watery winter sun shone down from an almost cloudless sky, but its bright rays contained precious little warmth; she shivered as she set Firefly at a gallop and headed for the northern gateway.

Mindful of the promise which she had made to Linford, she did not attempt to leave the park, but skirted the boundary wall for a while, and then cut back across the park in the direction of the home wood. Not once since that afternoon, when she had paid a visit to Ben Hughes's barn, had she attempted to ride through the wooded area on her own.

She experienced a frisson of fear as she turned Firefly on to one of the many tracks which criss-crossed the densely tree-covered landscape, and cursed herself silently for such cowardice. After all, who was there to hurt her now?

The thought had only just reassuringly crossed her mind when she detected a sudden movement on her left. She brought Firefly to an abrupt halt, and could only watch in a kind of frozen paralysis as a large, shadowy figure emerged from behind a sturdy oak. He drew his mount across the narrow path in front of her, effectively blocking her way, and she found herself staring down the barrel of a serviceable pistol.

An impulse to turn tail and run, engendered by the very natural inclination for self-preservation, was rapidly quashed by common sense. No, that would not answer, Rachel swiftly realised. Before she had fled more than half a dozen yards, she would no doubt feel the searing red-hot pain of a bullet in her back. Her heart pounded against her ribcage, but her eyes gazed levelly at the evilly mocking face of the Maitlands' errant groom.

'So, it was you all along, Renfrew,' she said in a voice

which remained amazingly unwavering. 'How foolish of me to have supposed otherwise!'

Rachel's mind was working rapidly. He had not attempted to shoot her, yet. If she could keep him talking long enough, perhaps someone, the gamekeeper or one of the other estate workers, might happen along. A forlorn hope, she knew, but her only one.

'Before you put a period to my existence, may I be permitted to know one thing?' She stared deeply into wickedly mocking dark eyes. 'What did I ever do to give you such a virulent hatred of me?'

Thick lips curled into a cruel smirk. 'It ain't you I hate, but yer 'usband. I'd do anything to get back at 'im for what he did to me and mine.'

Antipathy oozed from his every word, leaving Rachel in little doubt as to his state of mind. But what on earth could Linford have ever done to inspire such vindictiveness?

She was destined, however, not to have her curiosity satisfied, for at that moment a sound to her left drew Renfrew's attention, and she turned her head in the direction of his piercing stare, but could detect nothing. In all probability it was merely an animal foraging for food, a deer, or perhaps a fox, but the faint noise was sufficient to put Renfrew on his guard. He looked back at her, wielding the pistol threateningly.

'Move!' he ordered, drawing his mount to one side so that she could ride ahead of him. 'Keep to the track by the edge of the wood. And don't think of calling out, my lady, unless yer want a bullet in yer brain.'

Rachel did not doubt for a moment that he would carry out his threat. Even if by some chance someone did come riding along the bridle-path which skirted the edge of the wood, she had no intention of calling out. To do so would be to sign her own death warrant. If Renfrew's intention had been to kill her, he would have done so by now. No, she thought, eyes narrowing, he had some other nefarious scheme in mind. . . But what?

They came to the edge of the wood and, at Renfrew's prompting, rode along the bridle-path for a short while, without catching sight of a soul, and then turned down the track leading to the old barn on the land which Sam Hughes farmed.

Considering he had only worked in the area for a matter of months, Renfrew certainly seemed to know his way about very well, Rachel reflected as they reached the stone-built structure that had once housed Ben's injured animal friends.

Dismounting, Renfrew ordered her to open the door and to lead the horses inside. With hands not quite steady, Rachel obeyed, tethering the animals to a metal bar fixed into the end wall, whilst gazing about her. When she had visited the barn months before with Ben, it had been such a wonderful place, but now it seemed unfriendly, and smelt of damp and decay.

She swung round to find Renfrew standing directly behind her, a look in his eyes, as they wandered over her elegant habit, which made her blood run cold. 'Why have you brought me here?' she demanded, betraying none of the fear and revulsion she experienced at his insolent inspection of her figure. 'If you had intended to kill me, you would have done so by now.'

'I might, still, if yer don't do as yer told,' he hissed, placing the pistol to her shoulder and drawing it down over the curve of her left breast. 'Get down on the floor!'

Dear God, not that! She would die rather than have him violate her. On impulse, she made a vain attempt to reach the door, but before she had covered half the distance, his fingers had snaked painfully round her arm and she was thrown to the floor.

'Try that again, and I'll knock yer senseless!' he threatened. 'I've done it afore, remember? Now, put yer 'ands behind yer back!'

Rachel had little choice but to obey. Her futile attempt to escape had, no doubt, put him on his guard. He would not grant her a further opportunity. Kneeling down behind her, he bound her wrists tightly before tying the other end of the strong cord to one of the sturdy upright beams which supported the roof.

She leaned her back against the hard wood, trying desperately to control the ever-increasing hysteria at what he might do next, and felt untold relief when he rose to his feet and moved across the dirt floor to throw himself down on the pile of hay in one corner.

She watched him delve into the pocket of his rough homespun jacket and draw out a flask, whilst slipping his gun into the other, and stared into those dark, pitiless eyes. 'What do you intend doing with me, Renfrew?' she forced herself to ask again from a suddenly dry throat.

His unpleasant smile returned before he placed the flask to his lips and took a large swallow of its contents. 'Can think of quite a few things I could do whilst I'm waiting for yer 'igh and mighty 'usband to come up with the blunt for yer safe return.' Once again his cruel eyes appraised her with a slow insolence. 'Yer a fine, spirited filly—I'll give yer that. He'll pay 'andsomely for yer return.'

'I dare say he would. . .providing, of course, I return unsullied,' she responded, greatly daring.

So, extortion was his game, was it? The villainous wretch! Growing anger replaced fear, and restored a semblance of order to her wayward thoughts. 'You don't for a moment imagine, surely, that Linford would part with so much as a penny unless he was certain I had suffered no harm? And you hardly excel in delicate consideration to the fair sex, Renfrew.'

He guffawed, evidently genuinely amused. 'Now, yer mustn't 'old those other times against me, ma'am. If yer 'adn't riled me that day at the wood, and the other time at the forge, looking down yer pretty little nose at me that way, I'd never 'ave tried to shoot yer, or gone after yer on the ridge. It ain't wise to rile me.'

'Evidently not,' she agreed drily. 'But at the risk of doing so again, might I be permitted to know how long you intend keeping me here?'

His brawny shoulders rose in an indifferent shrug. 'Don't see why not. We'll stay 'ere until dark, then I'm taking yer to a safe place over Penley way. And if yer a good girl, and do as I say, I'll make sure me friends don't 'arm yer.'

Rachel gazed across at him consideringly as he continued to imbibe liberally from his flask. He appeared far less threatening now, and seemed inclined to talk; so she risked having her curiosity satisfied on several points by remarking casually, 'You seem to know your way about these parts very well, Renfrew.'

'Aye, well enough.'

'But I understood you hadn't been in Hampshire long?'

'I've lived 'ere afore.' He leaned back against the wall, yawning broadly. 'When London got a bit warm, as yer might say, seemed the right place to lie low for a bit. Fell in with a couple o' rogues quickly enough, but I 'ad to keep out o' trouble.'

'So that's why you took the job as Harry Maitland's groom?'

He guffawed again. 'What a block'ead! Spied 'im at a cock-fight one day. Seemed the sort of simple cove to fall for a 'ard-luck story. Got me friends to rough 'im up a bit, then I pretends to come to 'is aid. Worked like a charm! And I got a decent supper out of 'im.'

Poor Harry, she thought, animosity welling suddenly.

What a way to have one's kindness repaid! She could not keep the contempt she felt from creeping into her voice as she said, 'But you cannot keep out of trouble, can you, Renfrew? It follows you about like a stray dog.' She eyed him narrowly, measuringly. 'Your attack upon me proved to be your undoing. Mr Stubbs recognised you, Renfrew. And Mr Stubbs, let me tell you, used to be a Bow Street Runner.'

'I know well enough what he were,' he growled angrily. 'And where he be, now. It were yer 'igh and mighty 'usband brung 'im 'ere. And it were 'im, I don't doubt, put a stop to me other little money-maker. He's got a lot to answer for, and he'll pay dearly for it an' all. So shut yer gab, woman, and let me sleep!'

Rachel didn't need telling twice: she knew better than to anger him. But his words puzzled her. What little money-maker had he been referring to? Knowing him as she did, she doubted it would have been anything lawful. She pondered over this as she leaned back against the solid wooden support, but quickly turned her mind to her immediate problem. How on earth was she to get herself out of this evil rogue's clutches?

She turned her head in the direction of the small, grimy window. It was still light outside, possibly no later than three o'clock. If she had by this time been missed, she doubted very much that Linford would instigate a search.

No, he wouldn't become concerned until the light began to fade, and then he would send people out only to those places where he expected her to be found: to neighbouring houses, or, possibly, to Linfield. By which time, of course, she would be on her way to Penley, where escape would be nigh impossible with Renfrew's friends guarding her. No, if she was going to make the attempt, it must be soon. . .but how?

The cord binding her gnawed into her wrists painfully,

and her fingers were icy cold. Renfrew, the hard-boiled wretch, had even removed her gloves before tethering her like an animal to a stake, and had strewn them across the dirt floor, out of reach.

She turned a malevolent gaze on to him. His empty flask lay beside him on the hay. His eyes were closed, and he was breathing steadily and heavily. How she wished she were a man! She would dearly have loved to repay him for the many hurts he had inflicted on her.

Thrusting these vengeful thoughts aside, she gazed about her, searching for something, anything, that would aid her cause. There were plenty of small farming implements dotted about the place, even a scythe, but they were all out of reach.

Frustrated, she was about to abandon the idea, and try to resign herself to her fate, when she noticed a piece of glass, possibly a fragment from the jar that had contained the salve which Ben Hughes had used on his patients. But could she reach it?

There was very little slack in the cord which tethered her to the beam but, by stretching her right leg out as far as she could, she managed to make contact with the fragment with the toe of her boot. It took some little time before she had the glass manoeuvred into such a position that she was able to reach it with her fingers; then she wedged her precious fragment hard into a niche in the beam.

Renfrew's reassuringly loud snores were sufficient to cover the slight rasping sounds as she rubbed the cord back and forth across the fragment's sharp, jagged edge. It took a few minutes only, but to Rachel, whose arms ached unbearably, it seemed to take an age before one piece of rope frayed, and then blessedly snapped.

She was on her feet in an instant, but before she had taken more than a step or two towards Firefly, Renfrew's snoring stopped abruptly, he mumbled something under his breath, and those cruel, dark eyes were suddenly glaring at her.

Her reaction was lightning-fast. Stooping, Rachel picked up a stout piece of wood and, before Renfrew had fully regained his faculties, brought it down hard on the side of his head.

'There, that's given you your own!' she said, with wicked satisfaction, as she watched him slump over on to his side.

Tossing her weapon to the ground, Rachel delved into the pocket of his coat and relieved him of his pistol. Whether he was unconscious or merely stunned, she was not sure, but she wasn't staying around to find out.

Taking the added precaution of depriving her captor of his mount, so that he could not possibly follow her, she was about to lead both animals towards the door, and blessed freedom, when she heard the unmistakable sound of a horse, ridden at speed, drawing ever closer. Dear Lord, no, not one of Renfrew's degenerate friends, surely? Fate couldn't be so cruelly unjust!

The pounding in her temple was like the echoing of those hoof beats, loud and threatening. But she had not come thus far, only to be foiled at the last moment! she thought resolutely. Spurred by determination, she pressed herself against the cold stone wall by the door.

She was vaguely aware that Renfrew had moaned: he was regaining consciousness. She was aware, too, that a second rider was approaching, but her immediate problem was the person who had just brought his mount to a halt on the other side of the wall.

Her hand shook as she raised the heavy pistol. She had never handled a firearm in her life before, and had no idea whether or not she would be able to fire it, but it brought some comfort, just holding the cold metal in her hand as she listened to the sound of a firm tread drawing ever nearer. Then the latch was raised, the door creaked on its rusty hinges and a booted foot appeared in the opening.

# Chapter Sixteen

The clock chimed the half-hour as Linford entered the library. His business with his steward had taken longer than planned, and he had been forced to forgo the pleasure of eating his midday meal in the company of his wife. But, no matter how he longed to spend all his time with her, he must not neglect his duties.

In the spring, though, he would be quite content to leave the running of the estate in his steward's capable hands, and take Rachel abroad for a very belated honeymoon to visit all those places she longed to see. Yes, he mused, he had every intention of spoiling his lovely wife, of indulging her every whim. And not before time!

The door opened and his butler, his expression suggesting that there was a most unpleasant odour attacking his thin nostrils, entered the room. 'The person you escorted into Hampshire several months ago, my lord, has taken it upon himself to call again to see you.' He sniffed loudly. 'In the company of another such individual.'

The Viscount's lips twitched. He had no need to enquire further into the identity of one of his visitors, nor into the occupation of the other, for that matter. It would take a miracle to alter Peplow's low opinion of poor Mr Stubbs or, indeed, of any other person engaged in a similar profession. 'Show them in, and then remain to serve refreshments.'

For Peplow's benefit, his lordship welcomed Mr Stubbs very warmly before being introduced to his companion, Mr Phelps, a stockily built young man in his late twenties, whose alert, sharp eyes betrayed his affiliation with Bow Street.

He waited only until the butler had carried out his duties and had left the room, and then enquired into the reason for their visit. Before he could have his curiosity satisfied, however, an interruption occurred in the form of his conscientious housekeeper, who entered the room looking very grave.

'I'm sorry to disturb you, my lord, but I think you should know that her ladyship has not returned from her ride.'

Linford glanced at the mantel-clock, and then back at his housekeeper, who was staring fixedly, almost malevolently, at Mr Stubbs.

'We've met before, haven't we?' Stubbs enquired, his shrewd grey eyes keenly scrutinising the woman's features.

'Yes, sir, we have,' Mrs Litton replied in freezing tones. 'It was you, if I'm not very much mistaken, who escorted me to Bow Street after my husband's accidental death.'

'Ha!' Stubbs barked triumphantly. 'The Sharpe case!' He turned to the Viscount. 'Never forget a face, you see, m'lord. It were the same with that there groom. I knew I'd seen him somewhere before. That's why I returned to London. Not a wasted journey, either—discovered some very interesting facts. Mr Phelps, be good enough to enlighten his lordship.'

The young Bow Street Runner consulted his notebook. 'The individual in question is wanted in connection with robbery and the brutal attack upon a person in the early hours of the morning of 27th of February, last. The victim died from his injuries, but the attack was witnessed by an individual who was able to give a description of the assailant. Thomas Renfield is being sought by Bow Street on a count of murder.'

Mrs Litton gasped, drawing all eyes to turn in her direction. 'Renfield was the name of the family boarding with me at the time of my husband's death, my lord. I feel certain the son's name was Thomas.'

'And Renfield was the name of the family my father evicted many years ago.' The Viscount looked frowningly across at the young Bow Street Runner. 'So you have reason to believe that the groom Renfrew, and Thomas Renfield, are one and the same person?'

'From what Mr Stubbs has been telling us—yes, sir. Not a doubt about it.'

Linford looked up at his housekeeper, who had suddenly grown very pale, and asked her to sit down. 'It would seem, Mrs Litton, that we may well have discovered the identity of your blackmailer,' he remarked, drawing two pairs of interested eyes to gaze at him fixedly, and then went on to furnish his visitors with details of the blackmail demands.

'That ties in very nicely with all the rest,' Mr Stubbs reflected after a moment's thought. 'We have reason to believe Renfield left London early in March. He found work with the Maitlands. And the blackmail demands started in April. . . But can he read and write, I asks m'self?'

'Yes, he can.' The answer came from Mrs Litton, who had regained a little colour. 'His mother, if my memory serves me correctly, was a lady's maid before she married. She taught both her husband and son to read and write.'

'And that groom would have accompanied the Maitland ladies whenever they visited here. He must have caught sight of you crossing the stable yard to the buttery or wash-house, and recognised you. And if he is, indeed, the son of my father's evicted tenant, he would, no doubt, bear a grudge against my family. And might well take his revenge by. . .'

Linford's words trailed away as he once again glanced at the clock on the mantelshelf, and then looked back at his housekeeper. 'Why are you so concerned that my wife has not returned from her ride? It is still relatively early.'

'Because, my lord, her ladyship requested me to come to the small salon at two o'clock. And her ladyship is always punctual.'

'Yes, she is,' he agreed, betraying concern by a slight frown. He rose to his feet. 'In all probability, she has met up with Lucy Maitland and they have ridden off together somewhere, but I'll send men out to search for her.'

He was halfway across the room when he heard the sounds of an altercation in the hall. 'What the devil. . .?' he muttered, throwing wide the door to find Ben Hughes grappling with two footmen, and a very distraught Peplow hovering nearby.

'I'm sorry, my lord. But—but he just burst in. I couldn't stop him.'

'That's all right, Peplow. Release him.' Linford took hold of the disturbed young man's arm and led him into the library. 'It's all right, Ben,' he assured him. 'You wanted to see me?'

Ben's frightened eyes scanned the other occupants of the room. He received a frowning glance from Mr Phelps, and a rather startled look from the housekeeper, but Mr Stubbs, recognising him instantly, rose to his feet and smiled warmly.

'He's all of a muck-sweat, m'lord. What's upset him, I wonder?'

'We shall endeavour to discover just that.' His lordship turned to Ben, and gained his attention by patting his arm.

'It's all right, old fellow. I'm always pleased to see you, you know that. Now, what is it you wanted to see me about?'

'L-lay. . . Bad man! Bad man. . .!' Ben managed, wildly staring out of the window.

Linford cast a frustrated glance at Mr Stubbs, who scratched his head in some confusion, and then looked back at Ben. 'Are you trying to say you have seen the Maitlands' groom?' He received a nod in response. 'Where? Here in the park? Was her ladyship with him?'

Nodding excitedly, Ben took a hold of the Viscount's sleeve, drew him over to the window and pointed in a westerly direction.

'Dear God!' his lordship muttered. 'He's got her in the home wood. Quick! There's not a moment to lose.'

'Wait a moment, sir,' Stubbs said, arresting the Viscount's progress to the door. 'The lad shook his head. Her ladyship ain't there.' He turned to Ben. 'Did the groom take her ladyship somewhere, lad? Do you know where?'

In response, Ben prodded his great barrel of a chest with one large finger. Mr Stubbs, frowning in bewilderment, turned to the Viscount, who was also looking perplexed.

He came back towards them. 'Ben lives at the forge now. What motive could Renfrew have for taking her there? Besides, Rachel would never go with him anywhere. . .at least, not willingly. So where's he taken her?'

He turned his violet eyes to Ben once more, who was still prodding his chest vigorously. 'What's he trying to tell us? His what. . .?' His lordship stiffened suddenly as an idea occurred to him. 'Has that groom taken her ladyship to your barn?'

The nod was all that was needed to galvanise them into action: Mrs Litton took Ben down to the kitchen where she furnished him with ale and a large portion of game pie; Mr Phelps, accompanied by Jem, rode post-haste back to Linfield to locate the colleague who had accompanied him and Stubbs into Hampshire, and who had remained in Linfield to make enquiries into the whereabouts of Thomas Renfield; and the Viscount and Mr Stubbs, armed with his lordship's fine pistols, rode off in the direction of Ben's old barn.

Mr Stubbs's hired mount was a sluggish brute, and the Viscount, in torment over his wife's well-being, soon grew impatient, and galloped on ahead. He quickly arrived at his destination.

The place looked deserted, but he remained very much on the alert, scanning the area around the building. Renfield, no doubt armed, might still be inside the barn, or close by. . . And Rachel? A spasm of pain ran through him, but he refused to dwell on what might have happened to her at the mercy of that ruffian. So long as she was alive. . .

Dismounting, he moved towards the door, and very slowly raised the wooden latch. Trying desperately to brace himself for what he might discover inside, he was about to enter when a crystal-clear and beloved voice arrested him,

'If you take another step forward, I will shoot you dead!'

The relief was almost more than he could bear, but he managed to say with remarkable aplomb, 'And here I was, thinking you would be pleased to see me.'

'Dominic!'

Rachel threw herself on to his broad chest. The Viscount's arms locked protectively about her, and for a few moments he soothed her, murmuring words of endearment into her hair, but then, wisely, removed the heavy pistol, pressed against his heart, from her clutch, and slipped it into his pocket for safety.

The precautionary action brought Rachel back to reality with a start. After hurriedly assuring him that she was unharmed, she warned him about Renfrew who, hidden from view by the barn door, was swaying slightly as he rose to his feet. In a few giant strides the Viscount had bridged the distance between them and, drawing back his powerful arm, dealt his wife's abductor a punishing blow to the jaw, which sent him crashing to the floor once again.

'A nice flush hit, m'lord. Yes, very neatly done,' came an amused voice from the doorway, and Rachel swung round to see Henry Stubbs, an appreciative smile curling his lips, enter the barn. 'I trust you are unharmed, my lady?'

'What. . .? Oh, my wrists are a little sore where he bound them, but that is all. But what in the world are you doing here, Mr Stubbs?' she asked in some confusion.

'I happened to be paying a visit on your husband, my lady, when word reached us that Renfield, here, had been sighted in your company. Let me help you, my lord,' he went on as Linford, using the cord which had tethered his wife to the beam, began to bind Renfield's hands and feet.

Rachel, still bemused, sat herself on the wooden table, and waited until both men had securely tied the, still, unconscious Renfield, before demanding an explanation.

'Ben must have caught sight of us and followed us here. What a stroke of luck he happened to be in the wood!' she exclaimed when she had learned what had taken place at the Hall in her absence. 'I wonder what he was doing there?'

'I never got round to enquiring into the reason for his being on my land. I'm just exceedingly grateful that he was.' Linford, smiling crookedly at her nonchalant attitude to the whole affair, came towards her. 'What a redoubtable female you are, my love!' he declared, a hint of pride creeping into his voice. 'Most women would have succumbed to a fit of the vapours long since.'

'As I had little choice but to accompany him, I don't see how vapours would have improved my lot.' She gazed across at the recumbent form. 'It was he who tried to shoot me in the wood and who attacked me on the ridge, simply because I had angered him,' she explained, shaking her head in disbelief at such unwarranted retaliatory actions.

'He took a terrible risk coming back here, though. I cannot imagine today's visit was his first, either. He must have come to the estate on several occasions, hoping to catch me on my own. Though I suppose the opportunity to make some easy money was reason enough. And I suppose, as he bears a grudge against your family, Linford, there's some excuse for his behaviour.'

'Don't waste your sympathy on the likes of him, my lady,' Stubbs advised her. 'He's a bad lot. Belongs in Bedlam, so he does, but he'll hang now. He's added murder to his long list of crimes.'

'Which includes extortion,' his lordship put in. 'We have every reason to believe that he was the one blackmailing Mrs Litton.'

Rachel gave a sudden start. 'So *that's* what he meant! He said you had put a stop to his little money-making scheme. He intended extorting money out of you for my safe return, too. Which reminds me, Mr Stubbs,' she went on. 'He was taking me over to Penley this evening to the house of some friends of his. I can't be sure that these others were involved in Renfield's schemes, but I thought you should know.'

'Thank you, my lady. We'll look into it.'

Jem arrived with the Runners, and Linford soon afterwards escorted Rachel back to the Hall. After returning their mounts to the stables, they walked hand in hand round to the front of the house. His lordship, reaction setting in at last, suddenly pulled her into his arms as they reached the front door.

'I cannot bear the thought that something might happen to you. The mere thought that one hair on your head might be harmed fills me with such cold fury.'

Rachel could feel him trembling with suppressed emotions, and looked smilingly up into his concerned face. 'Now that, my lord, is a shocking untruth,' she teased in an attempt to lighten his mood. 'You dislike my hair intensely. I have it on the best authority that you loathe red hair.'

'I don't need to enquire from whom you gleaned that piece of nonsense,' he rejoined. 'But let me assure you, madam wife, that far from disliking your hair, I think it the most beautiful—'

He broke off as the door was suddenly opened and, looking beyond the concerned face of his major-domo, caught sight of a figure hovering in the hall. 'Talk of the. . .!'

Following the direction of his amused gaze, Rachel hurriedly disengaged herself from his hold, and dashed into the hall to embrace their visitor warmly. 'Hetta! What a lovely surprise! How long have you been here?'

'We arrived not an hour since.'

'We?' his lordship echoed, sauntering towards them.

'Yes, Cheffy's with me. He's in the library. Dozing, I don't doubt. Though how anyone could sleep when the house is in such an uproar defeats me.'

'A slight exaggeration, Hetta,' her nephew returned suavely, gazing about him. 'The place seems fine to me.'

'When we arrived it most certainly was not!' she assured him in strident tones. 'There were servants rushing about everywhere, and Bow Street Runners invading the place, demanding to know if you'd returned. And I'll take leave to inform you, Nevvy, that at this precise moment there's a halfwit sat at your kitchen table, eating you out of house and home! Now, perhaps one of you will be good enough to tell me what is going on?'

'Oh, is Ben still here?' Rachel's eyes glinted with unholy amusement. 'I'll see him first, then I must change. Would you just look at the dirt on this habit! I'll leave you to explain things, Dominic,' she added, heading towards the door leading down to the kitchen area. 'You're so much better at doing so than I.'

By the time Rachel, becomingly attired in pale green velvet, joined them in the library, Lady Barnsdale had been apprised of the afternoon's events. One glance was sufficient to reassure her that Rachel was none the worse for her ordeal, and she attained much gratification at seeing her young friend, with wifely familiarity, perch herself on the arm of the Viscount's chair. 'Not much wrong there, Cheffy,' she said in what she believed to be an undertone.

'Told you so,' he responded, not attempting to lower his voice at all. 'Just needed a little time to get to know each other. That was all.'

The Viscount glanced up at Rachel, who seemed to have taken an inordinately keen interest in the hearth all of a sudden, and whose cheeks mirrored its glowing warmth, and then turned his attention on to his old friend.

'Your perspicacity never ceases to amaze me, Cheffy. . . Yes, that was all we needed. Which in a way is not very good news for you, Aunt,' he continued, transferring his amused gaze to her. 'I'm afraid there's no possibility of Rachel moving in with you now. Unless, of course, it's for a short visit, and we are both invited.'

'Oh, don't fret yourself on that score, Nevvy,' she returned without preamble. 'I shan't be inviting either of you to Bath.'

This drew Rachel's head round. Lady Barnsdale was famed for her forthright manner, but this seemed rather abrupt, not to say a little rude, even for her. She glance at her strangely smiling husband before staring enquiringly across at her old friend, who for the first time in living memory betrayed definite signs of blushing.

'I no longer reside there, you see,' Lady Barnsdale added in response to the puzzled look.

'That no doubt accounts, in part, for the lack of correspondence from you.' For a few brief moments the Viscount fixed his violet eyes on Mr Cheffingham, who was also betraying signs of unease by toying with his neckcloth, and then rose to his feet and moved languidly across to the bell-pull. 'Champagne, I think, to celebrate. Don't you agree, my love?'

'If you say so,' Rachel answered, looking totally bewildered. 'Though I hardly think leaving Bath, and informing no one, is cause for celebration.'

'Are you going to enlighten her, Aunt Hetta, or shall I?'

'If you were a woman, Nevvy, I swear you'd keep a broomstick under your bed,' she informed him laughingly, and then looked across at his wife. 'After Cheffy's visit here a few weeks ago, he returned to Bath and told me about the attack upon you, Rachel. I was all for coming here to look after you, but Cheffy wouldn't have it. Told me to let well alone. Assured me that everything would work out fine, and advised me not to interfere.'

She smiled wanly. 'You were right, my dear. Bath didn't suit me at all. I was at such a low ebb, not knowing what to do for the best. So Cheffy took it upon himself to decide for me.'

Rachel cast him a warm look of approval. 'So you whisked Hetta back to Surrey where she belongs. That was well done of you, Cheffy!'

'He certainly did,' Hetta concurred, 'but not immediately.' That tinge of colour returned to her cheeks. 'I don't know if I've ever told you this before, but Cheffy's brother is a bishop. Yes, I know it's hard to believe,' she went on at Rachel's astounded look, 'but true, nonetheless. We travelled to Derbyshire to his home, and there attained a special licence.'

Rachel didn't wait to hear more. She flew across the room to embrace her friend warmly. 'Oh, Hetta, I'm so happy for you!'

'I, on the other hand, feel quite aggrieved,' his lordship put in haughtily, drawing a startled look from each member of the happy group. 'You ought to have attained permission from the head of the family first, Cheffy. Most remiss of you!'

'Fiddlesticks!' his aunt responded. Rachel was of a similar mind, but Cheffy looked decidedly ill at ease.

'Fact is, m'boy, didn't know quite how you'd take it.'

Linford dropped his affronted pose and, smiling broadly, gave the older man a hearty slap on the back. 'I couldn't be more pleased, old friend,' he assured him. 'You ought to have tied the knot years ago. Don't know why it's taken you so long.'

'Truth of the matter is, m'boy, the notion never entered my head until your little wife put it there.' Cheffy admitted with brutal candour. 'Then, the more I thought about it, the more sense it seemed to make. After all, we've known each other long enough to be sure we'd suit.'

'Yes, very true. And there's certainly something to be said for extended courtships,' the Viscount remarked gravely, but with a decided twinkle in the depths of his violet eyes.

'Why, just look at me! A prime example to set before any would-be incautious youth. Married in haste, I foolishly assumed my bride to be a sweet, biddable girl. Years later I believed myself in love with an unquestionable lady of grace and charm. . .but, alas, found myself riveted to a headstrong, green-eyed virago.'

Rachel contented herself with flashing him a fulminating glance from beneath her lashes, but Mrs Charles Cheffingham was not so easily satisfied.

'Yes, and you so unhappy with your lot!' she scoffed. 'Come, a little honesty if you please, Nevvy. You wouldn't change a hair on her head.'

'No,' he admitted softly, gazing lovingly at Rachel's fiery curls, 'not one single strand.'

# *Historical Romance*™

## Coming next month

# RAKE'S REFORM
### *Marie-Louise Hall*

Mr Jonathan Lindsay was most surprised when he was
confronted by the passionate Radical, Miss Janey Hilton.
Upon learning that he was an MP she begged him to
release a young boy who was to be hanged for a crime he
did not commit. Taken aback by her astonishing beauty
and forceful ways, he agreed to help. But he also had an
ulterior motive—he had made a bet with a friend that he
could seduce Janey! He knew he could do it but then the
unthinkable happened—the rakish Jonathan fell in love!
He knew he had to call off the wager. But would it be a
case of too much, too late, when Janey discovered his
horrendous deception?

# THE YOUNGEST MISS ASHE
### *Paula Marshall*

Sir Simon Darrow had known and liked Meg Ashe since
she was a child, and, secure in his acceptability, his blunt
proposal totally lacked romance—he was stunned when
Meg refused him, and went instead to her aunt in Paris.

Eight years later, as the widowed and very wealthy
Comtesse de Mortaine, Meg returned, trailing an
apparently slightly soiled reputation—to find Simon still
unmarried and not prepared to accept Meg's decision
never to marry again...despite his misgivings!

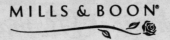

## MILLS & BOON®

*In Sultry New Orleans,*
*Passion and Scandal are...*

# Unmasked

Mills & Boon are delighted to bring you a star studded
line-up of three internationally renowned authors in one
compelling volume—

## Janet Dailey
## Elizabeth Gage
## Jennifer Blake

Set in steamy, sexy New Orleans, this fabulous collection of
three contemporary love stories centres around one magical
night—the annual masked ball.

Disguised as legendary lovers, the elite of New Orleans are
seemingly having the times of their lives.
Guarded secrets remain hidden—until midnight...
when *everyone* must unmask...

Available: August 1997                    Price: £4.99

# FREE!

## FOUR FREE
### specially selected
### Historical Romance™ novels
## <u>PLUS</u> a FREE Mystery Gift
## when you return this page...

Return this coupon and we'll send you 4 Historical Romance novels and a mystery gift absolutely FREE! We'll even pay the postage and packing for you.

We're making you this offer to introduce you to the benefits of the Reader Service™– FREE home delivery of brand-new Historical Romance novels, at least a month before they are available in the shops, FREE gifts and a monthly Newsletter packed with information, competitions, author profiles and lots more...

Accepting these FREE books and gift places you under no obligation to buy, you may cancel at any time, even after receiving just your free shipment. Simply complete the coupon below and send it to:

MILLS & BOON READER SERVICE, FREEPOST, CROYDON, SURREY, CR9 3WZ.

READERS IN EIRE PLEASE SEND COUPON TO PO BOX 4546, DUBLIN 24

## NO STAMP NEEDED

Yes, please send me 4 free Historical Romance novels and a mystery gift. I understand that unless you hear from me, I will receive 4 superb new titles every month for just £2.99* each, postage and packing free. I am under no obligation to purchase any books and I may cancel or suspend my subscription at any time, but the free books and gift will be mine to keep in any case. (I am over 18 years of age)

H7YE

Ms/Mrs/Miss/Mr_____
BLOCK CAPS PLEASE

Address_____

_____

_____

_____ Postcode _____

# JASMINE CRESSWELL

**Internationally-acclaimed Bestselling Author**

# SECRET SINS

## The rich are different—they're deadly!

Judge Victor Rodier is a powerful and dangerous man. At the age of twenty-seven, Jessica Marie Pazmany is confronted with terrifying evidence that her real name is Liliana Rodier. A threat on her life prompts Jessica to seek an appointment with her father—a meeting she may live to regret.

**AVAILABLE IN PAPERBACK
FROM JULY 1997**